THE
DINING
CLUB

ALSO BY MARINA ANDERSON

Haven of Obedience

THE DINING CLUB

MARINA ANDERSON

FOREVER

NEW YORK   BOSTON

This Forever edition is published by arrangement with Sphere, an imprint of Little, Brown Book Group, London, England.

Forever
Hachette Book Group
237 Park Avenue
New York, NY 10017

www.HachetteBookGroup.com

Printed in the United States of America

RRD-C

First published as a serialized ebook in the UK by Sphere, 2013
Published as a serialized ebook in the U.S. by Forever, 2013
Published in paperback in the UK by Sphere, 2014

First Forever trade edition: September 2014
10 9 8 7 6 5 4 3 2 1

Forever is an imprint of Grand Central Publishing.
The Forever name and logo are trademarks of Hachette Book Group, Inc.

The Hachette Speakers Bureau provides a wide range of authors for speaking events. To find out more, go to www.hachettespeakersbureau.com or call (866) 376-6591.

The publisher is not responsible for websites (or their content) that are not owned by the publisher.

Library of Congress Cataloging-in-Publication Data

Anderson, Marina, 1947–
    The dining club / Marina Anderson.
        pages cm
    ISBN 978-1-4555-7823-8 (paperback) — ISBN 978-1-4555-7824-5 (ebook) — ISBN 978-1-4789-5559-7 (audio download) 1. Man-woman relationships—Fiction.   I. Title.
    PR6052.I7775D66 2014
    823'.914—dc23
                        2014010761

*This book is for Tracy, who understands
the importance of tea and cake!*

ACKNOWLEDGMENTS

I am immensely grateful to my wonderful editor, Jenny Hutton, for all her help and support, and also to Catherine Burke and her team at Sphere, who were always there for me.

THE
DINING
CLUB

PART ONE

Desire

ONE

Lying on her back with her eyes closed, Grace tried desperately to hold on to the final seconds of her orgasm for a few moments longer, but she couldn't. The last flickers died away, and with a sigh of exhausted contentment she opened her eyes and looked up at her lover. "You're wonderful!" she exclaimed.

"And you're insatiable," David retorted dryly, as one corner of his mouth lifted in one of his rare half-smiles that she always found incredibly endearing.

"I wish I was, then we could spend a whole day and night making love."

Wrapping his arms around her and pulling her onto her side so that her head rested against his chest, he kissed the top of her long, dark tousled hair. "That sounds like a very good idea to me too," he admitted.

She licked lightly at his chest, loving the salty taste of his sweat, mingled as it was with the distinctive but subtle aftershave that he always wore. When she got back to her own small studio flat in Central London she knew that she would smell of it too. She liked that; it always helped her relive their lovemaking again when she was alone in her bed.

David's two-bedroom apartment was one of twenty in a Grade II–listed building on the outskirts of London. The whole apartment was decorated in shades of cream and brown, with the exception of the kitchen, which was black and white. It was always immaculate, thanks to his cleaners. Grace knew that if she lived there it wouldn't remain immaculate, but she loved it. It was an oasis of calm in her chaotic world as a young, up-and-coming theater director.

"What are you thinking about?" asked David.

"Your flat," replied Grace with a laugh.

"How very unromantic of you!"

"Do you mind?"

"Why should I mind? I'm not a romantic either, I'm afraid," he said lightly.

She snuggled closer to him. "I can be."

His arms loosened their hold on her and he rolled onto his back, staring up at the ceiling. "Yes, I imagine you can," he said thoughtfully.

Grace realized that he was doing it again. Time after time, just as they were becoming closer emotionally, usually after sex, which was the most incredibly satisfying sex she'd ever had, he would close himself off.

He was subtle about it, never leaving her feeling alone or used, but she was used to working with actors. She understood nuances of tone and body language, and that was definitely what he did.

She was too wise to try and talk about it. They'd been together for six months now, and he was the most attractive, charismatic and charming man she'd ever been in a relationship with. He was also an incredible lover, easily the most thoughtful and attentive one she'd ever had. Her pleasure always came first, and unlike other men who'd been in her life and bed, he never left her unfulfilled while he satisfied himself.

She knew that she was beginning to fall in love with him, but also knew that he wasn't in love with her yet. He seemed totally committed to their relationship, she hadn't heard any rumors about other women since they'd met at a theatrical fundraising evening and ended up in bed the same night, and as far as she knew he spent most of his free time with her. All the same, he definitely wasn't in love with her.

David glanced at his watch. "Time to shower and get you back home, before your clothes turn to rags. Not that you're wearing any right now of course! You did say you wanted to be back by midnight, didn't you?"

Grace nodded. "I've got an early meeting tomorrow with some possible sponsors for a new play I want to put on, if I can find a fringe theater that's free in the next six months."

"That's what I thought; shower or bath for you? I'd suggest we share the shower, but we haven't enough time," he said, and flicked lightly at her left nipple until it started to harden again.

"Stop it! We don't have time, and anyway I'm exhausted."

Sitting on the edge of the bed, David glanced back at her. "Really? You don't think you could, even if we tried?"

"I know I couldn't!"

"Interesting," he murmured, almost to himself, and then he lay back down on the bed again, his fingers lightly touching her now soft nipples. Slowly he rolled them between his fingers, and Grace felt her body start to stir again.

"I can't, truly I can't," she repeated, pushing his hands away. "And we don't have time."

"Relax, this won't take long," he assured her, and then his tongue was lapping at the areola, while his fingers continued to work on the slowly hardening nipples themselves.

Despite herself she began to squirm on the bed, her eyes wide as she looked up at him. He was watching her very closely, his expression tender and yet also watchful. She'd never seen that look on his face before.

Under his expert touch her nipples were now rigid, her breasts swollen and despite her previous exhaustion she could feel another orgasm building slowly deep within her. She moaned softly, her legs moving restlessly as she waited for the pleasure to come.

Then, without any warning, David closed his teeth around the tip of her left nipple and bit hard on it. With a scream of shock she started to push him off her but then, to her total disbelief she realized that her whole body felt hard and tight, tensed for the blissful moment of release. She couldn't believe it.

She waited for David to do something, anything, to trigger that final moment of ecstasy, but instead he stopped touching her and when she opened her eyes he was watching her with such tenderness that for one brief moment she could almost have believed that he loved her.

"What happened just then?" she asked in bewilderment.

He looked faintly amused. "I proved you wrong, that's what happened! You weren't as exhausted as you thought, were you?"

"No, but why didn't you finish what you'd started? I wanted..."

"What did you want, Grace?" he asked with interest.

"I wanted to come, you must have known that!"

He nodded. "I did know, but I also knew you wanted to get back home because of your work," he said with apparent regret.

"You hurt me," she added.

David shook his head. "Not really; I shocked you but you enjoyed it, didn't you?"

Grace wished she could deny it, because it didn't seem right, but it was the truth. "Yes," she admitted quietly, "and I didn't want you to stop."

"I thought we might go away next weekend," he said after a few moments spent watching her body as she continued to shift restlessly on the bed.

"Next weekend?"

"Yes. Why the surprise?"

"It's the weekend you always have to work."

"I've decided I deserve some time off. We can stay at a club that's managed by Andrew, a friend of mine. I have a feeling you'll really enjoy it."

"Hopefully we'll both enjoy it?"

"That's the general idea of a weekend away isn't it?"

"What sort of a club is it? If it's a sports club I'd rather not. I know you enjoy squash, tennis, badminton and every other game under the sun, but I don't."

"I may not be romantic, but I do realize that a sports club wouldn't be a romantic break for either of us!" he retorted.

"Then what kind of a club is it?" Grace felt there was something he wasn't telling her.

"I want it to be a surprise for you, but if you don't want

to come then of course we won't go. I only want to please you, darling."

Grace wasn't sure herself why she wanted details, but it seemed strange that he hadn't suggested a hotel.

"Is it a private club?" she asked. "You know, members only, that sort of thing."

"In a way, but as I'm a member they will let you in! It's in a beautiful building, there's a sauna, swimming pool, steam room and the food is excellent."

"What's its name?"

"It's called The Dining Club," said David quietly.

"So it specializes in fine dining?"

"You could say that."

There was something about the look in David's eyes at that moment that Grace found unsettling, but she didn't know why. What she did know was that if she asked one more question he would rightly think her very ungrateful and might drop the whole idea.

The prospect of them spending an entire weekend together was very appealing. With her work schedule frequently involving evenings, and his days often starting with working breakfasts, it would be the first time they'd managed two whole days and a night together.

"No Internet access, no long business calls?" she said teasingly.

"Certainly not; it's a place to relax and indulge ourselves."

"That sounds wonderfully decadent," she said with a laugh. "And where is this oasis of calm?"

"You'll find out when we get there, but it's not a long way to travel. Better take a couple of evening dresses though; they've got a very strict dress code for the dining room."

Grace looked at him in genuine horror. "Evening dresses? I don't possess an evening dress of any kind! I've got some very smart trousers and tops, but..."

"Sorry, but it's evening dresses for the women, suits and ties for the men."

"Well," muttered Grace as she left the apartment and followed her lover to his car, "I hope it's worth all this fuss and money."

"It will definitely be worth it," David assured her, closing the passenger door behind her and walking around to the driver's seat. "If you like it as much as I hope you will, we'll go there again, so the money you spend on dresses won't be wasted."

***

When he walked her to her door and kissed her goodnight, David seemed reluctant to let her go. "I'm really looking forward to our weekend break," he whispered as his mouth moved up her neck. "I'm so pleased you decided to come. I wonder, *would* you do anything for me, Gracie? Anything I asked?"

Before she had time to ask him what he meant, he'd gone, leaving her standing under the porch light, the unasked question going around in her head long after she had left.

Alone in her own bed later that night, Grace still felt uneasy about the forthcoming weekend. "It's only a club," she told herself, "a rather stuffy club by the sound of it, but a club. Grow up, Grace. With David at your side for two whole days and one long night, the Dining Club should give you the best weekend of your life so far."

As she started to fall asleep, back in his apartment David was talking animatedly on the telephone. For him the weekend couldn't come soon enough.

TWO

A mber stood in the arched entrance to the vast dining room and looked around. It was her job to make sure that everything was perfect for the evening's visitors. She was the hostess and if anything was out of place, or the ambience wasn't to David's liking, he would make his displeasure very clear later on, when they were alone together. Although normally that excited her, there were times when he could make sure that his displeasure didn't cause her any pleasure at all.

Walking slowly around the tables she checked the silver cutlery, the crystal wine glasses and the red damask napkins that provided the only touch of color in the room, apart from a single red rose in a slender silver vase in the center of table five.

Table five, her table, or rather their table. She was relieved that David, who could do almost anything, couldn't read her mind. She knew that in his view it was merely the top table, belonging to no one, just as he belonged to no one, at least not yet. He most certainly didn't consider it Amber's table, of that she was in no doubt.

All was well. Only the menu cards were missing, and that was because David was still putting the finishing touches to them.

With a sigh of contentment she walked back to the arched entrance for one final look at the room, the cream walls and matching cream chairs in stark contrast to the dark wooden floor and dark mahogany dining tables.

As she walked back to the archway she saw David coming toward her. Unlike her he wasn't yet dressed for the evening, and was wearing a pale blue open-necked shirt and dark blue casual trousers. He must have just showered, she realized, as his light brown hair was still trying to curl.

He was clearly deep in thought, as though his mind was a million miles away. Perhaps it was, thought Amber. She really had no idea what David thought about when they weren't together at the monthly weekends, and she knew better than to ask. He was the most private and controlled person she'd ever met, except sexually.

Her breathing quickened as she thought of the weekend that lay ahead of them; so many surprises, so many unexpected delights that would leave her sated and exhausted but longing for the next month. David was ingenious because, thanks to the way the monthly dining weekends were run, no two weekends were ever the same.

"Is that the dress you're wearing tonight?" he asked.

"Yes, if you approve."

"What time is it?"

"Ten o'clock. I thought I should get your approval before you went back to your office until this evening."

"God, is it ten already? I must go and pick up Grace. Here are the menus." He handed them to her and as their hands touched he looked at her more carefully. "That dress is excellent," he said. "It sets the tone perfectly. And it suits you," he added.

Moving behind her he put the palm of one hand against the exposed, velvety skin of her back. The backless dress was made out of black silk, a fishtail design with an intricate flowered neck and a diamond-encrusted front collar. The silk bodice was draped and then pulled around and up at the back, meeting the collar at the nape of her neck.

"I like the draping effect," he said, his fingers now stroking the nape of her neck as he pushed her long honey-blonde hair to one side. "It's perfect, and the bondage effect makes me wish I could stay longer so that I could take full advantage of it." As he spoke he twisted her hands behind her back, gripping her wrists tightly together with one hand while pushing her up against the wall.

Then, with his free hand, he pulled her left breast out of the bodice of the dress and squeezed it hard. She let out a tiny sound of surprise mixed with excitement.

"You're not to make any noise," he said quietly. "Not one sound. Do you understand me?"

Amber nodded, swallowing hard as she fought to obey. His long fingers were now squeezing her rounded breast with increasing pressure. At first it was comfortable, then uncomfortable, and then as he kept his eyes on her face, he gripped it with all his strength and red-hot pain lanced through the delicate tissue.

She had difficulty in keeping silent, but then the pressure was released, and bending his head he licked tenderly at the marks his fingers had left behind on the soft globe. Amber trembled, because she knew this was only a temporary respite. Sure enough a few seconds later his fingers began to tighten around the aching flesh once more, and this time the pain came more quickly.

The only sound in the room was that of Amber's breathing as she struggled to stop herself from crying out, not with the pain but with the wonderful hot, liquid pleasure that was starting to flood through her body. As her climax rushed through her she closed her mouth tightly, knowing that any sound would mean David would walk away, and she needed him inside her now.

When her body arched away from the wall, David, who'd been watching her eyes closely, roughly pushed up the long folds of her dress and inserted two fingers inside her damp, needy opening.

She was soaking wet, and when his fingers located the tiny raised G-spot just inside the entrance and lightly massaged it, she convulsed with pleasure and a tiny whimper escaped from her lips.

Without a moment's hesitation, David bit down hard on the breast that was still imprisoned in his hand, but although it was her punishment it merely served to extend her orgasm, although now she shuddered in silent ecstasy.

Half-slumped against the wall she realized that he was still watching her, and he touched the side of her face with the back of his hand. "So wonderfully decadent," he murmured. "If only I could stay, but I must go and collect Grace."

"Who is Grace?" she asked, trying to rearrange her dress and regain some of her more usual poise.

David smiled at her. "Grace is to be my guest at table one tonight. She's a theater director, and she's very special to me."

Amber was stunned. "You mean, you're bringing her here to try and complete the whole trial?"

"Yes, it's been a long time since I've brought my own guest. I'm looking forward to it."

She couldn't believe what she was hearing. It had been over two years since David had brought anyone to the Dining Club, and after such a long time she'd felt secure in their relationship. She was shocked to the core by the realization that there was now going to be a potential rival on the scene. "Presumably she spends her life telling people what to do," she said, trying to gather her thoughts together. "That might make it difficult for her to let anyone else take over during our evening entertainment."

David caught hold of Amber's chin and turned her head toward him. "If she finds the weekend challenging, that will make it all the more interesting for us, won't it?"

His fingers were strong, and she didn't want any more marks to spoil the way she looked this evening. "Yes, I know, I was only…"

David's startlingly blue eyes stared off into the distance and he released her. "Don't prejudge my guest, Amber. And don't try to change things to make it more difficult for her than it should be during her first visit. I'm sure you don't want to annoy me, and that would annoy me, very much."

Amber certainly didn't want to annoy him, and in one way she was pleased. If the weekend were extra interesting thanks to this Grace woman, then David wouldn't be bored. A bored David wasn't the best of companions.

"Everything will run as usual," she assured him.

He grinned at her, suddenly looking almost boyish. Her stomach tightened with renewed desire. She was in thrall to every facet of this man, especially his imaginative and dark sexuality.

After David had left to get Grace, Amber started to put the menus on the tables, and as she glanced at them and began to read the choices, she smiled to herself. She didn't need to worry about this Grace. David had brought other women to the Dining Club, and none of them had ever got beyond table three. If anything, having her here would add piquancy to the situation.

As usual, it was going to be a wonderful weekend.

—

Grace was still packing when David arrived. At over 6' tall, he always made her little studio flat seem small. "I can't zip my case up," she said, letting him in. "The dresses take up so much room!"

David glanced at a dress lying over the back of the sofa bed in the living area. "Is that one of them?" he asked, raising his eyebrows.

"Yes, and it took me hours and hours to find it so I won't take kindly to you telling me you don't like it."

Picking it up he frowned slightly, then held it against her. "Is green really your color?" he asked doubtfully.

"No, but I was running out of time and patience."

"So was the dressmaker by the look of it," he said with a laugh. "Never mind, let's get away. We can do something about that later."

"Like what? Unpick it and start again?" snapped Grace.

"Just pack it will you," he said with amusement. "I thought women enjoyed buying dresses."

"I'd have thought you knew me well enough to know I'm one of the exceptions," she retorted. "I'm much happier in..."

"I know what you're happiest in, and that's nothing at all! Now, give me the case and we'll be on our way."

As he concentrated on easing the silver Lexus in and out of the London traffic, Grace slowly began to relax. At last they were on their way, and had a whole weekend ahead of them.

"Tell me more about this club," she said. "How many members does it have?"

"Not many, there are only eight bedrooms, although quite a few members don't stay overnight, they leave after the Saturday evening is finished."

"You mean they leave after dinner?"

She saw a small muscle was jumping in his left temple. "Yes, dinner and the entertainment."

"You make it sound like a holiday camp!" laughed Grace.

"Sorry, I'm trying to do it justice without giving too much away, but I promise you it's nothing like a holiday camp!"

"I don't know why you're being so secretive about it."

"I want to surprise you when we get there. It's not easy when you keep asking questions."

"Perhaps I don't like surprises."

"Surely you do? I'm certain you'll like this one anyway," he said, and reaching out his left hand he squeezed her right knee reassuringly.

Within five minutes of reaching northwest London, they stopped at a private gated entrance to a wide, tree-lined road with large houses set well back and surrounded by shrubbery-lined drives.

"Very swish!" said Grace.

David, who was quickly let through by a man sitting to the side of the gate, glanced at her. "I'm pleased you approve!"

"Now is that sarcasm or irony?" mused Grace aloud.

David drove slowly down the wide, gently curving road until he reached a walled front garden with security gates and high iron railings at the entrance to the drive. Opening his window he punched some numbers into the black box on the side of the gates and they swung open.

As he drove through, Grace glanced back and felt a twinge of unease as she saw the gates closing softly behind them. She looked at her lover, but he was concentrating on parking the car in front of one of the garages set to the side of the large, three-story house, his expression closed and inward looking.

It was only when he was taking their cases out of the boot that he looked at her. "Are you all right, Grace? You look nervous."

She shook her head. "I'm fine."

Putting an arm around her shoulders he gave her a quick hug. "Now we're here you can relax and enjoy yourself," he said as he rang the doorbell.

While they waited for someone to let them in, Grace noticed a tiny black plaque with the words "The Dining Club" on it, set in the top panel of the white front door.

"They're not big on advertising," she said to David, "that must be the smallest plaque you can get."

"They never advertise; they don't need to," explained David, and then the front door opened.

An exceptionally beautiful girl and a strikingly hand-some young man picked up their cases. David ushered her in, then greeted the very tall, muscular dark-haired man waiting just inside with a warm handshake. "Andrew! Great to see you again."

Andrew smiled. "It's always a pleasure to see you, espe-cially when you bring a guest. You must be Grace," he added, turning to her. "I've heard a lot about you."

He was so relaxed and friendly that Grace's initial ner-vousness started to wear off. He was taller than David, about 6'3" she thought, with broad shoulders and a strong upper body. His dark hair was quite long and unruly, his large, brown, thickly lashed eyes warm and welcoming.

Looking around the vast, marble-floored entrance hall with its high ceiling and wide, winding staircase leading to the upper floors, Grace wondered who actually owned the Dining Club. With only a few members and, as far as she knew, only one dining room, she had no idea how it could be a profitable concern.

"What did you want to do about lunch?" asked Andrew. "As you know the dining room doesn't open until seven, but naturally we can send anything you want up to your suite and…"

"That will suit us very well, thanks," said David. "I'll phone down later. Right now I think we'd like to go to our rooms and get settled in."

"Of course. I'm sure you'll find everything you want in your rooms, but if anything has been forgotten then…"

"I doubt if that will have happened, you know me too well," said David, and Grace saw a quick glance pass between the two men, a glance that had an air of complicity about it, which made no sense to her at all.

At the bottom of the stairs she looked to her left and through a partly opened door saw what she assumed must be the dining room. It looked huge, with small tables set well apart that all appeared to be set up for three people.

"That's odd," she remarked as she and David went up to their suite.

"What is?"

"It looks as though all the tables in the dining room are set for three people. You aren't likely to have three people dining out together very often. Two people or four, yes, but not three!"

"Here we are, number one," said David, inserting a key into the heavy, cream, paneled door and totally ignoring her remark. "Now our weekend break can really begin. In you go. I'll bring the cases."

Grace walked in ahead of him, and heard the lock click softly behind them.

THREE

The room they walked into was so elegant that it took Grace's breath away. It was a large bedroom and sitting room combined, with a king-size curtained bed taking up most of the right-hand wall, its long, creamy peach-colored drapes falling in elegant folds to the deep, pale moss-green carpet. The two tall windows had matching curtains, draped along the top and then hanging in columns to the floor, while the rest of the room had a peach-colored chaise longue and three matching large velvet armchairs that looked big enough for two people to sit in. Close to one window were two small delicate cream chairs with circular backs. The glass-topped coffee table in the middle of the room had a small vase of peach and white roses standing in the middle.

"It's beautiful!" she exclaimed, drinking it in and mentally storing it up for use in a period play sometime in the future. "Absolutely out of this world!"

David smiled. "I hoped you'd like it. Take a look at the bathroom—it's through this door here."

Opening some double doors he stood back to let her go through first. Her initial thought was that it was a drawing room, but then she realized that the floor wasn't covered in carpet but in tiles cleverly designed to look like carpet. In an alcove on the right a deep, claw-footed bath was flanked by a large, soft chair, but one without arms, which she assumed was to make it an easy place to leave your towel or discarded clothes. She certainly wouldn't dare throw her clothes on the floor, she thought to herself. On the other side of the room there was a small alcove with a basin and shelves, and directly opposite the bath there was an ornate mirror that ran from the ceiling to the floor.

"I don't know what to say," she confessed. "It's all out of this world. I imagined it would be far more modern. The house looked new from the outside."

"Some of the suites are modern. I guessed, given your line of work, you'd appreciate the thought that had gone into this design. And of course it's very comfortable," he added with a laugh.

"Have you stayed here a lot?" asked Grace, as they went back into the main room.

"A few times over the past three years."

She wondered if his other girlfriends had liked it as much as she did. She imagined they would have. It was hard to think of any woman not liking it. The entire suite could have been designed as a backdrop for sensual pleasures.

David was opening a small fridge that was concealed by one of the panels in the wall by the door. "I think it's time we had some champagne."

Grace wandered over to the window, looking out at the trees, the immaculate expanse of lawn and carefully tended flower borders that made up the garden. All at once she felt the touch of an ice-cold glass against the back of her neck. She turned and David handed her a champagne flute. "To our weekend at the Dining Club," he said.

She'd only taken one sip when he gently took the glass out of her hand, put it down on the window ledge and, turning her to face him, cradled the sides of her face and neck in his hands as he bent to kiss her.

The kiss was soft at first, and then he gently sucked on her lower lip, drawing it into his mouth for a few seconds before releasing it and then repeating the action. She relaxed into his hands, and felt his tongue sliding beneath her upper lip, running from side to side as she moved her whole body into his.

The pressure from his mouth increased, and as she opened her mouth wider he sucked softly on her tongue. She began to tremble with desire, her body melting and merging with his. Slowly, steadily, the kiss became firmer, more demanding and she could hear his breathing quickening.

"I want to kiss you all over," he said softly, and with deft hands he quickly pulled her T-shirt over her head and removed her bra, so that her rounded breasts were free.

She leaned her back against the frame of the nearest window as he unzipped her jeans and pushed them down around her ankles, making it difficult for her to move, even if she wanted to. Slowly, gently he licked and sucked at her rapidly hardening nipples until she started to moan softly. Then his head moved lower and he knelt down, easing the tops of her legs apart, but still leaving her jeans around her ankles.

Grace's breath caught in her throat as he parted her pubic hair with his fingers, nibbled lightly on her outer sex lips and then separated them before licking upwards with his tongue, which moved in long, firm sweeps.

She could feel her juices flowing now, and he sucked at them before swirling the tip of his tongue around the whole rapidly engorging area. Her moans of delight filled the room and then, as she felt the first tingles of an orgasm beginning he thrust his tongue deep inside her for a few wonderful seconds before moving his head and biting hard at the soft flesh at the top of her left thigh.

With a cry of shock she tried to move, but she was trapped by the window frame and her own jeans. "What are you doing?" she cried. "That hurts. Let me go!"

Ignoring her words he simply returned to licking the soft, wet channel of needy flesh, before lightly touching her clitoris with the tip of his tongue.

To her surprise her excitement began to rekindle, but then he bit her again, at the top of her other thigh, and she started to struggle to free herself.

"Relax," he murmured. "This can feel good, I promise you."

"I don't like it! I . . ."

She stopped, as a strange sensation started to build deep inside her. It wasn't the way her orgasms usually began, it was a deeper, more intense feeling, and gradually she felt her body tighten and almost without thinking she thrust her pelvis forward wanting, needing, something, anything, that would enable her to climax.

To her astonishment, the moment her hips moved, David released her, moving away and leaving her both frustrated and shocked.

"That will do for now," he murmured, "we'll finish later on."

"You bit me!" said Grace accusingly.

David shook his head. "I nipped your skin, and you liked it."

"I didn't like it."

"But your body liked it. Be truthful, you want to come, don't you?"

Confused and bewildered she nodded, her cheeks flushed with shame. Kissing her lightly on the forehead he began to help her get her clothes back on. "Later," he murmured.

"I don't want to wait until later. Don't you understand? I didn't come!" protested Grace.

"You weren't meant to come. Now let's drink our champagne, and I'll explain more about this weekend."

Feeling thoroughly frustrated, Grace finished straightening her clothes. David was already seated on one of the large chairs by the glass-topped table. As she walked past him he caught hold of her, pulling her down into the chair with him.

She tried to wriggle free. "Let me go, you've annoyed me."

"My darling Gracie, I wasn't trying to annoy you. I suppose I was half-testing you and half-preparing you for this evening. Come on, drink some champagne with me."

"What do you mean, 'preparing me' for this evening?" she asked, finally taking a sip of the champagne but refusing to snuggle up against him.

"As you've clearly suspected from the beginning, this isn't going to be an ordinary weekend break," said David, resting one arm along the back of the chair so that his fingertips brushed against the nape of her neck.

"You'd better explain exactly what you mean," responded

Grace, wishing that he'd stop touching her as she was still aroused but unsatisfied.

He nodded in agreement. "We've been going out together for six months now, and I felt the time was right to introduce you to another part of my life. It's a very important part, and obviously I'm hoping that you'll share my enthusiasm for it, but I'll understand if you don't. I'll be sorry, but I'll understand."

Grace took another sip of her champagne. "I don't know what you're talking about, but I have a feeling it's something I definitely need to know, especially as..."

"Especially as what?" he asked quietly.

She sensed that to tell him how much she cared for him would be a mistake. "As I thought we knew each other pretty well already. No one likes to discover their judgment of someone is totally wrong, especially me, as I need to be a good judge of character in my line of work."

"Grace, most people keep parts of themselves hidden from the rest of the world. Haven't you any deep, dark secrets or feelings that you never vocalize?"

"No, I haven't. Tell me about this weekend before I get up and walk out of here," she retorted, her anxiety rising with every word he spoke.

His fingers stopped moving against the nape of her neck. "This club isn't really a dining club. It's a club for people with specialized sexual needs and desires. They come here so that they can enjoy themselves safe in the knowledge that they're surrounded by like-minded people."

Grace frowned. "Why do they need a dining room for

that? There are plenty of clubs in London that cater for all kinds of sexual tastes."

"True, but sometimes people need a place to bring someone they're involved with who doesn't know some of their, shall we say, more unusual sexual needs. This is a safe place for them to find out if that person can ever be happy sharing their world, or if the relationship is doomed to failure because they can't."

Remembering the way her lover's teeth had closed over her soft inner thighs, causing her moments of genuine pain, Grace began to understand what he meant. "Can you explain more about the dining room?"

"There are four tables, five if you count the top table, but you don't need to get involved with that. Each table is numbered from one to five. As you noticed, every table seats three people. This is because at every table there are two people like you and me, who are here to discover whether they are well suited sexually or not, and either another Club member or one of the staff. Needless to say, all of the staff here have a very wide range of sexual skills.

"Tonight you and I will sit at table one. If the evening goes well, and you want to come back next month, we'll sit at table two. This means that each month there is only ever one new guest, as all the visitors either progress up the tables or choose to leave. If two people leave after the same weekend, then a member of staff fills in at the higher table. We like to keep the novices coming, for the benefit of our members."

"Is every novice, as you put it, female?" queried Grace, who although shocked was surprised to realize that she was also beginning to feel a sense of totally unexpected excitement.

"No, we do have female members, and sometimes they bring along a new male partner, but it's predominantly women who are our guests."

"Much more fun for all you men then," remarked Grace.

David turned so that he could look directly into her eyes. "Everyone gets pleasure from the dining trials. Sometimes people fail, or choose to stop something one evening, and then of course they're free to go. They can't come back to the Dining Club, there is only ever one chance to succeed at all the levels, but I promise you that women can get more pleasure here than they have ever imagined in their wildest dreams."

"If they'd had wild dreams they probably wouldn't need to come here," retorted Grace.

David stood up and walked away from her. "I'm sorry if you feel like that. I truly thought you'd find it an intriguing premise. Rather like a series of short plays if you like, erotic ones of course, but fascinating for someone as creative as you.

"I also thought, sadly wrongly it would appear, that you cared enough for me to want to do this. Believe me, if you succeed, we will be closer than ever. There won't be any secrets between us anymore."

"I didn't know there were before," she pointed out, her voice trembling.

He sighed. "I realize that, and I regret it, but I had to be sure about us. It's only because I care for you so much that I now want to be totally honest with you."

Grace felt as though her whole world had been turned upside down. "I don't think you understand how hurt I am," she said softly.

He turned and looked at her, his eyes puzzled. "You mean my explanation hasn't helped at all?"

"No, I understand that. What I don't understand is why we have to do this when we were already so happy. We have a great sex life. You're the best lover I've ever had, and we suit each other in almost every way. Stupidly it seems, I thought that would be enough for you. Why do you want to change things?"

His expression softened. Taking hold of her hands he pulled her to her feet and held her close to him. "I have to change things. We have been happy, but if you don't want to share in this side of my life then no matter how hard I try to make it work out, I know I'll get bored eventually. For me, the sex we're having isn't enough. It's great sex, and I love seeing you in the throes of orgasms, and of course it's good for me too, but I need more. We're only touching the surface of my sensuality and, I believe, yours too.

"I'm sure that once you get into this, you'll enjoy it. Think about how you felt earlier, here in this very room. Remember the way your body responded and how you reacted the other night in your flat, after you'd thought you were too tired for more sex.

"There's a whole world of sexuality that you've never explored. You've never had the opportunity to discover the whole truth about yourself, and here you will. You won't like everything, no one does, but you will find out what satisfies you the most, and in the end you'll need it as much as I do. The more you explore your sexuality, the more things that you discover give you pleasure, the greater our life together can be.

"Trust me, we're alike in this. I wouldn't have brought you here if I didn't believe that. The trials and tasks will take you to heights of pleasure you can't even begin to imagine yet. What we've done together is only the start of an amazing sensual journey."

She tried to pull away from him. "How can you talk about trials and tasks when you're talking about sex? That's not love."

"Grace, it's my kind of love," he said quietly.

She knew that he was telling her the truth. This wasn't merely a club where people changed partners and played out fantasies. For him at least it was a place of safety where he could be sure that the person he was with, and perhaps even wanted to love, shared his sexual tastes.

Realizing that this might well be the key to making him love her as she loved him, a terrible thought struck her. "What if you're wrong about me? What if I fail because I don't enjoy all these things you're talking about—and right now I can't imagine anything worse than having sex with strangers, not even the kind of sex I'm used to—what will happen to us?"

An expression of sadness crossed his face, and she realized she'd never seen him look sad before.

"You leave the Dining Club, and we part as friends," he said softly. "We'll have had some great times along the way, won't we? But there wouldn't be any point in keeping the relationship going, as it won't be able to grow. Don't worry though. I'm not wrong about you. Your body soaks up pleasure like a sponge. Now you'll have the opportunity to experience ecstasy beyond your wildest dreams."

His deep voice enveloped her like a cloak, but part of her knew that it was a cloak of darkness.

"I'm afraid," she whispered against his chest.

His hands caressed her hair, his fingers stroking her scalp. "There's nothing to be afraid of; I'll be with you all the time. Even if I'm only watching, I'll be there."

Leaning back she looked up at him as his hands slid down into the small of her back. "But if I fail, it will be over for us, won't it?"

"Yes," he admitted reluctantly, "but I don't want that to happen."

"Neither do I," responded Grace, shivering at the realization of what she'd just learned about this man she'd fallen in love with, and beginning to realize what lay ahead of her if she agreed to go through with the weekend in order to try and gain his love. "I don't want to lose you," she repeated, "but I'm scared."

"Do it for me, Grace, for both of us. Trust me, you'll never regret it."

He fixed his eyes on hers, as though trying to see into her soul, and Grace stood motionless, struggling with conflicting emotions as she tried to decide whether she wanted to leave now, or stay and take part in what the Dining Club was offering: a dangerous journey of sexual self-discovery for the sake of love.

PART TWO

Bound

FOUR

O nce she'd made her decision, a clearly delighted David suggested that he should show her around the Dining Club, and introduce her to some of the people who worked there. Walking down the long, curved staircase they found Andrew in the hallway, filling in some forms. He smiled at them.

"Having a look around?"

Grace couldn't help noticing the way his T-shirt clung to his chest, showing very well-defined muscles. Combined with his overall build and dark floppy hair he would have made the perfect Stanley in *A Streetcar Named Desire* she thought to herself, her mind switching into work mode for a moment. She imagined he was very popular with women, and his quiet charm was intriguingly at odds with his physical appearance.

"Yes, Grace wanted to meet some of the people here before this evening, didn't you darling?" said David, looking across at her.

"Yes," she said hastily, aware that daydreaming about Andrew wasn't something she should be doing right now.

"You'll find everyone is very friendly," he assured her. "Very friendly indeed," he added, as his eyes swept over her.

"That's a relief," she said with a nervous laugh.

"Well, I'm sure you've got a lot to do, so we'll go and meet the twins," said David, sounding less than pleased with the friendliness of Andrew.

"I look forward to seeing you at dinner," said Andrew, as David hurried Grace along a narrow passageway with concealed lighting set all along the sidewalls, as well as in the low ceiling. At the end was a white painted door, which he opened before stepping aside to let her through.

A soft gray carpet covered the center of the floor, with bleached wood around the sides. The walls were a pale coffee color, the long soft sofa a darker shade of coffee with chocolate-colored cushions. Several very large chairs had been placed around the remaining perimeter, all matching the sofa. One entire side of the room was made up of windows from floor to ceiling, and gray curtains that matched the carpet were drawn back at the sides.

Through the windows Grace could see a part of the garden that had been invisible from their suite. It was a secluded walled area, with sunbeds around a small pond, which had a decorative fountain in the middle.

"Why don't you sit down," said David, gesturing toward the long sofa, which was unoccupied.

Grace did and, seeing the other women in the room wished fervently that she'd worn something a little more formal than her black boot-cut jeans and coral-colored V-neck top. Sitting in a chair opposite her, arms wrapped around each other like small children, were two very young, blonde women, who were clearly the twins that David had mentioned.

One of them was wearing a halter neck sleeveless turquoise dress that finished halfway down her thighs and had beading below her breasts, while the other was in a similar dress but in a very pale pink. It was strapless and longer than her twin's, although to compensate it had a thigh-length split down the left side.

"Grace, meet the twins, Amy and Laura," said David with a smile. "Amy will be sharing our table at dinner tonight, isn't that right, Amy?"

Amy nodded, but her attention was on her twin and Grace saw that she was stroking the top of Laura's slim, tanned thigh, letting her long, beautifully manicured nails scratch lightly on the skin. Laura, who had opened her eyes just long enough to look at Grace, had now closed them again, and the only movement she made was the occasional wriggle.

"Say hello to my guest," said David sharply. "I don't like rudeness, Amy, as I may have to help you remember later this evening."

Amy's eyes flew open and she smiled sweetly at Grace. "Hello, Grace. It's lovely to meet you." She then looked to David for approval.

"Laura?" he said smoothly, apparently unaware that she was shuddering in the chair as a result of her twin's attentions. She struggled to open her eyes, but managed it eventually. "Hello, Grace, I hope you like the Club," she gasped and, like her twin, she then looked at David for approval.

"That's better, girls," he remarked, finally sitting down next to Grace. "The twins have been working here for almost a year now," he explained to her. "They've still got a lot to learn, but they're quick and as you can see they know how to enjoy themselves in their spare time!"

One of them, Grace wasn't sure which, giggled but the other didn't. Instead she studied Grace thoughtfully. "Jeans aren't allowed here," she said at last.

"Don't be silly, Laura," said Andrew, walking in through the door. "Grace doesn't work here; she's a guest. Only members and staff have to follow the rules. Visitors are free to wear what they like. Hope you like your suite," he added, smiling at Grace. "I forgot to ask just now."

His smile was friendly, his tone relaxed and cheerful, and Grace realized that she really liked him. She thought he was probably a couple of years younger than David, maybe twenty-eight or twenty-nine, and he had a boyish charm about him that was very endearing.

"It's a beautiful suite," she replied. "I might copy it to use in one of my plays sometime."

"Let's hope your budget is a large one then," said David dryly.

"Is there anything you wanted, anything we'd forgotten?" Andrew continued.

"I thought you said you were busy," remarked David, and although his voice was smooth Grace thought he looked tense, and not particularly pleased to see Andrew again so soon.

"I found I'd finished. David, do you fancy a swim?"

David smiled, and relaxed again. "Great idea! You'll be fine with the twins for company, won't you Grace?"

Taken by surprise, Grace didn't feel she could object

without sounding rude, although the twins' behavior made her feel distinctly uncomfortable. "Of course," she said, hoping she sounded more cheerful than she felt at the prospect.

"Good, see you later then. We won't be long."

"I'll take good care of him," promised Andrew, smiling at Grace again.

As the door closed behind the two men, the twins disentangled themselves and sat bolt upright, side by side on the one chair, their heads tilted as they surveyed Grace with interest.

"Are you here for dinner tonight?" asked one of them. Grace nodded.

"As David's guest?"

She nodded again.

"You must be special," said the other twin. "He's only ever brought two other people in all the time the Club has been open."

"And we've only seen one of those," they chimed in unison.

"I'm afraid I can't tell which of you is which," apologized Grace as she digested this interesting piece of information.

"I'm Laura," said the one in the pink dress. "I've got bigger breasts than Amy."

Grace couldn't help but smile. "I'll take your word for it!"

The twins looked at each other in surprise.

"You don't have to do that!" they said in unison. "We're meant to entertain you while the men are talking business. You can find out for yourself." With that, Laura peeled down the top of her dress so that her large, creamy white breasts were fully exposed. Amy quickly unfastened the clip at the

back of the halter neck on her dress and let the top half
fall forward so that her breasts were on show as well. Then
they got up and came across the room to join Grace.

"Move over," said Laura. "You can sit in the middle of
us. I was telling the truth wasn't I? My breasts are bigger."

Grace was so shocked she didn't know how to react.
She couldn't believe this was happening to her. It was like
a bad dream, except she knew she wasn't going to escape
by waking up.

She was now sandwiched between the twins, who were
both naked to the waist, and clearly expecting her to comment on their exposed breasts. She tried to speak, but her
mouth had gone dry and it took her a few minutes to form
the words.

"Yes, they probably are," she agreed at last. "You're both
very slim apart from that though," she added, anxious not
to hurt their feelings.

"You're meant to feel them," laughed Laura. "Don't be
shy. This isn't a club for shy people!"

"Shut up!" said Amy. "She's only just arrived. She doesn't
know…"

"Sorry," apologized Laura. "Do feel though. I love having
my breasts touched, and it's so long to wait until tonight."

"Tonight?" queried Grace.

"You are so dumb, Laura," said her twin. "You're lucky
David isn't here. He'd be seriously annoyed with you."

"Just cup my breasts," continued Laura, ignoring her twin.
"They're double G, and totally natural," she added proudly.

Grace knew that she had to react, had to take part in what
appeared to be nothing more than mild fun for the twins,

because clearly what lay ahead that evening was going to be much more of a challenge than this. As Laura pushed her upper torso toward her, she reached out one tentative hand.

"Not like that," murmured Amy softly. "You must look more confident."

Grace opened her mouth to say that she didn't feel confident.

"She likes this," whispered Amy, putting a hand beneath one of her twin's breasts. "Try, Grace, you have to try."

With trembling hands, Grace cupped each of the large, soft globes in her hands and then lifted them slightly.

Laura sighed luxuriously. "You can play with them."

Grace shook her head and went to get up. She just couldn't do it.

On the other side of her, Amy drew nearer and pushed a section of Grace's long, chestnut brown hair behind her left ear. Then, under the pretext of stroking the hair she whispered "There's a camera in here, and we're being filmed as part of your first test."

Grace froze in mid-movement. She wanted to jump off the sofa and run out of the house, to escape now, before even worse things were demanded of her. But then she thought of David's words urging her to trust him, to do whatever was asked of her for both of them, and she knew that she had to go ahead. If she wanted David to love her, and stay with her, which she did, then she had no choice. As Laura whimpered and wriggled she concentrated her mind on David, and releasing one of the breasts she lightly teased the nipple, rolling it between her thumb and index finger until it grew rigid.

Laura arched her back and moaned softly, while Amy continued to play with Grace's hair. "She'd like you to lick it now," she whispered.

Grace started to draw back. "If you want to pass this weekend, just do it!" hissed Amy.

Looking down at the swollen globe resting in her hand, Grace realized to her astonishment that she herself was becoming excited, so she lowered her head and flicked her tongue lightly across the taut nipple.

"Perfect," groaned Laura.

It was then that Grace remembered what David had done to her in her flat a week earlier, and without further thought she closed her teeth around the tender, tight bud and nipped it, before swirling her tongue around the reddening tip.

"Oh yes!" exclaimed Laura, and her whole body shook as she climaxed.

"You're not meant to let visitors give you orgasms until tonight," said Amy smugly.

Laura's left hand flew to her mouth. "I forgot, but that was such bliss I couldn't help myself anyway." Pulling up the top of her dress she looked at Grace admiringly. "You're good for a beginner," she admitted. "Very good."

Grace was trembling herself, and her own breasts felt tight and needy. Next to her, Amy laughed softly.

"You had fun then, didn't you? I think David has got it right this time. I wish I was joining you after dinner. It will be seriously interesting!"

"Is this what it's like?" asked Grace.

The twins got off the sofa and returned to their

armchair, where once again they sat entwined, only now their fingers were still and rather than touching each other they were content to sit and study Grace.

"We're not allowed to say," said Amy. "What do you do in the real world?" she asked politely.

"I'm a theater director."

"That's cool," said Laura, still basking in the afterglow of her orgasm. "Do you work in London?"

"Yes, fringe theater mainly."

"You'll be used to scene setting, improvisations and that kind of thing then," mused Amy. "I imagine that will help you here."

Grace, whose body was feeling restless after playing with Laura's breasts, nodded. "You make it all sound fascinating."

At that moment she heard the sound of a gong being struck. Immediately the twins got out of the chair and straightened their clothing. "We have to go now," they said, speaking in unison once more. "There's a lot to do before tonight," added Amy.

"Good luck tonight," said Laura, as the two of them walked slowly toward the door.

"Will I need it?" asked Grace, half-laughing.

Amy turned to look at her, her light-blue eyes glittering in the shadows. There was something catlike about her now, a feline quality totally at odds with the almost child-like persona she'd displayed earlier.

"That's a secret, and anyway, only Amber knows about tonight. Bye!"

"Wait! Who's Amber?" cried Grace, but she was too late. The twins had gone, and she was now alone in the room, with only the memory of how she'd felt when her teeth had closed around Laura's exposed nipple to keep her company. As she sat waiting for the men to return, little did she know that in a small office at the back of the house, Andrew and Amber were watching the film of her with the twins, as they worked out the final, sophisticated details of Grace's imminent first trial at the Dining Club.

FIVE

I hope the twins were good hostesses," said David, when he and Grace were finally back in their suite. "You hadn't been alone long before I got back had you?"

She shook her head. "No, they'd only just left, and they were very…"—pausing for a moment she tried to think of the right word, knowing as she did that their time together was on camera—"interesting," she said weakly, still unable to believe all that had happened to her while she was with them. Remembering what she'd done to Laura's pliant young body she swallowed hard.

"Good. Amy's a bright young thing; she'll do well. She wants to be a solicitor, but chose to have a year out first. Laura isn't quite as academic. Her ambition is to travel and marry a rich man."

Grace smiled. "A nice rich man, or any rich man?"

"Any rich man I imagine. Niceness isn't something most girls worry about if money is their first concern."

"They should, it's very important."

"Of course it is, but people's ideas of niceness aren't always the same. Some men think a 'girl next door' type of young woman is nice. I prefer women with edge."

Grace shook her head. "You're deliberately being obtuse. I meant nice as in thinking about the other person, caring about their feelings, and making them feel loved and cherished."

"There are other ways of making a woman feel loved and cherished," he said gently, "as I hope you'll come to understand better after your visits here. If you care about someone, it's wonderful to teach them new pathways to pleasure. It's exciting for a man to watch a woman he cares about discover things about herself that she would never have dreamed of if she hadn't met him."

Grace's dark eyes, which were usually sparkling, as though something had amused her, lost their animated look. "You're just talking about sex!" she exclaimed.

Running a hand through his wavy brown hair, David shook his head. "Don't you feel loved and cherished after sex?"

"Yes, but there's far more to it than that. Women need tenderness; desire comes through feeling that you're cherished, not the other way around."

"How do you know that, Gracie? How can you be so sure that what you've always been led to believe is, in reality, the only way women can start to feel desire? Society often makes women feel guilty about their own sexuality. It's more accepting when it comes to men, but why? I want you to forget everything you think you should feel, and be open to new experiences.

"You work in the arts, you like to push the boundaries with plays you put on. If you direct a Jacobean tragedy, you try to do something new with it, play up an aspect of it that's been missed before. Don't you see, that's what we try to do at the Dining Club? I want you to discover things about yourself that you've never even considered before. You can experience pleasure such as you've never imagined if you allow yourself to. It's only society that's dictated what should and what shouldn't feel good to you. Here you get the chance to find out for yourself, and find the aspects of sexual pleasure that you've been missing out on."

"But what about love?" asked Grace.

"How can anyone define love? It means different things to different people, and at different stages in their lives. I believe that love, if it exists, comes through physical and mental closeness, and the ability to share moments of pure, unadulterated sexual ecstasy."

"Don't you believe that love exists?" asked a shocked Grace.

"I hope it does, which is why I've brought you here. I want to experience love, love as I understand it, and I believe you can help me through your experiences at the Dining Club.

"I want to love you, Grace, but if that's going to happen I need you to have absolute trust in me."

Grace was sure she could hear a note of underlying sadness in his voice, a tiny speck of vulnerability that he'd never revealed before, and moving across the room she put her arms around him. He quickly gripped her tightly too, so that they were locked in an embrace.

"You do trust me, don't you my darling?" he said softly.

"Yes," she whispered.

"And you understand what I've been saying?"

"I understand it, but I don't know if I agree with it all," she confessed.

"That doesn't matter. As time passes, and you experience the trials, that's when you'll be in a position to discover whether you agree with me or not. As long as you understand, I know that the rest will follow."

"I hope so," she said softly.

"So do I," replied David, and Grace could tell that he really meant it.

They stayed locked in their embrace for a long time, until Grace realized how time was passing and that the evening would soon be upon her. Swiftly she collected all she needed from her suitcase and went through into the bathroom, leaving her lover standing by the window, lost in his own thoughts.

It was six-thirty. Amber and Andrew took one last look around the dining room before Andrew went to strike the gong for dinner.

"Perfect," said Amber contentedly. "This is a beautiful room. So calm and relaxing."

Andrew smiled. "I always think that it's rather cruel on the newcomers, so misleading when you think about what's to follow."

Amber nodded. "That's what makes it so perfect. I hope Grace enjoys the meal, because I doubt if she's going to enjoy her first evening as David's special guest."

Andrew frowned. "I hope she does. She might resist a little at first, most people do, but I know he's very keen on her and I doubt if he'd have made a mistake."

"He's been very keen on other women, but they didn't

come here very often. The second one only ate here once. I'll never forget her face when she had to..."

"Amber," said Andrew gently, "you can't keep him to yourself forever. One day he'll fall for someone who likes it here and fits into his whole life. Then I hope he marries her and they're very happy. He's a nice man, he deserves to be happy."

"He's not the marrying kind. He needs the stimulation of the Dining Club to stop terminal boredom. He's said as much himself. You can't honestly imagine him marrying can you?"

"Maybe not marrying, but wanting to be with one woman all the time would suit him."

"Only one woman?" she asked sharply.

Andrew shrugged. "Probably not, but he'd like to live with a woman full-time. I suppose he'd use the Club when the need arose, or rather the two of them would use it."

"I doubt if any woman would want to come here knowing I'm in charge," Amber pointed out.

"True, but then you won't be here forever will you? None of us will be. I'll go and sound the gong."

Alone in the room, Amber realized that she was shaking with fury. Andrew was wrong, she knew that really, but his words had scared her. No matter how involved David became with other women, he'd always need her specialized skills and abilities as a hostess. No one could replace her at the Dining Club, and certainly not the admittedly lovely but clearly relatively sexually unsophisticated Grace. Why, she'd even turned up this morning in jeans and a cropped top. Clearly she had no idea of how important clothes were when it came to keeping a man like David keen.

Running her hands down her black dress, she then checked that there weren't any stray strands of hair falling from her French pleat before moving gracefully to the top table. Tall and curvaceous, with her fair skin lightly tanned she was, she knew, a truly beautiful woman. If she had her way, in a few months' time Grace would be nothing more than a distant memory to David.

———

At the sound of the gong, Grace took a final look at herself in the long bedroom mirror, as David adjusted the knot of his dark blue tie, which he was wearing with a white shirt and blue Armani suit. "Are you sure this dress isn't over-the-top?" she asked anxiously. "It's not something I'd ever have chosen."

"I know, which is why I chose it for you. Your dresses were nice, but I realized I hadn't explained quite how formal dinner is here and brought this along in case of emergencies. You look beautiful in it, truly beautiful," he added.

Grace blushed. She felt beautiful. The pale lemon chiffon dress, with lace over the bottom half, fitted her like a second skin. Thin spaghetti straps exposed her creamy shoulders, and a small piece of trailing lace encircled the top of her left arm, like a bracelet made out of material. She thought it looked as though she was about to undress. It was also very sexy, and made her feel sexy too.

"It's amazing," she admitted. "I look..."

"Ready to be ravished," murmured David, standing close behind her so that their eyes met in the mirror. "Unfortunately we have to eat first, but I doubt if I'll be able to control myself after that!"

"I thought that the first trial was after we've eaten?"

"Yes, that's what I meant. Now, let's go down shall we?" He ran one finger across the exposed, sensitive skin of her chest, pushed the lace arm bracelet a fraction lower and then, with an arm around her waist, guided her out of the door. "At last the evening begins," he murmured to himself, and hearing his words Grace's pulse quickened with a mixture of fear and excitement.

The dining room was almost full when they walked in, and Grace realized that David had been right. The dresses she'd bought wouldn't have been right, but the dress he'd bought for her was perfect. Because of the cut and fit it even made her walk differently, and she loved the sensuous feel of the material against her skin.

David led the way to table one, where Amy was already sitting. Her dress was the same color as the one she'd worn earlier in the afternoon, but it revealed more of her legs, and around her neck she had a matching fabric collar, studded with tiny diamond chips.

"Gorgeous dress!" exclaimed Amy, as Grace sat down. "Where did you get it?"

"David bought it for me," said Grace, and she saw a look of surprise cross Amy's face for a fleeting second, before her expression changed to one of amused understanding, which made no sense at all to Grace.

A tall blonde woman then came over to them from the

top table, introducing herself as Amber. "I'm in charge of this part of the Dining Club," she explained, "and it's always a pleasure to meet a guest of David's. He so rarely brings anyone here. I hope you enjoy your evening. You'll find everyone is very friendly, isn't that right, David?"

He nodded. "Oh yes, extremely friendly!" Grace didn't miss the brief, knowing glance that passed between the two of them before Amber glided away again, and there was something about it that increased her nervousness.

"She's beautiful," said Grace. "A classic beauty too, like one of Hitchcock's heroines."

"I hope not, they either end up dead or half-dead with fear!" replied David. "Now, shall I order some champagne?"

The three of them chatted quietly during dinner. David surprised Grace by feeding her olives and tiny slivers of smoked salmon from his fingers at the start of the meal, and later on did the same with the asparagus tips that accompanied the lamb cutlets.

The subdued lighting and quiet murmur of intensely private conversations in the dining room were an arousing background to these small acts of sensuality, and Grace was thoroughly relaxed and enjoying herself when Laura, Amy's twin, arrived at the table with some cards in her hands. "The dessert choice," she explained, handing them to David.

Amy sat up very straight, her eyes on Grace. David glanced briefly at the cards, put three down on the table and passed the rest back to Laura, who then stood waiting for their order.

"Grace, these dessert choices are coded," he said quietly.

"Each of them hints at the type of trial you want this evening. Here, look at them and you'll see what I mean."

Grace's stomach tightened with fear. For a short time she'd forgotten what lay ahead, but now there was no way out. If she wanted to keep David, and after their conversation earlier she knew without a doubt that she did, then she had to go through with this. All around her other women were also looking at cards and making choices. One looked excited, but the others looked as nervous as Grace was feeling.

"Tantalizing Tiramisu, Obedient Orange Sorbet or Controlled Chocolate Delight," she read aloud.

"I think you should leave the Controlled Chocolate Delight for another month," said David quietly. "Choose from the first two."

Grace began to tremble. "I don't want either," she whispered. "I don't know what they mean. I don't think I can do this."

"Then you simply refuse the dessert, my darling, but of course you know what that will mean for us."

"I'm scared; doesn't that matter to you?"

"Don't be scared. You don't have to choose anything, you know that. If none of them appeal to you, then all you have to do is tell Laura. There's no pressure on you, Gracie, it's only that..."

Trembling, Grace looked at him, and saw the regret in his eyes. She wanted to go on, to take the final step into the unknown, but the descriptions on the cards didn't give her enough of a clue for her to dare to choose anything with any confidence.

"The tiramisu should be nice," murmured Amy, leaning close to Grace so that no one near could hear. "Choose that. You'll be fine."

As Grace hesitated, Amber came to their table. "Is there a problem?" she asked.

Looking up, Grace saw that Amber had guessed what was happening and was enjoying it. She also noticed that Amber had rested one hand possessively on David's left shoulder. "No, I'm spoilt for choice, that's all," she said brightly. "I think I'll go for the Tantalizing Tiramisu. It sounds fascinating."

Laura wrote it down and went away and Amy smiled and touched Grace's arm encouragingly while Amber merely nodded before walking off. All around them groups of three were getting up from their tables and making their way out of the dining room.

"Well done," said David. With a sigh of relief he pushed back his chair. "We're in the study for dessert tonight aren't we, Amy?"

Amy nodded.

"Aren't you coming too?" asked Grace.

"No, I'm hardly ever involved at a guest's first trial. My skills are for the higher tables. Good luck though," she added more quietly, "and try to enjoy it. It's one of the best choices you can get." With that, Amy hurried off to join another group.

Grace felt bereft as she watched her go. Now she knew that whatever lay ahead she had to cope with it on her own, because she was certain that no one else was going to help her in any way at all.

Silently David guided Grace out of the dining room, down the hallway and along a short corridor. He then opened a concealed door and she stepped inside.

"Hello," said Amber, getting up from a chair to greet her. "Do come in. Andrew and I are both so pleased you chose the tiramisu."

Grace took a step backwards, feeling her heart racing and aware that the palms of her hands were damp with fear, but David was standing behind her, and before she could say anything he'd locked the study door and dropped the key into a jar on a high shelf.

"Welcome to your first trial, my darling," he murmured. "I'm sure we're all going to have a wonderful time."

SIX

The lighting in the room was turned off, leaving it in darkness apart from the light provided by the many jasmine-scented candles, whose perfume filled the air. Flickering shadows moved on the walls, and Grace stood motionless, wondering if this was how a fox felt when it was caught in the headlights of a car. She wanted to run, and yet she was hypnotized by the all-pervading air of sexuality that filled the room.

Andrew held out his hands. "Come here, Grace," he said, smiling at her. "Don't be nervous. This will be a wonderful evening for you. Tantalizing Tiramisu is one of my favorite scenarios, because it gives the woman so much pleasure."

Pleased to see him, she allowed him to draw her close, and then as he turned her around and his lips caressed the sides of her neck in tiny, circular motions she jumped with shock. It felt all wrong. She only wanted David to kiss her in that way. She shivered, and his hands moved to the tops of her arms, as he drew small circles with his fingers, while his tongue continued to move over the delicate flesh of her neck.

Grace was mortified to feel her body start to soften, and she was very aware of David standing on the far side of the room, watching her keenly. When Andrew began to unzip the back of her dress, kissing each bone of her spine as he peeled the top down, she felt heat spreading between her inner thighs.

Someone gave a tiny moan, and it took her a few seconds to realize that the sound had come from her.

Reaching in front of her, Andrew spread his fingers over the undersides of her swelling breasts, and he scratched lightly on them with his nails for a few seconds before cupping them again.

Grace was shamed by the speed with which her body was responding. She looked apologetically at David, but it was clear from the rapt expression on his face that he didn't mind in the least. He was enjoying seeing Andrew give her pleasure. She felt that this was wrong, that if he really loved her he would be jealous, and was deeply ashamed of the way her body was responding to a stranger's skilled touch while the man she loved was watching.

"That's enough," said David as Andrew finished unzipping the dress, easing the cloth bracelet section down her arm, stroking the soft flesh of it as he did so, until the dress fell to the ground around her ankles. "It's time we explained what the trial is all about."

Standing alone and naked except for a pair of cream-colored French knickers, her breasts tight and her nipples rigid, Grace waited, trembling, to hear what he had to say.

"Since you chose the Tantalizing Tiramisu, I'm sure you've already guessed that this evening you'll be teased and tantalized sexually," he said with a brief smile. "It's something you're almost certain to find exceedingly pleasurable, judging by your response to Andrew taking your dress off. From the point of view of the trial, it's an interestingly quick and encouraging response. You see that illuminated clock on the wall, opposite the sofa?"

Grace hadn't noticed it in the semidarkness before, but when she looked she was surprised by the size of it. It was very large, and each minute was marked with a bright red line. She nodded.

"We'll be in here an hour," continued David. "In that time we will all, plus Laura who will join us later, take it in turns to give you pleasure. However, you're only allowed two orgasms in the hour. The minutes are marked very clearly so that you can see how well you're doing, and you'll hear each minute click by if you listen carefully.

"If you climax more than twice, then you will fail the trial. You can't control what we do to you, nor can you stop us unless you want the trial to end. It's not as easy as you might imagine," he added, "especially as we don't tolerate disobedience. If we tell you to do something to yourself, then you have to obey."

"What if I don't have two orgasms?" asked Grace nervously.

"I don't think that's something you're going to need to worry about!" replied David. "If you've no other questions, we'll start the clock now."

"But that's not fair!" she exclaimed.

His brow darkened. "What do you mean?"

"Andrew's already aroused me before the clock has started."

"He was merely relaxing you," said David. "Amber, start the clock now."

With a brief glance at Grace, Amber did as he'd ordered,

and before Grace knew what was happening Andrew had lifted her up and placed her facedown on the large sofa, which was covered with soft downy pillows.

"Rest your head on your arms," he said quietly, "and close your eyes."

Grace's mouth was dry with fear. Her naked breasts were squashed against the soft pillows, and her lower body sunk into the bolster Amber pushed widthways beneath her. She waited, eyes closed and body tensed, for something to happen.

A sudden drop of warm liquid on her spine made her jump, and her eyes flew open.

"Keep your eyes closed," David reminded her sharply. She realized he must be standing in the nearest corner of the room, watching her intently.

"Apologize," said Amber.

Grace's body stiffened. "Why should I? I wasn't expecting..."

"Obedience at all times, Grace," murmured Andrew, and then his hands began to massage the scented oil into her body.

"I'm sorry," she said, as her breathing quickened.

His fingers were spread out, so that he covered the maximum amount of skin possible, pressing firmly with every upward stroke and then more lightly as his hands returned to their original position. When his fingers covered the sides of her body she moaned with pleasure, and felt a soft tingling begin low down and deep inside her.

"Turn over, but keep your eyes closed," said David.

She started to move, but Andrew flipped her over in one

swift movement before letting his oiled fingers glide down the sides of her neck and along the tops of her breasts. Her whole body felt hot and restless, and she moaned with the pleasure of it.

"She's certainly responsive," said Amber, and Grace could hear the satisfaction in the other woman's voice. It was then she realized that she must try not to become aroused so fast, or she would never last the hour with only two climaxes. She knew her own body, and that she was multiorgasmic. It would be easy to fall into the trap of letting herself be carried away far too soon. Desperately she tried to distance herself from the wonderful sensations.

David saw what she was doing. "Can't you keep your thoughts to yourself, Amber? You've ruined all Andrew's good work now," he said, but he sounded amused, and Grace heard Amber laugh quietly in response. She hated her then, for her obvious closeness to David, and her casual dismissal of Grace's desperate efforts to discipline her own body.

"I don't think so," said Andrew, spreading Grace's arms and legs out until her body formed an X-shape.

Grace could smell the scent of sandalwood as he continued his massage. Now he concentrated even more on her breasts and also the top of her stomach. Because her eyes were closed the sensations were all the more intense. By the time Andrew started to vary the pressure as he stroked her, Grace's whole body was tingling and hot.

He molded his hands around her breasts, lightly at first but then more and more firmly until the pressure was too much and she made a small sound of protest. Ignoring this, he continued to grip the burgeoning flesh tightly and her hips started to move restlessly on the bolster.

Only then did his grip loosen, and now his hands moved to her belly, where once again he pressed very lightly at first but then harder, his long, lean fingers digging into the mound of flesh just above her pubic bone.

Grace groaned as the first darts of hot pleasure began to spark, and she felt the familiar coiling sensation between her thighs that preceded her orgasms. Now his hands were on her thighs, parting them so that her sex was fully exposed.

Gently, stealthily, his hands gripped the tops of her thighs, his thumbs splayed out so that they could tease at the most delicate area of flesh at the very top of her inner thigh. Despite herself, Grace arched her body upwards, suddenly frantic for a more intimate touch as her swollen, aroused body longed for some kind of stimulation between her thighs that would release the pent-up tension.

"Stop!" she protested. "Please, just let me have a minute's respite."

"Be quiet, Grace!" said David harshly. "Don't try to change what's being done to you. That's not allowed."

"She doesn't really want him to stop," said Amber. "She's desperate to come."

"That's true," agreed David. "Tell us if that's true, Gracie," he added, with a touch of such calculated cruelty that Grace wanted to weep. "Tell us," he repeated more firmly.

"Yes," she sobbed, hating herself and them for what was happening to her body. "Yes, it's true."

"What is?" he persisted.

"I want to come," she admitted, and hearing herself say the words served only to increase her longing for release.

She could hear herself whimpering with a mixture of pleasure and frustration, and heard too the sound of Andrew's breathing and Amber's soft laughter.

"It's only been fifteen minutes," said David, yet even his warning couldn't stop her overwhelming need for satisfaction. Tiny cries escaped from her mouth as she moved her hips around, but Andrew was skilled at this game and never went near the hard, swollen nub of pleasure that Grace wanted, needed, to be touched.

For several more minutes he continued to stroke, press and caress her body and then, just as she thought she couldn't bear it any longer, something light brushed against the creases at the tops of her thighs. It felt like a piece of silk, and again her hips jerked upwards.

This time Andrew's hands parted her sex lips and someone else—she had no way of knowing who as her eyes were still closed—drew the silken cloth upwards against her clitoris so that it was brushed three times with the softest of touches and then Andrew pressed down hard with the heel of one hand against her pubic bone while his tongue swirled around the frantic center of her pleasure.

Grace's body jackknifed in a spasm of intense, almost overwhelming release and she cried out with pleasure as her long-delayed orgasm was finally allowed to explode. As it slowly died away her body continued to shudder, because the soft silken cloth was still being trailed between her thighs and it seemed as though the hot, sweet rush of release would never end.

Finally Andrew moved off the sofa, Grace lay still and the room fell silent. "Twenty minutes," said David calmly. "You can open your eyes now."

Feeling exposed and ashamed, Grace decided to keep them closed.

"I said open your eyes," instructed David.

Reluctantly she obeyed him. He was standing at the foot of the couch, looking down at her sweat-streaked body with detached interest. "You enjoyed that didn't you?" he asked.

"Yes," she whispered, unable to make out his expression in the shadowy light from the candles.

"Good. I'm not sure you're totally satisfied though. I think you're going to find it very difficult to last forty minutes with only one more chance of release. What do you think?"

Grace knew that he was right. Now that the last tremors of her climax had died away, she still felt aroused and receptive. She knew that David would be well aware of this, as he had often pleasured her multiple times before having his own orgasm. She bit on her lower lip. "I don't know," she lied.

"Oh I think you do," he said, then sat beside her on the couch, his long, familiar fingers brushing her dark hair off her hot forehead. "You're so beautiful," he murmured, "beautiful and insatiable. It's an irresistible combination."

"Then why isn't it enough for you," she asked softly. "Why do we have to come here and..."

He pressed three fingers tightly against her mouth. "Because it's exciting and challenging. It's impossible to be bored if you belong to the Dining Club."

"But you've never bored me," she protested.

"No whispering," said Andrew with a laugh. "What next, David?"

"I think it's my turn now," said David. "Put the cushions on the floor, Amber."

Taking hold of Grace's hands he helped her off the couch.

Shamed by the way her wanton body had behaved, she kept her eyes averted from Amber and Andrew as David gestured for her to sit on a pile of cushions in front of a large chair, then watched him as he took off his clothes. The sight of his lean but muscular torso made her mouth go dry with desire.

She'd never been as obsessed with a man as she was with David. He was everything she'd dreamed of, or so she'd thought before he'd revealed his other life, and his need for the Dining Club.

Once he was naked he sat himself behind Grace, and she could feel his erection nudging against the base of her spine. He put his feet flat on the floor, so that his knees were raised.

"Put your legs around the outside of mine," he instructed her, "then let your knees fall away to the sides." Once she'd done this he hooked his feet under her ankles and moved his legs to open hers even wider, leaving her sex fully exposed to the watching Amber and Andrew.

"She's still very moist," remarked Amber, sitting down next to them and cupping Grace's sex in one hand.

Grace felt herself flushing with humiliation, trying not to think of how she must look to Amber and Andrew.

"Good," said David, "I was counting on that."

Grace's breath caught in her throat as Amber touched her lightly on the inside of her sex lips before moving away and peeling off her dress. As Grace had guessed, she was totally naked beneath it.

"I'll sit with Andrew and watch," murmured Amber, crouching behind Andrew who was seated on the end of the couch.

"Remember to listen to the clock, Grace," David reminded her.

She couldn't see it from where they were sitting, but she could hear it very clearly. "How much longer before the hour's up?" she asked.

"Thirty minutes, just thirty of those warning clicks," he said. "Remember, failure now means you can never return here with me, and you know what that means."

She did know. It would mean the end of their relationship, the end of any chance of him learning to love her as she loved him. She wondered how he could be cruel enough to remind her of this now, when he was already putting some lubricant on his hands and reaching forward around the lower half of her body.

"Caress your breasts," he whispered in her ear. "Play with them in the way you like me to play with them. Pull on the nipples, make them long and hard. Start now, so that we can work together."

Grace swallowed hard. She was already aroused, but she could hear the click of the minutes, and in the quiet semidarkness the sound seemed to get louder all the time.

"Start now," he whispered, "so that we begin in unison."

Knowing she had to obey, Grace began to caress her nipples, and as they swelled she gently grasped the tips and tugged on them.

"Good," said David. "Now relax against me and give yourself up to the sensations." There was no gentleness in his voice now, he was giving her instructions, and she knew that she had to obey. Part of her was dismayed by this, yet another part was aroused. She was ashamed to realize that his detached yet skillful ministrations were arousing a darkly excited pleasure in her.

Grace leaned the upper half of her torso back against him, and felt his tongue licking her ear in gentle swirls. She shivered with delight, and then his hands were parting her sex lips, and his thumb and forefinger lightly circled her already swelling clitoris. All at once she knew what he was going to do.

"No, don't!" she protested loudly. "That's not fair. You know how quickly I come when you do that!"

"Quiet now or we'll have to gag you. Arguing isn't allowed."

She began to panic. A loud click told her that another minute had passed, but she knew she mustn't orgasm yet, there were still too many minutes left on the clock. "Please," she begged him, and she heard Amber give a low laugh.

"She's so sweet when she begs," said the blonde. "If she passes this trial, she'll be begging even more next month."

Tired of waiting, David started to gently rotate Grace's swollen clitoris between his thumb and forefinger, and with the lubricant he'd put on his fingers mixed with Grace's own juices it quickly swelled more. It was soon one expanding mass of delicate nerve endings, which she was terrified would bring her incredible pleasure far too soon.

"Now for the spin," said David.

She didn't dare protest, but as he began the slow rotating movement that always drove her out of her mind with pleasure she knew that she wouldn't last very long.

The pressure was light at first, yet despite that her whole body tightened, and the tips of her nipples were hard and painful between her own fingers. Pleasure lanced through her body, streaks of it moving from her breasts to her pubic mound and she groaned in ecstasy as the tight, throbbing heat grew behind the core of all her pleasure.

David's breathing quickened, and she felt a drop of moisture fall from his straining penis onto her back. He was almost as near to coming as she was, but that didn't help her as he increased the amount of pressure on her clitoris and the speed of the rotating movement.

"Come now," he murmured against her ear. "You need to come, I can tell. Let the pleasure start. Let it consume you. Think how good it will be when that tightness explodes and…"

His voice had exactly the effect that she knew he'd intended, tipping her over the edge, and Grace heard herself scream with a mixture of ecstasy and despair as her orgasm rushed through her overstimulated body. She arched backwards so that she was pressed tightly against her lover. Her lover, but also the man who had cleverly triggered her release far too soon. As her toes uncurled and the tension in her body ebbed away she wanted to cry at her own weakness, and David's subtle cruelty.

"That only took fifteen minutes," said Amber, her husky voice breaking the silence in the room. "That means she has to last fifteen minutes without another climax."

"She's probably too exhausted to climax again," said Andrew, his voice kind and reassuring.

David laughed shortly. "I very much doubt it. What do you think, Grace?"

Grace didn't answer.

Pulling her across the tops of his thighs, David looked down at her. "I asked you a question. You're expected to reply."

Staring up at him she couldn't see any trace of the man she'd fallen in love with. His eyes were expressionless. He could have been a stranger, and yet unbelievably she didn't think she'd ever wanted him inside her more.

"I'm sorry," she whimpered. "I truly don't know."

"Well, we'll soon find out. I think it's time to bring in Laura."

SEVEN

Within seconds of David pulling on a tasseled bell rope, Laura walked into the room, and Grace realized that the others didn't want to waste any of the fifteen minutes that were ticking away.

As Amber talked to Laura, Andrew pushed a wicker rocking chair into the center of the room. It had rounded metallic edging and a very small cushion on the seat. The two men then led Grace toward the chair, both of them caressing her upper body as they did so.

Out of the corner of her eye, Grace saw that Laura was peeling off a skintight black and white basque while listening attentively to Amber. Then as Grace was placed in the rocking chair, Laura came and stood by David.

"You know what to do?" he queried. She nodded. "Good. Then you'd better get started. She's very ready, it shouldn't take long."

Even the words made Grace's body tremble. He was right, and they all knew it. Her body was very ready for more pleasuring but she had to stop it from happening. She couldn't fail this early on, not the first month. The prospect of losing David was unbearable.

Andrew stood behind the chair, then pulled Grace's arms up and fastened her wrists together behind her head with a Velcro strip. "Put your legs over the sides of the chair now," he said quietly.

As she obeyed, Grace felt the air on her hot flesh, and then she jumped with surprise as Laura knelt down in front of her. "What does she like best?" she asked David, her fingers straying up and down Grace's exposed inner thighs.

"Your special trick will suit her," said David.

Grace heard another click, and knew she was a minute closer to safety. As Laura put her head between her thighs, Andrew began to caress Grace's breasts, which were thrusting upwards because of the way her hands were bound. His fingers moved over her flesh in a steady rhythm, and he kept sliding two fingers on each side of her painfully hard nipples, so that he could squeeze them gently.

Grace was so busy struggling against that pleasure that she jumped with shock when Laura closed her mouth over her vulva, sucking on it for a few seconds while at the same time making the chair rock slowly back and forth.

"Open her up now," said David, and Grace whimpered with fear. She'd heard another minute pass, but had no idea how much longer she had to last. She felt Laura's fingers opening her sex lips, and then came the touch of the small, pointed tip of her tongue. Laura lapped at the exposed clitoris with firm sweeps and Grace felt her belly begin to tighten.

Her breathing began to quicken and she heard Amber say "This won't take long." The words should have been a warning, but they only aroused Grace more, as she struggled to control her body's response to the dual stimulation from Andrew's hands and Laura's skillful mouth and tongue.

"Four minutes left," said David, his voice thick with excitement. "Time for your party piece, Laura."

Grace's hips were twitching, trying to move upwards to the source of the pleasure, and she heard herself panting as the need for release from the hot tightness grew and grew.

Her whole body felt swollen, her breasts were aching, her lower belly trembling with need. She could feel the heat building behind her clitoris, which Laura was now encircling with the very tip of her tongue in a swirling motion that made Grace groan with despairing pleasure, a pleasure that was constantly increased by the gentle rocking motion of the chair.

"I said it was time for your specialty," said David, and Grace could hear the excitement in his voice too.

"Nothing more," she pleaded. "Please nothing more. I'll come, I know I will."

"Two minutes left," said Amber gleefully.

"Don't do anything more, please Laura," cried Grace, unable to keep silent, but she knew that Laura would obey David, and her words counted for nothing.

"Be quiet, Grace! If you say another word you'll fail the trial anyway," said David sharply.

Laura paused for a second, her tongue motionless, and then she moved her head a little to one side, sucked lightly on Grace's frantic clitoris and very gently pressed a finger against the delicate area just below it, around the opening to the urethra.

Grace gave a moan of frantic pleasure as a deep throbbing began and heat suffused the whole area. "No, don't do that!" she shouted, but Laura continued sucking and licking

Grace's tormented bud of pleasure while relentlessly increasing the pressure of her finger.

Grace's body could take no more. Her hips thrust upwards, the darts of pleasure merged into one and with a cry of despairing ecstasy she climaxed. Her whole body was racked by spasms of forbidden pleasure, and she sobbed aloud at her body's weakness.

Andrew released her wrists, Laura moved away and Grace was left alone, her body still trembling from the intensity of her climax. She'd kept her eyes closed during the trial, but now she opened them and saw David standing in front of her.

"I tried," she said, tears forming in her eyes. "Truly I did, but I couldn't last any longer. I wanted to succeed and..."

"You did succeed," he said gently. "You succeeded by fifteen seconds. Didn't you hear the click before you came?"

Grace shook her head, and now the tears rolling down her face were tears of relief. Hastily she brushed them away with her hands, not wanting the others to see.

"Don't cry," he said softly. "You were amazing. I was so proud of you." Carefully he helped her out of the chair, wrapped a soft toweling robe around her then drew her close to him. His arms were tight around her body, and she could feel his erection through the robe. "I've never wanted you so much before," he murmured.

Looking around, Grace saw that they were the only two people left in the room. "Don't you mind watching other people do that to me? Why do you need...?"

"You loved it too," he said softly. "Don't pretend you didn't. You've never had orgasms like that before have you?"

"No, but..."

"I can't wait much longer," he said, his voice thick with longing.

Almost before she knew what was happening, he'd removed her robe and was naked himself. Then he sat down in the rocking chair, where she'd suffered such delicious torment, and putting his hands around her waist he lifted her onto his lap so that she was facing him. "Put your legs over my shoulders," he said huskily, and as she obeyed he pulled her even closer to him until he could slide his rock-hard erection deep inside her.

To her surprise, Grace realized that now she wanted him too. After all he'd put her through she'd been left feeling angry and bewildered. But her anger, combined with hearing the urgency in his voice, and knowing that he was desperate for her, were proving incredibly arousing.

Using his feet to control the movements of the chair David built up a steady rhythm with his hands gripping her around her rib cage, and she threw back her head in wild enjoyment as she was at last filled by him, by the man she loved.

She tightened her internal muscles around him, forcing his pleasure to spill quicker than usual and then screamed aloud with what was almost a cry of triumph at the final rush of hot, all-engulfing pleasure that spread through her body as they climaxed together.

David gave a muffled groan. She lowered her legs and then they wrapped their arms around each other, waiting for their breathing to slow and the last flickers of pleasure to die away.

"I knew I was right about you," murmured David a little

later, as he helped her put her dress back on. "You were amazing, my darling, absolutely amazing."

———

When she woke the next morning, Grace couldn't remember how they'd got back to their room. She realized she must have been so exhausted that she'd slept the sleep of the dead. Beside her, David was still sleeping, and in sleep he looked younger, more vulnerable, than usual.

Gently she brushed a lock of hair off his forehead, and immediately his eyes opened. "Good morning, beautiful Grace," he murmured, and she snuggled up close to him.

"Do we have lunch here before we leave?" she asked.

David yawned and stretched himself before kissing her lightly on the mouth. "You're always hungry, although after last night it's not surprising!"

She felt herself blushing, and he smiled. "There's no need to blush. You were fantastic. We all had a wonderful time. I told you there was nothing to worry about."

Remembering all that had happened, and what she'd allowed strangers to do to her, Grace wasn't sure she agreed with him, but she knew he was right about one thing. To her own astonishment, she had enjoyed most of it, and she knew it would take her time to come to terms with what she was learning about herself.

"It wasn't easy," she said quietly. "Do you like watching your girlfriends having sex with strangers?"

"I like watching people learn about their sexuality, discovering new things about themselves," he replied. "And

I only bring very special women here, for obvious reasons. How about we share a bath now?"

Grace was tempted, but there was something she needed to know before that happened. "Maybe later," she replied. "Right now I want to know about table five."

David rolled onto his back, his arms behind his head, and sighed. "I don't know why you're so interested. It needn't concern you at all. In any case, Club rules forbid it until table four has been completed. Only then does table five have any meaning."

"That's not fair. It's obviously important, and if it's going to be my final challenge then I want to know in what way it's different."

"It's the rules, Grace, and anyway it's irrelevant right now. You have three more weekend trials to complete before table five will mean anything to you. All I can say is that table five is best described as an optional extra. Does that satisfy you?"

"No, it makes me more eager to know about it! But you give me your word that then you can tell me?"

"Surprisingly," said David slowly, "I'm beginning to have a feeling that I may have to tell you. Now, how about that bath?"

Three hours later, with David wearing a sports jacket, open-neck shirt and casual trousers, and Grace in the pale green A-line dress she'd originally intended to wear the previous evening, they went down to the dining room.

Only one other table was occupied when they sat down. "Where is everyone?" asked Grace in surprise.

"They've probably left. Some of them come quite a distance and have a long drive back. Amber and Andrew will join us though. I'll ask Laura to get us some drinks. She's usually working on Sundays."

A few minutes later, Laura came into the dining room. She was wearing a conventional waitress's uniform, except for the fact that the skirt was very short and over her white top was a black strapless boned corset. Grace felt very uncomfortable seeing her, remembering only too clearly what Laura had done to her the previous evening, and how she'd given her such incredible pleasure.

Laura though looked tired and heavy-eyed as she took the drinks order.

"I hear you had a problem last night," said David. Laura shook her head. "No, I didn't. It was only that…"

"Amber told me all about it. I hope it doesn't happen again, or your time here will come to an end I'm afraid."

"It was Amber's fault, she made me…"

"Laura!" David's voice was sharp, and the blonde twin chewed nervously on her bottom lip. "I'm sorry," she said apologetically.

"I'm sure you are. We'd like some wine please. White zinfandel for Grace and a sparkling water for me. I'm driving this afternoon unfortunately."

He smiled at Laura then, but she only nodded and scurried away.

"Whatever's the matter with her?" asked Grace.

"She disobeyed an order later last night and had to be punished for it. Amber has had problems with Laura before, but the twins add something to the Dining Club. I hope we don't have to let them go."

"Did Amy cause a problem too?"

"Not that I know of, but aesthetically it wouldn't be the same to keep one of the girls. The Dining Club would have to train up another pair of twins if Laura doesn't improve. I imagine Amber will keep her under control though. She's very strict with the staff. That's why the standard is so high."

"What's it all got to do with you?" asked Grace. "You don't run the Club."

"I'm one of the financial backers for the Dining Club, so naturally I'm interested in what's happening," he said smoothly. "I try to keep a sharp eye on all my financial investments."

Grace, who hadn't liked Amber at all the previous night, thought that the change in Laura since she'd last seen her was so huge that she dreaded to think what punishment the blonde woman could have inflicted on the younger girl.

"I meant to be here to greet you both," said Andrew, coming into the dining room. He smiled warmly at Grace, kissing her on both cheeks before sitting down at the table with them. As he started to ask her questions about her work, Grace's worries about Laura were quickly forgotten.

Eventually Amber joined them as well, and over Sunday lunch of roast beef followed by lemon mousse, conversation flowed easily.

At two o'clock David glanced at his watch and turned to Grace. "We'd better be going. I have to drop you at your apartment, and then I have a business meeting."

Grace, who'd been expecting him to spend a few more hours with her, couldn't hide her expression of disappointment.

"Haven't you seen enough of each other for one weekend, Grace?" asked Amber, getting up and standing behind David, her hands resting on his shoulders.

Grace didn't like this possessive gesture, or the way Amber was looking at her as though she was an amusing toy who was no longer needed. "No," she said shortly.

Amber massaged David's shoulders. "You feel tense, David. Didn't the weekend relax you enough?"

"Stop it, Amber," said Andrew sharply. "I'm sure Grace is tired of us being around by now."

In fact, Grace wasn't tired of Andrew at all. The more she saw of him, the more she liked him. He was always so relaxed and laid-back, and unlike David he was easy company. With Andrew what you saw was what you got, and she liked what she saw. David didn't let you see very much, but she realized that was probably why she was so obsessed with him.

Half an hour later the two of them were driving out of the gates of the Dining Club. "I take it you'll be coming with me next month?" asked David.

"Yes, I will, if that's what you want too?"

He glanced across at her. "It's definitely what I want, but it won't be quite as easy next time. The first test is always pure pleasure."

Remembering how she'd struggled to control her desires, and how she'd wept in his arms when Saturday night was over, Grace wondered how he could call her experience pure pleasure, but she knew better than to say anything. If she really wanted this man to love her, then she needed to know what his deepest desires were, and whether or not she would be able to fulfill them.

"I'll remember that. Will I see you next weekend?"

David shook his head. "I wish we could meet, but I have to work. I'm sorry about that, and I don't expect any sympathy from you about how hard businessmen have to work," he added teasingly.

A part of her wondered if he was testing her, trying to assess if she was becoming needy. She'd always known, instinctively, that he wouldn't like that.

"That's lucky really," she replied. "I've got a busy week coming up, but I need to meet up with Fran sometime. Now I can do it at the weekend, so it suits me very well."

"Good," he said, squeezing her knee lightly and smiling at her.

She was surprised, and rather pleased, to note that he didn't actually sound as happy with her reply as she'd expected.

Once at her flat he carried her case inside, pulled her to him, kissed her hard on the mouth as his hands cupped the sides of her face and then released her. "I'll be in touch later in the week," he promised. Then before she could say any more, he was gone, leaving her alone with her vivid memories of Saturday night.

Later in the evening she started to think about her next visit to the Club. After everything that had happened to her this time, she wondered what she would have to do in four weeks' time. Clearly the experience would not, as David had said himself, be pure pleasure, and she now knew exactly what that meant.

She remembered how she'd struggled to control herself, begging Laura not to touch her because she couldn't discipline her body any longer. The fear she'd experienced on entering the trial room was still vivid in her mind, but so too was the intensity of the orgasms they'd teased from her.

Even thinking about it started to arouse her again, and she realized that she was excited at the prospect of what lay ahead. Excited, yet at the same time scared. To make matters worse, the fear itself seemed to have become an aphrodisiac.

The whole weekend had showed her a side of herself that she'd never known existed, but whether she would still enjoy the experience the next time, when everything was going to be more intense, and they would doubtless be testing her reactions to different methods of arousal, she didn't know.

All she knew as she lay in bed that night, her fingers lightly caressing her body to try and ease the sexual tensions her thoughts were arousing in her, was that despite being nervous she was rapidly becoming consumed by an overwhelming desire for her next visit to the Dining Club. Yet at the same time she was filled with anxiety as to whether or not she would be able to endure, let alone pass, the trial that awaited her.

PART THREE

Crave

EIGHT

Grace slept through the alarm the following morning, which meant she was half an hour late for the meeting with her friend Fran, who had written the play Grace was hoping to put on by the end of the year. Their meeting was in a small hired studio at Covent Garden, and she grabbed a doughnut and plastic beaker of coffee on her way in.

Luckily Fran had the key, and was sitting on a black plastic chair looking decidedly fed up when Grace finally burst into the room. "I was about to phone you," she said by way of greeting. "You did suggest ten this morning didn't you? It's now ten-thirty and my backside is numb from sitting on this horrible chair!"

"Sorry," apologized Grace, "I overslept."

"Busy weekend?"

Grace's mind flashed back to the moment Laura had brought her to a shattering climax, and she felt the blood rush to her cheeks. "It was rather. Now…"

"Were you with your rich financier boyfriend?" asked Fran.

"What do you mean?"

"Oh come on, David White, who could give us enough money to put my play on at the Young Vic if he wanted to. Only he wouldn't want to, because he doesn't understand the problems facing artistic people, especially in a recession."

Grace was so taken aback she didn't know how to respond. "What does it matter to you who I go out with?" she asked, after a pause to muster her thoughts.

"It doesn't really, but I'm a bit shocked. He's the polar opposite of all we believe in. I only know you're going out with him because you were mentioned in a tabloid gossip column yesterday."

"What did it say?"

"Something about the incongruous pairing of an up-and-coming, groundbreaking stage director and her rich financier boyfriend, and it named you both. At least it means you're getting yourself noticed I suppose."

"Not that it's any of your business, but he happens to be a patron of the arts. That's how I met him, at a fundraising event for the new Going Places theater company."

"You are naive," said Fran. "It's almost certainly a useful tax dodge for him. Anyway, it won't matter. You should be careful not to get too emotionally involved. The article said he's fiercely private and has never shown any interest in settling down."

"Settling down sounds so boring and conventional it's not something I'd want to do either," she retorted.

Fran looked surprised. "My goodness, you really must like him to be that defensive. Is he good in bed? Men like that are usually total control freaks and pretty selfish that way, or so I'm told. I've never been out with one."

"No, you haven't, so you don't know a thing about him or people like him. Let's leave the gossip and get on with the work shall we?" snapped Grace.

"Oh come on, there's no need to be so intense about

it all. You haven't been going out with him long have you? Apparently he went out with that actress Isla Roberts last year. Mind you, rumor has it she's never got over him, so he must be good at something!"

Grace wasn't aware that David even knew Isla Roberts, let alone that he'd taken her out and wondered if the tall, willowy redhead had ever visited the Dining Club. She tried to picture her being pleasured by Laura's clever tongue, but her imagination failed her. Isla had always struck her as being very shy, as many actors were when they weren't performing.

"Hello!" said Fran loudly. "Turning up late is bad enough, but daydreaming once you arrive is even worse. Drink your coffee and then perhaps you can tell me your thoughts on who would be right for the two leading roles, providing you can concentrate, that is!"

Taking a deep breath, Grace pushed the images of Isla at the Dining Club that were rushing into her mind firmly away. "I'm sorry, I just had a heavy weekend. I thought perhaps Mark Lewis might be good if he's available by the time we get a venue."

"Mark Lewis? He's tall and slim. Martin, who we need to cast, is short, stocky and useful in a fight. Mark Lewis looks as though he'd fall over in a strong wind! Get a grip, Grace."

Slowly Grace was drawn back into the world of work, a world that had previously consumed almost every waking moment of her time, but try as she might memories of her weekend at the Dining Club still flickered in the background of her mind, like an old film on a projector screen.

At the same time as Grace was struggling to concentrate on work, Amber and Andrew were sitting in the study of the Dining Club. They were working on scenarios for the next month's meeting, and Amber wasn't happy. She had a bad feeling about Grace, who'd done far better than most people did at their first trial, and could clearly prove to be more of a challenge than she'd expected.

The two of them had left Grace's next trial until last, and when Andrew handed Amber the blank form she knew exactly what she'd like to put on it, but knew too that it wouldn't be allowed for only the second trial.

"No ideas?" asked Andrew.

"Plenty, but none of them will be of any use yet," she replied.

"What's the matter?"

"I'm worried, that's what's the matter," she retorted.

"In what way?"

Sometimes, thought Amber irritably, being handsome and nice didn't make up for being unobservant. "Because she could be a threat to me and my position here, of course."

Andrew laughed. "I rather doubt it. She found her first trial difficult; she's not likely to want to take you on even if she does complete all five trials successfully."

"I wish I shared your confidence, but I don't. She's very determined, in work as well as play, from what I read when I Googled her. That's what will drive her on. She'll push herself to the limit rather than fail, and I think David wants her to succeed."

"Of course he does. He's falling in love with her."

Amber looked at him in astonishment. "David doesn't fall in love, he falls in lust."

"That's not true. He's fallen in love twice before, which is why he's brought two other women here. Admittedly he doesn't fall in love easily, but it does happen. He doesn't like to admit it though. I agree that he really wants Grace to succeed, but that's because he loves her. He still won't break the rules."

"That would be stupid of him, since he made them up," said Amber. "But you're wrong about him. I know him better than any woman, and love isn't in his nature. All the same, the sooner Grace fails the happier I'll be. I think she'll struggle next time. Bondage and submission aren't going to make her happy, especially as I'm going to use Will rather than you, Andrew. Will is brilliant at bondage. I'll save Amy for the third weekend, in case Grace does get through next time."

"Be careful, Amber. Remember, David will be there again, and he'll probably take part as well because he likes that theme. If you go too far you'll damage your own cause."

"I'll run the scenario past him next weekend. He wants a meeting then, and Laura has to be disciplined."

"I thought you'd done that."

Amber gave a slow smile. "David wants to make quite sure she's learned her lesson. He doesn't want to have to train up another pair of twins. He'll stay overnight, and that will give me a chance to please him in ways little Miss Grace would never think of."

"He's staying over despite Grace?" Andrew's voice showed his surprise.

"Yes, so as you can tell he's not intending to give me up for love!"

Andrew put a hand on Amber's left wrist. "He's never going to love you, Amber. You have to accept that."

Furious, she snatched her arm away. "I know that. I've just told you that he'll never love anyone."

"Then what's the point in you falling in love with him?"

"I'm not," she lied. "But I do like this life, my work here and the things we do to please each other. I don't want to lose any of that. What would I do without the Dining Club?"

"I'm quite sure that Grace, who's beginning to build a good career for herself in the theater, won't want to give all that up and run this place instead," said Andrew reassuringly. "It wouldn't make sense. She's only here to please David, like the other two he brought. They weren't a threat, they didn't get anywhere near the top table."

"It would make sense if she loves him, and I think you underestimate her as well. She's tougher than she looks."

"This is meant to be a place of pleasure," said Andrew.

Amber smiled. "I know that, but sometimes the pleasure is mixed with pain, and that's where Grace will fall down. That's something I can make sure of, and I think I'll use Laura's punishment time as a trial run for one or two of my ideas."

"Suit yourself then," said Andrew. "I must get back to the office now, or my secretary will wonder what my dentist is doing to me!"

After he'd gone, Amber returned to the study and picked up the form for Grace's next visit. It was still blank, and she slid it into the top drawer of her desk. She'd fill it in after David had finished overseeing the disciplining of Laura. If she had her way, she thought with a smile, Grace wasn't likely to pass her second trial at the Dining Club.

The following Saturday, Grace and Fran had spent the day together discussing a possible alteration to the ending of the play. When Fran finally left the flat it was early evening. Glancing at her watch, Grace saw that it was six-thirty, and realized that exactly a week had passed since she and David had sat down to dinner at the Dining Club.

She hadn't seen him since their return, and was missing him, but knew that he'd said he would be busy working this weekend. However, he'd phoned her twice in the week, and the second time he'd told her that he had tickets for the Opera at Covent Garden the following weekend and suggesting they also have a meal first.

She was looking forward to that, and hoped they'd go back to his flat afterwards, as she was missing him terribly. Since the previous weekend she'd thought more about sex than at any other time in her life, which was shaming but also exciting. She was even looking forward to their next visit, wondering what her trial would involve this time.

Little did she know, as she settled down with a glass of wine to watch the final season of *The Killing* that her lover was already back at the Dining Club. This was lucky, because if she had known, and been able to see what was happening, she might not have been quite as eager for her next visit.

Across London, Laura was lying on a high, narrow bed in the center of one of the smaller bedrooms. Heavy curtains had been drawn across the windows, leaving the room in semidarkness.

Her wrists were fastened to metal rings on each side of the bed, her legs held apart by a spreader board, and she couldn't speak because of the gag in her mouth. She had no means of communicating with anyone except through her eyes.

She was sobbing softly, her body taut as Amber and Will worked on her with their clever, knowing fingers, hands and mouths. Every time she climaxed, she was punished and the mixture of pain and pleasure meant that there was never any respite for her tormented flesh.

Watching her hapless, shuddering body from the corner of the room, David noted every nuance of expression in Laura's pleading eyes and mentally replaced the softly moaning twin with Grace.

As the unfortunate girl strained against her bonds, he pictured Grace in the same situation, her gentle curves tightening as she struggled to escape her clever tormentors. He swallowed hard, aroused almost beyond control at the thought.

Suddenly a desperate muffled scream filled the room, and David was drawn back to what was happening at that moment. He realized that Will, who was standing over Laura with a slim riding crop in his hand, the end trailing over the blonde girl's heaving belly, was looking to him for guidance. Laura was shuddering violently, clearly still recovering from yet another pain-tinged orgasm, and Will wanted to know whether to continue or not.

"Go on," said Amber, her voice cold and emotionless. "She needs to understand the gravity of what she did last weekend."

David crossed the room and looked down at Laura, whose tear-filled eyes looked pleadingly up at him. Removing her gag he wiped away a teardrop. "Have you learned your lesson, Laura?" he asked quietly.

"Yes, yes I have. I promise that I have," she sobbed. "Please make them stop. They're hurting me."

"But your body likes it, doesn't it?" he said, putting his hand between her thighs and running a finger up and down the soft, damp channels inside her outer sex lips. She jerked beneath her bonds, and when he pulled back the hood that was covering her clitoris and swirled his finger around the retreating bud she cried out again. "Don't, please don't! I mustn't come again. I don't want more punishment."

"Make her come," urged Amber. "It was her stupidity that ruined table two's test last weekend, and now that has to be run all over again."

After a moment's reflection, David shook his head. "I'm sure she's learned her lesson now. Will, you can take your pleasure with her before she's released though. She should enjoy that. No pain this time, only pleasure," he added as reassurance for the still whimpering Laura.

Will didn't need telling twice, and as he moved to cover Laura's body with his own, David turned on his heel and left the room, with Amber close behind him.

"That should make certain we don't have any more problems with her," said David. "Remember though, there always has to be pleasure as well as pain. Sometimes I think you forget that, Amber."

"Of course," agreed Amber. "Now shall we go upstairs to my room?"

David hesitated, but he couldn't get the image of Grace, bound and gagged, lying helpless beneath his hands, out of his thoughts. "I've changed my mind," he said shortly. "I'd better get back. I've some important business calls to make tonight. I'll see you at the next official weekend."

Amber looked at him in disbelief. "Didn't watching Laura turn you on?"

"Of course, but as I said, I need to leave."

"Don't you want to see the outline for Grace's next visit before you go?" persisted Amber.

David shook his head. "I imagine I've just seen most of it while watching Laura, haven't I?"

"It's similar," she admitted.

"Then that's fine. You've never let me down yet, Amber, and I have every confidence in you. You're the perfect hostess for the Dining Club. Believe me no one appreciates your skills more than I do." He kissed her hard, his hands tight on her shoulders, the fingers digging into her hot flesh, before walking away down the corridor.

It was then that Amber knew for certain that Grace was just as dangerous to her as she'd feared, and would have to be stopped.

NINE

Closing the zip on her weekend bag, Grace wondered where the past month had gone. Despite only seeing David twice, the time had flown by. After the opera, they'd gone back to his flat and he'd made tender love to her for longer than ever. He'd also held her close all night, something he'd never done before, and when she'd woken on the Sunday morning he'd been propped up on one elbow gazing down at her tenderly.

Their second meeting had been a more public one. He'd taken her to the opening of a new art gallery owned by a friend. The press had been there, but when a photographer had approached them David had swiftly turned away, and no photo was taken.

It had been a good evening though, and this time they'd gone back to her flat where he'd taken her quickly, almost roughly, and the unexpected urgency and change in his approach had excited her so much she'd come with shaming speed. He hadn't spent the night with her, but instead had dressed and left within an hour. When he left he'd told her that he couldn't wait for their next visit to the Dining Club, and the look of excitement in his eyes had aroused her so much that she'd asked him to stay longer but he'd only smiled and shook his head.

Thinking about this she felt a tremor run through her, as

she began to wonder about what lay ahead this time. Then her doorbell rang twice, and picking up her case she went downstairs to where she knew her lover would be waiting for her.

David was unusually quiet on the drive, and Grace began to feel less excited and more nervous. "Is anything wrong?" she asked.

"Of course not. Why?"

"Nothing, you're just rather quiet."

"Sorry, the traffic seems extra heavy this morning."

It seemed the same as usual to Grace, but she kept that thought to herself. "I didn't bring any dresses. You said you'd choose one again didn't you?

"Yes, and I have. You'll like it. How are you feeling?" he added. "Excited?"

"Excited and nervous," admitted Grace. "I suppose it will be a different sort of test this time?"

"Naturally, but I'm sure you'll do really well. I think I should warn you that there'll be two of you having the same trial, because of a problem last time. The lady at table two last month couldn't finish the trial due to a mistake made by one of the staff. It made more sense for the two of you to take the test together this time, as the same staff will be needed for you both."

Grace was horrified. "I don't want another guest to be there!" she protested.

"I don't see why not. It will be company for you. Of course, as she's already experienced what it's about, you won't be in competition with her. She'll be expected to do better than you, so if anything she's the one who should be upset, but I'm sure she won't complain. Guests rarely do," he added.

"That means that the man who's brought her to the Club will be in the room as well, and able to watch me!" exclaimed Grace.

David swung the car into the private road that housed the Dining Club and waited to be let through the gates. He rested his left hand lightly on her knee. "He'll be too busy watching his own companion to watch you."

"He might enjoy watching both of us," said Grace with horror.

The gate was opened and David drove slowly down the road toward the Club. "He might, and I might as well, come to that. Be grateful, Grace. In a couple of months' time that will happen anyway. This will give you quite an advantage for that weekend."

"I don't think..."

"Darling, I really hope you're not going to disappoint me," he said softly.

In the silence that followed his remark she felt a moment of overwhelming fear. "No, of course not!" she said hastily. "I only meant..."

"That's good to hear," he said, smiling warmly at her as he parked in his usual place before getting out of the car. "Perhaps we'll have a swim before lunch this time. That might relax you."

Struggling to cope with all that he'd told her, and to adjust to what she was learning about him, Grace got out of the car and waited by the front door with him. Before she'd learned more details she'd been strangely excited, almost eager for her trial, but now she was very nervous.

Once they were inside a well-built, fair-haired young man led them up to the suite they'd had before. "I thought you'd like the same rooms," said David.

"You were right, I love this suite," exclaimed Grace, the sight of the familiar fabrics and furniture calming her nerves. "It's so beautiful, like something from the Edwardian era."

"Would you like a swim? We can eat up here afterwards rather than downstairs."

The prospect of spending more time alone with David than she had the previous month cheered Grace up even more. She quickly changed into her burgundy and black bikini, put on a white toweling robe that was hanging in the en suite bathroom and then followed David down some back stairs that led directly to the pool area.

The large kidney-shaped pool had half a dozen chairs around the sides, and huge sliding glass doors all down one side. These not only let in a lot of light, but also allowed people strolling in the grounds outside to look in.

Grace was a strong swimmer, as was David, and soon they were both powering up and down the pool. No one else was using it, and after they'd done a few lengths David grabbed hold of her around the waist, lifted her legs so that she was floating on her back and then put a hand in the small of her back to push her stomach up out of the water. Next he nibbled at the bare flesh, while his fingers drummed between her thighs, against the tight material of her bikini bottom.

She moaned at the delicious pleasure as tendrils of excitement snaked through her body. Totally relaxed she felt his fingers ease the edges of her bikini bottom to one side so that he could stroke her swelling sex lips and she gave a tiny cry of excitement.

Quickly he guided her to the side of the pool, and she rested her arms on the white tiles surrounding it while he continued to arouse her with his fingers. Finally he pushed the bottom half of her body high out of the water, put her legs over his shoulders and pushing the material to one side closed his mouth over her vulva.

She heard herself breathing heavily, gasping as he increased and then decreased the pressure from his mouth. It was as though he was drawing all the darts of pleasure toward his mouth while the warm water lapped at the rest of her body. For a fleeting second his tongue darted inside her, and she felt her body stiffen as her climax approached. Then, with no warning, he moved the bottom of the bikini so that she was covered once again, and then swam slowly away.

"Come back!" shouted Grace. "You can't leave me like this!" but he simply looked back over his shoulder at her, laughing at her desperation to climax. Her whole body felt heavy and the pressure behind her clitoris almost unbearable.

Furious, she pulled herself out of the pool, grabbed her towel and was about to walk out when David came up behind her and caught hold of her shoulders. "Lie on one of the chairs and finish yourself off," he whispered. "Let me watch you masturbate. I know how near you are. It won't take any time."

"What if someone comes in?" asked Grace, wishing that she didn't want to do as he asked.

"They won't. You know you want to do it," and he trailed his fingers down the sides of her body.

That was what decided her. Her whole body was so desperate for an orgasm, and she was so excited by his suggestion, that now nothing else mattered. Quickly she lay down on a recliner pool chair, pushed her right hand inside her bikini bottom and groaned as her fingers moved over the needy, slippery flesh until she found the vital spot near the stem of the clitoris that always triggered an orgasm for her.

She could hear David's rapid breathing as her fingers swirled around the clitoris before pressing more firmly against the tiny stem. Then, with a cry of delight she felt the familiar sweet explosion of release and shuddered as the shockwaves of pleasure rushed through her body.

"Wonderful!" exclaimed David, bending down to kiss her passionately on the mouth. Reaching up, she put her arms around his neck to draw him closer as her breathing slowly returned to normal, totally unaware of the small camera positioned high up near the ceiling in the opposite wall, recording every detail.

Later, after eating a salad that David had sent up to their room for her, she sat in a chair by one of the windows and idly replayed the scene in her mind as the sun streamed in on her. She felt relaxed and happy, and when David went off to talk to Andrew her eyelids grew heavy and the next thing she knew he was waking her from a deep sleep.

"Lightweight!" he said with a laugh.

Stretching luxuriously she smiled up at him. "Everything all right below stairs?"

"Fine. They're all set up for tonight's dining experience."

The total relaxation that had followed her sleep vanished, and Grace felt herself tense. "Should I be worried?"

"Of course not. Remember, you're doing this for us. Pleasure is the name of the game."

Remembering her first visit she wondered if he really believed everything that had happened to her then had been pleasurable, but she didn't say a word. She desperately wanted to enter his world, become so much a part of him that he would never want to leave her.

"Don't you want to look at your dress for the evening?" he asked. She did, and when he opened the wardrobe door she gave a cry of delight.

It was floor-length, red, and strapless, with a wide, white cummerbund just beneath the bust that was decorated with embroidered red flowers. Below that the material was tightly ruched until it met with a line of carefully embroidered white blossoms running diagonally from the left hip to what she thought was probably the top of the right thigh, and at the bottom of the dress the red silk was cut into a high v-shape. The gap had been filled with white satin covered in delicate lace. She'd never seen anything like it. Until she'd met David, clothes hadn't been that important to her. Now she was discovering how clothes could not only enhance how she looked, but also add to the sensuality of a special evening.

"I thought of you the moment I saw it," said David. "You'll look stunning wearing it. It's a shame you won't be wearing it for long, but you'll certainly make an entrance when we go down to dinner."

"What do you mean about not wearing it for long?"

"It's hardly the right dress for the after-dinner activities, is it?"

Her delight ebbed away, to be replaced by nerves, but nerves tinged with excitement. "I suppose not," she agreed.

"Believe me, you'll look even more beautiful later on tonight," he murmured, his mouth nuzzling the side of her neck, and she shivered, but whether with fear or desire she didn't know.

David had been right about her entrance to the dining room. They were the last to take their places for dinner, at table two this time, and all eyes were on her as she crossed the floor. "I wonder if they realize you're naked beneath it?" he murmured, his hand in the small of her back as he guided her to her seat.

No sooner was she sitting down than Amber was standing by their table. "What a beautiful dress," she said sweetly. "It suits your dark coloring, but then David has exquisite taste. He knows exactly how he likes his women to look."

Grace looked at Amber's ankle-length halter neck dress in pale lemon with a plunging neckline that revealed her tawny skin, and noticed too the long diamond and ruby earrings she was wearing with a matching necklace, and understood what she was being told. David chose Amber's dresses as well, and had probably been doing so for far longer than he'd known her.

Inwardly she was filled with jealousy, but she smiled as

she agreed with their hostess, hoping her eyes didn't give away what she was really feeling.

"I understand the dessert for your table has already been chosen," continued Amber.

Grace shook her head. "No."

"It has, my darling. If you remember I told you last month that you would have to leave the Controlled Chocolate Delight for another month," said David.

"I thought you meant for another time, and it's not what I want this weekend," she retorted.

Amber stood quite still, her face expressionless.

"No, I meant 'another month' in the same way as a doctor might say that he'd see you in 'another month,'" replied David calmly. "In any case, as I told you, there will be a second guest retaking the same trial, so it can't be altered."

The clinging bodice of the beautiful dress suddenly felt too tight, as though it was imprisoning her, and Grace felt panic rising in her. She'd forgotten that she'd be doing the trial at the same time as another woman. "I..."

"Do you have a problem with this?" David's voice was gentle, almost caressing, but his mouth was set in a tight line and when she looked into his eyes she could see that he was actually annoyed.

"You don't have to choose it," said Amber. "The Dining Club exists purely for pleasure. It would be silly to spoil your evening by doing something you didn't want to do."

At that moment Grace knew beyond any shadow of a doubt that Amber was her enemy. She wanted her to fail, to walk away from one of the trials, and there could only be one reason for that, and that reason was David.

"It's fine; I was confused, that's all," she responded. Her reward came both from the tender smile from David and the brief flare of annoyance that crossed Amber's beautiful face.

To her disappointment, Andrew didn't join them for the meal, and she realized she'd been looking forward to talking to him again, but she quite liked the newcomer, who introduced himself as Will and said he'd been assistant manager at the Dining Club for six months.

By the time the main course of fish in a light lemon sauce had been eaten and digested, Grace's nerves were on edge. As everyone began to leave the dining room she looked across to table three. To her dismay the petite red-haired young woman who was sitting there was crying softly. Her male companion had his arm around her, and was obviously trying to both comfort and encourage her, but it was quite clear that the woman didn't want to retake the trial that she'd started the month before.

"Why's she crying like that?" asked Grace. "If she doesn't want to do it, he should take her home."

"I'm sure he would, but she's crying because she's torn between wanting to do it for his sake and not doing it because it's not really what she enjoys."

"Why? What happens?" asked Grace, becoming more anxious by the minute.

"Don't worry, you'll be fine, my love," he promised her. "Remember many people don't complete the experience. She might be one of those. It's also a great shame that she's having to do some of this section twice. It's never happened before," he added, clearly annoyed that it had happened at all.

Just before they left the dining room he went across and spoke to the red-haired girl's partner. "It's all right, she wants to do it because they're hoping to get married," he said steering Grace out through a different door from the previous month and down some stairs to what she assumed must be a basement room.

"I don't understand why she wants to marry someone if what he enjoys makes her cry that much," retorted Grace.

"She might change her mind about him. It does happen." Opening a heavy wooden door he stood back to let her enter. All Grace could think was that she didn't want the same thing to happen to her.

For a moment she paused at the basement entrance. There was something about a basement room that was more frightening than an ordinary room. It was more cut off from the rest of the Club, and bound to be dark.

"Table three's guest will be here in a few minutes," said David, as she finally found the courage to enter and he closed the heavy, soundproofed door behind them.

As she'd feared the room was darker than any of the others Grace had been in, and in the middle of the floor there were two very high beds that looked more like doctors' examination couches than proper beds. In the shadows of the room she could see little tables and chests of drawers, and above the beds there was a large light that wasn't yet switched on.

Laura was there, looking more subdued than usual, as were Will and Amber. Stepping forward, Laura walked around the back of Grace and went to unzip her dress. Grace took a step away from the girl. Everything about the room, and the air of excited anticipation and heightened sexuality in it, scared her.

She looked across at David, hoping to see some reassurance and encouragement in his face, but it was totally impassive. Mutely she allowed the blonde girl to continue.

"It's time to take this gorgeous dress off," explained Laura. "It's really lovely. You looked beautiful in it."

As the dress fell into a pool around her feet, leaving her naked and totally exposed to everyone in the room, Grace instinctively covered her breasts and pubic mound with her hands.

"There's no need to be shy, Grace," said David. "You still look beautiful, don't you think, Will?"

"Stunning," agreed Will.

"I'll help you into your new outfit," continued Laura, bringing a short leather dress over to the waiting Grace. "It should fit you perfectly; it was made to measure."

Bewildered, Grace tried to step into the dress but Laura explained that it would only go on over her head, so she raised her arms and tried not to think about what she must look like to the watching people as her breasts lifted and the dress was pulled down her body inch by inch.

"It's very tight," she protested.

"It's meant to be tight," said Laura, tugging on the hem. "You have to wriggle a bit to help me."

"Let me," said David, and his strong hands quickly adjusted the skintight leather garment, making it very apparent that it wasn't a dress at all. Grace's breasts were thrust through openings in the front, part of her stomach was exposed through another opening and her buttocks were totally revealed at the back. It was so short that it ended just above her pubic mound, leaving her trapped and exposed.

"Now I'm going to lift you onto the bed," said David, his eyes bright with excitement. As he settled her in place, her buttocks slotting into a hole in the bed, she heard the door opening and the sound of new voices.

"It's table three," said David quietly. "You don't need to worry about them. They're not involved with your trial, although you and your fellow guest may find it interesting to hear each other's reactions. Interesting and stimulating," he added, pinching Grace's nipples lightly before dropping a kiss on her forehead. "Remember, this is all part of my world," he whispered before walking away.

Grace began to quake with fear. The low lighting, the way she was dressed and the air of suppressed excitement in the room scared her. Yet, despite her fear, the tightness of the leather outfit and the way it was pressing into her lower belly were combining to excite her body.

"Time to explain the trial, ladies," said Amber after a short pause for the other woman to take her place on the second bed. "As you know, it's called Controlled Chocolate Delight. Fortunately for you both, you don't have to control your own pleasure. We do that for you. During the next hour you'll be pleasured in many different ways. You may not enjoy them all, but that might come as a relief because every time you climax you'll be punished for as long as your orgasm lasts. The pain is intended to encourage you to control yourselves but, as many people discover, it often has quite the opposite effect.

"In fact, pleasure through pain is what your partners hope you'll discover during the course of the evening. As always, should you wish to quit the trial at any point you only need to say the word and you'll be released from this room. Naturally you would then have to leave the Dining Club immediately. No one can attempt the trial twice, meaning this is your only opportunity to learn if you can take pleasure from something that your respective partners enjoy. If neither of you have any questions, then we'll start the clock for the hour."

Stunned by Amber's words, Grace knew that she had to speak out. "I want to talk to David first," she said firmly.

Within seconds he was by her side. "Is there something you don't understand, Grace?"

"Yes, I don't understand how, if you truly feel anything for me, you can take pleasure in seeing me hurt. It doesn't make any sense. That's not what a loving relationship is meant to be about."

"I don't want to see you hurt," he said softly, one hand stroking her long, dark hair. "I want you to learn that immense pleasure can come through just a little pain."

"I don't believe that's true. It's cruel and you're being unkind," she retorted, on the edge of tears.

He bent lower, until his mouth was against her ear. "It is true, my darling. If you really loved me, then you'd trust me."

"I do love you! Why won't you believe that?"

"I want to believe it, but you're making it very difficult

for me when you won't even try something that I've told you I enjoy."

"You mean you'll enjoy seeing me hurt in front of virtual strangers?" she asked incredulously.

"No! The pain is nothing compared to the pleasure that follows it. You keep saying you love me, yet you won't trust me. Show me how much you love me, try it."

Grace was about to refuse when Amber spoke. "She doesn't want to do it, David. We must let her go. No one can be kept against their will, or coerced, and you're trying to…"

Hearing David's sigh of acceptance, Grace suddenly realized that she couldn't just let him go. She didn't want to lose him, and she certainly didn't want to return to her previous life never knowing if they could have been happy together. She would be left with nothing except her work, but he would continue visiting the Dining Club whenever he liked, and almost certainly would regularly enjoy the delights of Amber's beautiful, sexually sophisticated body.

Amber wanted Grace out of the way, which had to mean that she saw her, Grace, as a threat to the hopes she clearly had for making David hers and hers alone.

"It's all right, I want to go ahead now," she announced, and the look of relief that crossed David's face before he left her side was a reward in itself. Clearly he did care deeply for her, and wanted to love her. Now she had to hope that he was right and they were as sexually compatible as he believed.

On the bed next to her she could hear the young woman from table three whimpering, and realized that inadvertently she'd made it worse for her by delaying the start of the trial. She heard Andrew's deep voice coming from that side of the room, but it was Will who fastened her wrists into fur-covered cuffs set on each side of the bed. Then he pushed her feet up until her knees were pointing to the ceiling, fastened her ankles in the same way as her wrists and waited while Laura fastened soft leather straps around the tops of Grace's thighs.

Shocked and terrified, Grace twisted and turned in the restraints. No one had ever tied her up before, and she didn't like the resulting feeling of helplessness. All control had been taken away from her, and she was totally at their mercy. The feeling was worse than anything she'd ever imagined, and now she understood only too well why the red-haired young woman had been crying at the prospect of undergoing the trial again.

"What are you doing?" she asked Laura, her voice barely a whisper.

"It's a labia spreader," explained the younger girl. She parted Grace's outer sex lips and then her slim fingers were opening Grace up and she felt something small but quite hard fasten on each side of her outer labia, meaning she was fully exposed all the time.

"It helps during oral sex," Laura whispered, but Grace didn't find the words as comforting as they were clearly meant to be.

As soon as Grace was properly positioned Amber announced that the clock was starting, and as Laura gently stroked Grace's breasts, so tightly trapped in the leather openings, Will began to massage warm, scented oil into her equally exposed and gently rounded belly.

She could feel what they were doing, but because she was lying flat she couldn't see, and this made her nervous. She started to tremble, fearful of what might happen next. "It's all right," murmured David, coming to stand by her head. "They are only trying to give you pleasure. We want you to orgasm, remember?" His words, which seemed so kind, in fact only served to remind her of why they wanted her to orgasm.

She did remember, and she remembered too what was going to happen when she did, so she tried to fight against the tendrils of pleasure that were slithering through her lower belly.

Her breasts started to swell and tighten as Laura flicked her tongue against the sensitive tips of her nipples, before drawing each of them in turn into her mouth and sucking delicately on them.

In the meantime Will's clever tongue was sliding up and down her rapidly dampening inner channel, and when he pushed back the clitoral hood and swirled his tongue around the incredibly sensitive clitoris she felt a heavy throbbing begin deep in her pubic mound. Whimpering with rising excitement she felt her hips start to move upwards, and then Will pushed firmly against the flesh above her pubic bone, which increased the heavy, aching need inside her.

Lost in the sensations, it took her a few minutes to realize that David was now sitting on a chair at her side, and had reached beneath the raised bed. His fingers were spreading a cool gel between the cheeks of her bottom, which were imprisoned tightly in the hole in the bed, preventing her from wriggling away.

"What are you doing?" she cried, feeling his fingers moving insidiously toward her back passage, but he didn't answer. Instead he continued to spread the gel around.

Laura, who had briefly stopped caressing Grace's breasts, began to suck them again, but her mouth was now so cold that Grace gave a squeal of surprise. "I sucked on an ice cube," explained the twin, "doesn't it feel good?"

"I don't know. I can't think. I..."

She flinched as she felt David begin to insert a well-lubricated finger inside her anus. "Don't," she pleaded. "That hurts."

On the bed next to her, the other woman suddenly began to groan and cry, which increased Grace's anxiety.

"Relax and you'll find it adds to your pleasure. It will give you a stronger orgasm," he promised her. She could tell that his finger was now inside her, but he didn't move it around, instead he kept it quite still, pressed against one inner wall of her rectum. Within seconds she knew that he'd been right as the tension in her stimulated body continued to increase.

Beside her, the woman from table three was sobbing so loudly that it momentarily distracted Grace, giving her a moment's respite from her impending orgasm.

Despite this, she could feel how wet she was between her thighs, and wished she could close them, but the fiendish little straps meant she was fully open to Will all the time, and his hands had pushed her knees wide apart.

As Laura nibbled at one of her rigid, throbbing nipples, Will pushed his tongue into her damp, needy vagina and David moved his finger very slightly against the wall of her rectum, Grace felt as though her body was going to explode.

"They're both close to coming," she heard Amber say as she tried frantically to delay the pleasure, for fear of what would follow.

In the other bed her fellow guest was now gasping and crying loudly as her desire mounted, which increased Grace's excitement so much that she knew it was only a matter of seconds now before she climaxed.

Will's tongue was suddenly still, but her muted sound of protest stopped as he used his fingers instead, while at the same time climbing up onto the bed until he was crouching over her on all fours and she felt the tip of his erection nudging against her shamefully wet opening.

The swollen head of his straining penis remained at the entrance to her vagina, and now she desperately wanted him inside her, no matter what the consequences. Her body was so full, and under such tight pressure from the leather outfit she'd been put in, that it craved release from the throbbing, hot tension that was making every inch of her flesh frantic as she both longed for and yet feared the orgasm that was now so close.

As Will slowly thrust into her and David slid another finger inside her second opening she heard herself scream "Yes, oh yes!" as the first tingles of her long-awaited climax began deep inside her body.

"She's coming," said Will. "It's time now."

Grace realized what he meant, and knew that once her orgasm took hold something bad was going to happen. Desperately she fought to control herself, breathing through her open mouth and attempting to quell the shards of hot ecstasy that were travelling up her body, but her efforts were in vain.

As her teased and tormented body finally went into spasms Will, without withdrawing from her, leaned back away from her and Grace's initial cry of ecstasy changed to a shout of protest as a swift blow from a riding crop fell across the shuddering, trapped flesh of her belly. Pain seared through her tender flesh like fire.

"No!" she screamed. "That hurts. Stop, please stop!"

"It will stop when your climax stops," said David softly. "Wait a few seconds and you'll be surprised at what happens now."

As the pleasure from her long-delayed orgasm continued to flood through her body, and with the sound of the other guest's cries filling the room, Grace wanted to weep at the cruelty of a trial designed to spoil such a cleverly orchestrated moment of ecstasy.

Then the feelings inside her changed, and the spasms grew stronger. "Why won't it stop?" she cried, as waves of hot, dark pleasure continued to swamp her while the riding crop flicked relentlessly at her trapped, flinching belly.

"Because the pain from the crop is prolonging your orgasm," said David, his voice thick with excitement. "It's giving your body pleasure, as I knew it would."

When her orgasm finally ended and Amber put the riding crop down, an exhausted and whimpering Grace lay in a sweat-soaked daze. "You know I was right," David whispered in her ear, but she refused to answer him.

She didn't fully understand what had happened to her, and she didn't want to. Everything she'd ever believed about love told her that it was wrong to have had another man inside her while David was standing watching them. Yet shockingly, in a perverse way, the fact that David was watching had actually increased her pleasure.

As for the pleasure pain, she didn't want to admit even to herself how good those moments had felt. She knew that she'd never felt so totally sated before, and the knowledge both excited and disturbed her. Her whole world was being turned upside down here in this darkly erotic basement room. Furthermore, she knew that the trial wasn't over yet, and the most difficult part probably lay ahead of her.

Then, hearing the door to the room open and close she realized that the other guest had chosen to leave both the Dining Club and the man she'd planned to marry. The realization increased her fear, because unlike her, the other woman knew what else lay ahead in the trial, and had given up the man she'd hoped to marry rather than face it.

Now, if she chose to stay, she was the only one left for them all to pleasure and then torment. She knew that she had to go on, despite being well aware that the next part of the trial was going to be worse than the part she'd just endured. She had to gain David's love, and this was the only way to do it. She was more afraid of the trials now than before, but deep inside her a new fear was also growing.

If, at some point during the course of the trial, she failed a test, how would it be possible for her, with all that she was learning about her own sexuality, to go back to the life she'd led before she was introduced to the Dining Club? This realization only increased her tension, because no matter what lay ahead she knew that by remaining she would have to learn to embrace the life that David loved so much. Choosing to stay this time would mean there was no way back.

PART FOUR

Seduce

TEN

David was disappointed to see table three's guest leave the room. Her presence had clearly added both to Grace's arousal and her fear. Fear was, he knew, an excellent aphrodisiac, but he was confident that even without the unknown woman's presence he and the staff could make certain that by the end of her next orgasm Grace would understand and fully embrace the indescribable sensations of pleasure pain.

So far her trials had gone very well. The last time he'd brought a woman he'd cared for to the Dining Club, she'd failed on this very test, and his disappointment had been crushing. In her he'd thought he'd found someone he could love and be himself with, but he'd made a bad mistake. It had taken him several years to allow himself to get as close to a woman again, but now Grace meant more to him than she realized.

He was tired of living alone, and of the endless line of beautiful women who flitted in and out of his life. They were all sophisticated, intelligent and excellent company, but he'd known instinctively that they could never share his deepest sexual desires. Grace was different. Her work meant that she was very open-minded, she enjoyed her own sexuality and she was determined to succeed in a very difficult line of work. He wanted a woman who could be his equal in all things and yet was willing, at times, to become submissive to his darkest desires.

Amber was always an eager sexual partner, with a line in sexual depravity that more than matched his own. He could rely on her to satisfy him in that way whenever he visited the Dining Club, but in other ways she wasn't his type of woman. Her undeniable beauty was almost too perfect, and she had no warmth in her, and no humor.

Over the past two years he'd reluctantly begun to accept the fact that one woman could never be everything that he wanted and needed, but then he'd met Grace and had dared to hope again. So far she was proving him right, but the second part of the pain through pleasure trial might, he knew, see her walk out of the Dining Club and his life forever.

Despite the fact that she was succeeding as he'd hoped, he was honest enough to admit to himself that there was a small part of him that almost wanted her to fail before the end of all the trials. Watching Grace struggle with herself, trying to adapt to forms of sexuality that had previously been totally alien to her, he'd felt one or two totally unexpected moments of tenderness toward her. Once or twice he'd even wanted to protect her from the greatest excesses, and he didn't like that feeling.

Yes, he wanted to love her, but he wanted to do it on his own terms and in his own way. From the moment he was old enough to leave the home where he'd grown up he'd vowed that he'd never allow anyone to manipulate him emotionally in the way he'd watched his mother manipulate his father. His father had always said that his mother wasn't well, but David had known differently. She used her husband's love as a weapon, so that she got her own way in everything.

Then, as he made his way in the world, he watched male friends fall into the same trap. Besotted with the women they'd fallen in love with, they changed. The rounds of golf became few and far between, while nights out with their male friends gradually tapered off. Falling in love turned them into different people. Once, long ago, he'd nearly fallen into the same trap himself, and when he'd extricated himself from that relationship he'd sworn never to fall in love again.

He'd vowed that no one was ever going to be allowed to do that to him, but whereas with Amber there had never been any danger of her having emotional control over him, he was now faced with a very different situation. If Grace succeeded in becoming what he wanted sexually, would it mean that she could then wield the kind of emotional power over him that his mother had over his father?

It was a dilemma he'd never expected to have to face, and at the moment he had no idea how to deal with it.

"I think we're ready, and she's had a ten minute rest," said Amber, touching him on the arm and breaking into his train of thought.

He nodded. "Good. Andrew can get her down off the bed while I check that everything is to hand."

Within a few minutes, Andrew had removed the leather outfit from Grace and moved her to the side of the room nearest the small windows. Her lightly tanned body was still covered with small drops of perspiration, and fading red lines covered the area of her belly where Amber had used the riding crop on her, but she held her head up high and fastened her large, dark brown eyes on David's as she stood naked before them all.

"You'll enjoy a lot of this," he assured her as Andrew cuffed her wrists and then stretched her arms above her head so that he could fasten the cuffs to a metal ring set in a small beam in the ceiling. Her tightly stretched body and expression of wide-eyed apprehension aroused David instantly, but it would be Andrew who enjoyed her body while David carefully administered the dark side of her pleasure.

"Now the blindfold," he said quietly.

"No!" Grace objected. "I want to see what's happening to me." Andrew stepped back so that David could speak to her more privately.

Standing opposite her he put his hands on each side of her waist, his thumbs caressing her hip bones. Then he let his tongue travel slowly up each side of her neck in turn, before swirling the tip inside her left ear, something that he knew she loved. Her hips moved with delight and she gave a soft moan of pleasure.

"Remember, it's nearly all pleasure," he reminded her. "We blindfold you so that the pleasure is even more intense. There won't be any distractions. You've done the same thing with me," he added quietly.

"Yes, because I love and trust you. This is totally different."

"Different but just as exciting I promise you. You can refuse of course," he added diffidently.

"No, I don't want to refuse," she said quietly, but he

could tell by the look in her eyes that his words had hurt her, even though that hadn't been his intention.

"Then Andrew can go ahead and put the blindfold on?"

Grace nodded, and a relieved David moved away and watched as Andrew put the black velvet blindfold over Grace's eyes.

Now that she was suspended naked before them all, it was time for the pleasuring to begin. As Laura began to brush the front of her body with a large, plumed feather, Andrew carefully started to massage the suspended young woman's ankles and calves.

David watched as Grace's breathing began to quicken, and the skin over her neck and chest flushed as she became more and more aroused. He could see that she was battling to blot out the sensations, but knew that it would be impossible. The four of them were far too experienced to allow that to happen.

Andrew's hands reached the top of Grace's legs, and David noticed how she instinctively opened them, moving her hips forward to allow him to massage her inner thighs, but instead he straightened up and began to massage her taut arms.

He tenderly caressed the soft skin of her tightly stretched inner arms, and she uttered a small moan of pleasure. Smiling to himself, David moved quietly around to the back of Grace, signaling for Laura to use the feather on Grace's back now that her breasts were so swollen, with painfully tight nipples.

Laura drew the feather lightly between Grace's thighs, causing a sharp intake of breath from her, and then began to move it in small circles on her lower back and over her hip bones.

Grace started to moan softly, and it was then that Andrew moved his naked body until he was standing pressed against the front of her, allowing his straining erection to brush against the crisp, dark curls of her pubic hair.

Clearly torn between her need for a climax and her fear of what would follow it, Grace moaned "Please, oh please," but no one, least of all Grace herself, knew whether she was begging for an orgasm to release her from the wonderful sensations flooding her body or fear of the pain that would come with the release.

"Be careful, I'm not ready yet," David warned Laura and Andrew. Immediately Laura stopped moving the feather while Andrew reluctantly returned to massaging Grace's legs, but this time he worked on the top of her thighs. Every now and then he pressed his thumbs firmly into the inner creases. Each time he did this her breath would snag in her throat, and her whole body would quiver.

Watching her, David was almost overcome with a desire to make love to her there and then. He could tell that her body was more than ready to climax, but now she was fighting against it because of her fear, and for him that realization was incredibly exciting and arousing. With the help of a willing Amber he steadied her body as it jerked away from his touch, and then parted the cheeks of her bottom, covered two fingers with the Dining Club's special lubricant and inserted them slowly into her rectum.

Immediately he felt Grace's body shake with fear. "Relax, my darling."

"It hurts," she whimpered, but he knew that very soon the lubricant would warm the inner walls and for a short time there would be nothing but a strange, full pleasure from what he was doing. Gradually she stopped protesting, and instead began to gasp as the hot sensation spread through her back passage.

David waited a few more seconds and then, always a consummate judge of what was happening to a woman's body, gave Andrew the signal for him to proceed. Immediately Andrew pressed his body against Grace's, allowing his penis to slide up and down the slippery flesh between her sex lips.

Clearly desperate now, Grace moaned and sobbed, begging him to stop even as she thrust her hips forward to try and draw him inside her. David knew how much she must want to be penetrated, because she wanted the pleasure regardless of what was to follow. This was what he wanted, for her to lose herself in a spasm of ecstasy only to have it shattered by a totally new sensation.

Andrew glanced at him again, and once more David nodded as his own excitement mounted. His erection grew painfully tight and he felt his testicles drawing up beneath him in readiness for release.

Grace was whimpering and moaning with frustration now, and as Laura moved away, Amber stepped quietly to the side of Grace's tightly restrained and suspended body waiting, as was David, for the long-delayed climax to finally flood through her.

Grasping Grace's hips, Andrew pulled her lower body toward him, lifting her feet off the floor and placing her legs around his waist. Crossing her ankles behind his back she gave a small cry of delight as he slowly eased his way into her. Once inside he remained totally still for a few seconds.

"No, don't stop now!" she shouted, trying to move her body around in order to stimulate herself.

"You're sure about this?" asked Andrew quietly, and David felt a moment of fleeting annoyance. It wasn't Andrew's job to help Grace delay her climax. If they weren't careful the hour would be up and she would never receive this carefully planned example of pleasure pain that he wanted her to experience.

"Do as she asks," he said curtly.

Andrew immediately began to move in and out of Grace, at the same time allowing his left hand to move to the base of her stomach so that he could press firmly on the soft mound of flesh above her pubic bone. As he increased the pace of his thrusts, her breathing quickened and David heard the telltale gasps that often preceded her orgasms.

Gently he licked the bottom of her spine, swirling his tongue in the cleft at its base. With a cry of relief, Grace's body jolted in one huge spasm of overwhelming pleasure, and at the same time Andrew let out a muffled groan as he too climaxed.

As Grace's body continued to twist and turn, her legs still around Andrew's waist, David withdrew his fingers from her rectum and replaced them with a far thicker anal plug. As he pressed it in, she gave a cry of distress, but he knew that the contractions of her muscles would grip it tightly, meaning that the walls of her back passage were once again aroused by the lubricant that the Dining Club imported from the Far East.

Sure enough she suddenly began to twist and turn again, but this time she was whimpering with a mixture of pain and pleasure. Andrew kept her legs up in the air as Amber snapped two tight vibrating nipple clamps on Grace's swollen nipples. Again Grace cried out at the sudden pain, then shuddered as the vibrations caused her overstimulated body to spasm. Seeing this, David flicked the multistranded leather whip lightly over her buttocks, making them tighten around the anal plug.

"Stop!" cried Grace and she started to sob. "That's hurting me."

"Do you really want me to stop?" whispered David, allowing the whip to fall more heavily. He was keenly aware that, despite her protestations, her body was excited by the dark pleasure she was experiencing.

"Yes, no... I don't know!" she replied.

He flicked her buttocks sharply again and then, while she moaned pitifully, he ran his tongue along the red lines that were appearing on her flesh.

The moment he did this, Grace let out a shout of shock and ecstasy as a second climax engulfed her helpless body, which twisted and turned in Andrew's hands, brought to the peak of pleasure by the red-hot streaks of pain from the whip.

Finally, after what seemed endless minutes to those watching, she was totally still and the only sound in the room was her ragged, exhausted breathing.

"Release her," said David, "and then leave us."

"We never do that," protested Amber.

"There's a first time for everything," replied David. Knowing better than to argue with him, Amber reluctantly obeyed and a few minutes later David and Grace were alone in the room.

Setting the exhausted Grace down in the one large chair in the room and covering her with a warm blanket, David stripped off his clothes and settled himself beside her.

"I have to have you," he said huskily. "I know you're tired, but I need you."

"Do I have any choice?" she asked.

"Gracie, you know you've had a choice all along, but you chose to stay. I could tell you enjoyed everything in the end too, just as I'd hoped you would."

While he was talking he brushed her sweat-soaked hair off her face, gazing into her troubled eyes. "There's nothing wrong with gaining pleasure the way you did," he murmured, stroking her body tenderly.

"Even so, I don't understand how you could enjoy watching me with other people. I'd hate to watch you..."

Covering her mouth with his own he blotted out the rest of her sentence, pulling her onto his lap until she was sitting across his thighs, facing him. Then he lifted her up and onto his straining erection, while at the same time his fingers danced lightly over the incredibly sensitive skin of her perineum.

He felt her internal muscles contract around him as he pleasured her in this way that he knew she loved, and his climax came hard and fast. Exhausted, Grace collapsed against him, her body warm and damp. Wrapping his arms tightly around her, David wanted to tell her that he loved her, but he couldn't. He knew himself, his needs and his low boredom threshold too well, and two more trials still lay ahead of her. For a long time he stayed quite still, holding her close, and hoping against hope that she was slowly beginning to understand both his needs and her desires better. Then soon she might find that, like him, it was a way of life.

ELEVEN

"I f a man you loved asked you to do something you didn't
want to do, but you didn't want to lose him, would you
do it?" Grace asked Fran when the two of them met for coffee in Balham the following week.

"Do you mean something like potholing? If so, the
answer is definitely no. He'd have to go on his own. I don't
think couples have to share all their interests. Actually, I
think it's better if they don't."

"No, not potholing, something he couldn't do on his own."

"Something like mixed doubles at tennis or golf? I hate
sport, so again I'd have to say no."

"Fran, this is serious, and it's not about sport. It's more
about, well lifestyle I suppose."

"This isn't a general question is it, it's about your financier
lover? What does he want you to do, go to swingers' parties?"

Grace felt herself begin to blush. "No, but suppose
someone you loved did want you to do that. Would you?"

Fran shook her head. "No, I wouldn't. It's just not my
scene."

"How do you know?"

Fran looked surprised. "What do you mean?"

"If you've never been to a swingers' party, how do you
know it's not your scene?"

"Because I'm too private. I couldn't have sex with a

stranger. For me sex has to be part of a loving relationship. I'm not saying it's wrong, but I wouldn't do it."

"Not even to keep someone you loved happy?"

"God Grace, he *has* asked you to do it hasn't he?"

Grace shook her head. "No, he hasn't."

"I heard he's quite way out sexually," continued Fran, taking a sip of her latte and getting out her notebook.

"Where did you hear that?" asked Grace sharply.

Fran looked surprised. "My, you're touchy today, touchy and weird. I don't think he's good for you. I don't know where I heard it, but it was probably at some after-show party. Maybe someone had heard something from Isla after he ditched her."

"Sorry, I'm a bit tired," admitted Grace. "Now, that new place in Battersea will be free for your play when *Wanderlust* ends. I should go and see it for myself, it's had great reviews."

"I saw it, it's good. Not as good as my play, but good!" said Fran. "I take it you had a busy weekend then, if you're tired?"

"Yes, we stayed at a hotel and did a lot of swimming and walking," replied Grace, grateful that at least the swimming part was true.

"He looks fit. Presumably he's good in bed? You have a different look about you today," she added. "I'm trying to work out what it is."

"It's called exhaustion!"

"So, he's not way out but he wants you to do something you don't want to do," mused Fran. "That sounds like a good premise for a play."

"Don't you dare!" exclaimed Grace. "Anyway, it was a hypothetical question, not a personal one."

"Right, and my name's Albert Einstein! If you want to talk about it, then I'm willing. We've got the whole morning, and I can drink coffee until it's coming out of my ears. I could do with coffee stations, like petrol stations only cheaper, where I could fill up for a day!"

"It's all right, I'd rather we talked about the play," said Grace, wishing she'd never asked the question in the first place.

"Fine, but seriously, as your friend, I have to say that I think it would be a big mistake to let anyone persuade you to do something you didn't want to do just because you were afraid of losing them if you didn't do it. That's not how relationships work. You know that. If your financier is trying that kind of blackmail on you, then you should cut and run."

"I would," lied Grace. "Hypothetically though, don't you think that sometimes we don't try things because we're afraid, but if we can overcome that fear then . . . ."

" 'Feel the fear and do it anyway,' as that self-help book says? Maybe, but it depends on how it makes you feel about yourself afterwards, don't you think?"

Grace nodded. Without realizing it, with that one comment Fran had answered her question, because Grace was surprised to realize that she felt very good about herself indeed and it was only while they were talking that she'd made that discovery.

Furthermore, she only had to think back to the events of the weekend to become aroused once more. When she remembered the way the crop had stung her flesh and how the red-hot pain had changed to a type of pleasure deeper than any she'd known before she could feel herself growing damp between her thighs.

"I'm sure you're right," she said briskly, dragging herself back from her arousing daydream. "We've got to sort out casting now, because we need to find out who's free and who isn't. Have you still got the list we drew up last time?"

Fran had, and soon they were deeply immersed in their work, and for a time Grace was able to forget the Dining Club and all she was learning there.

Afterwards, when she was back in her apartment that evening, her mind returned to the conversation she'd had with Fran, and she realized she'd been stupid to talk about it, even obliquely. What was happening to her was far too personal and complex for anyone else to understand.

Too tired to make herself a meal she settled for cheese on toast, then sat down in front of the television to watch the news. It was nearly over, but as she went to switch channels her hand froze over the remote control as she saw David appear on the screen.

Astonished, she turned up the sound, just in time to hear the reporter saying that David had made a "rare public appearance" at a dinner for one of his charities, accompanied by his personal assistant, Louise Penfold.

Dressed in a black three-piece dinner suit with a white shirt and black, flower-patterned bow tie, David looked devastatingly attractive. His thick brown hair had been slicked back, emphasizing his cheekbones, and contrasting sharply with his blue eyes. He was smiling the half-smile that always made Grace's stomach turn over, and although he didn't linger for the photographers his personal assistant was clearly happy in the limelight.

She was tall, almost as tall as David, and her mass of tumbling blonde hair reminded Grace of Amber, while her elegant gray dress with red beading around the low-cut neckline was stunning. With her arm through David's she was obviously relaxed in his company, and Grace saw him smiling at her as they moved away.

She felt as though someone had hit her in the solar plexus. It was hard for her to breathe, and she realized that her hands were trembling. Although he'd spoken about his personal assistant, and even had to call her sometimes when he was with Grace, she had never expected her to be so beautiful. She'd imagined her to be middle-aged, very efficient and slightly masculine looking. Now she realized that she'd had no basis for this assumption, which had probably been born out of hope.

Rationally she knew it didn't mean anything. David liked beautiful things, and would therefore want an attractive woman as his PA. All the same, Louise Penfold wasn't just attractive, she was stunning, and yet he'd never said a word about her to Grace.

She wondered if Louise was the second woman he'd taken to the Dining Club before Grace, but even though that would mean she'd failed, it didn't lessen Grace's rising jealousy, which she realized was based on fear. She wondered why David hadn't mentioned the charity dinner to her and, even worse, hadn't invited her to go with him.

She felt as though her world was collapsing. None of

it made any sense. Why would he be taking her, Grace, to the Dining Club if he was close to another woman? Or was this Louise, rather than someone who had failed the tests, actually a replacement he had waiting in the wings in case Grace should fail?

It took her a long time to calm down enough to pull herself together. She'd overreacted, and she was honest enough to admit to herself that the reason for this was two-fold. In the first place, she was so in love with David that even the sight of him with a beautiful woman was enough to make her jealous, which wasn't the way she wanted to be, or had ever been before. In the second place, and possibly more disturbing still, she was in thrall to the thrill of the Club.

No matter how difficult she found it, or how far down a dark path the trials were leading her, she wanted to go on. She needed the monthly visits, because it was only then that her body became totally alive. She loved having David watch her as her body was satisfied in so many perverse ways, and she knew the reason for this too. Afterwards he was always emotionally closer to her than at any other time.

The slight barrier, the withholding of himself that she sensed at other times, vanished when they were at the Dining Club. When he had made love to her the last time, after everyone else had left the room, she had never known him to be so tender.

"Forget Louise," she told herself sternly. "She isn't the person you have to worry about. The only woman who can ruin things for you and David is Amber."

When she'd started out as a theater director a much

older, wiser director had watched her at work and afterwards had said that the one thing she should remember
when dealing with playwrights and actors was to choose
her battles wisely. In a moment of clarity she knew that this
applied to her fears about Louise and Amber too, and the
battle she was choosing was with Amber, because Amber
ran the Dining Club. By running it, and catering to all his
sexual needs as well as her own, she held the key to keeping David. Worryingly, this meant that she was also in a
position to make things very difficult for Grace.

Amber walked briskly into her office and found that
Andrew was there before her. He was sitting with his back
to the door, so engrossed in what he was watching on the
computer that he didn't even hear her come in.

Looking over his shoulder she saw that he was watching the tape of Grace pleasuring herself by the swimming
pool, rewinding to the moment of her orgasm time after
time. Realizing what this meant, Amber decided that she
could use the information to her own advantage.

"Enjoying yourself?" she asked sweetly.

Andrew jumped with surprise. "I'm watching David's
face. I don't think he's ever been as keen on anyone he's
brought here as he is on Grace," he explained.

"Right, so it doesn't have anything to do with the fact
that you fancy her yourself then?" she asked dryly.

"Maybe," he admitted. "There's something about her
that makes me want to get to know her better, but she's
David's, so I don't know why I torture myself."

"I wonder how she'll enjoy her next visit?" murmured Amber, her eyes fixed on the screen at the far end of her office, where the swimming pool scene was still running.

"She'll probably enjoy it more than her last one," replied Andrew. "I always think the pleasure pain session is a tricky one. It seems David has chosen better this time."

"Much better, and far too well for both of us, it seems."

"Maybe so," agreed Andrew, "but there's nothing we can do about it. The game has to be played to the end."

"And what if the end comes when she decides to challenge me for the top table?"

"Why on earth would she do that? She's only interested in keeping David. She already has a good career ahead of her. She wouldn't have time to run this place."

"You're falling for her, that's why you're underestimating her. Yes, she wants to keep David interested in her, but if she passes all four trials and learns about the fifth one, she'll go for it. She won't want me in his life if they become a couple, living together full-time. Beneath that wide-eyed air of innocent fragility she's a very determined character."

"I think you're seeing a problem where there isn't one," insisted Andrew. "She's in love with David, that's all that matters to her."

"Quite, and as she's in love with him do you honestly think she'll want him coming here once a month playing sexual games that involve us? No, she won't."

"Surely David isn't going to change his ways for her, no matter how fond he might be of her?"

"Exactly! That's why her only way of stopping him being with me will be to take my place. I know I'm right, and I know what I can do to stop it happening, which would suit both of us very well, because it would leave you free to try your luck with Grace."

Andrew leaned forward in his chair. "What can you do?" he asked with interest.

Amber smiled at his eagerness. "I'll make sure she fails before the end, preferably next time. That way, should it go wrong, I'll still have another chance of stopping her."

Andrew frowned. "How? You can't change the rules. David would figure out what you were playing at, and he'd be furious with you. You'd end up out on your ear due to your own stupidity, and I wouldn't be any further forward with Grace."

"I won't change the rules, but I can change the players. That's allowed. I shall put her in competition with Amy, and Laura and I will do the pleasuring. You know how insatiable Amy is, she can go on all night!"

"Grace might not be turned on by other women touching her."

"That's why I shall bring you in at the end, after spending most of my time with her. I don't think I'll have any problems. She's extremely receptive to pleasure."

"Possibly not to you, though," remarked Andrew.

Amber smiled at him. "You really do like her don't you? Well, if she fails she'll be free. I'm sure you won't have any trouble getting her to go out with you. You're not as obsessed with the Dining Club as David is. I expect you'd be happy to settle down with a nice young woman!"

"There's nothing wrong with that. I do like it here, but I don't intend to spend my life having sex with strangers, exciting though it is at the moment. I'll leave when I meet the right woman."

"Which is Grace."

Andrew's face flushed. "Yes, but she belongs to David and he's my friend."

"Hopefully she won't be his for much longer. I think you'd make a good couple."

Andrew shook his head. "I don't know if I can do that to a friend."

"You'll be doing him a favor. If she's not able to complete the trial, then she's not right for him. It's up to you though. You'll have to be there anyway. You and David will be in charge of the toys."

Andrew's face flushed with excitement. "Of course, it's meant to be the toys—if Grace chooses the right card."

"She'll choose it," said Amber confidently. " 'Playful Profiteroles' sounds quite a gentle evening, don't you think?"

Andrew laughed. "It's meant to be a more subtle evening," he pointed out.

"With a little competition too. All the games have to have some element of competitiveness. You know that. Amy never loses at games of this sort."

Andrew nodded. "That's true."

"I can see it's turning you on just thinking about it," laughed Amber.

"Does it turn you on too?"

"Not yet, but it will do when I watch her struggling with her own sensuality."

Andrew nodded. "All right, you're on. I'll help you."

Amber smiled. "You won't regret this; and we'll both get what we want."

Once Andrew had gone she let out a sigh of relief. With him on her side, she had nothing to fear.

Sitting down at the computer she started to outline Grace's next trial, and when she'd finished she could hardly contain her excitement at the prospect of Grace's next, and almost certainly final, visit to the Dining Club.

TWELVE

As David drove them to the Dining Club for the third time, Grace thought how quickly the two months had passed since her first visit. Watching his long hands on the steering wheel, the light hairs on the backs of his fingers catching the June sunlight that was coming through the car windows, she felt a rush of desire for him.

They'd only been out three times together since her last visit here, mainly because he'd been in America on business. Each time they'd ended up back at his flat, and the sex had been fantastic. As usual he'd been the perfect lover, but when she tried to talk about some of the things that had happened at the Dining Club, he'd changed the subject. Now, wanting him and wondering what lay ahead of her, she wondered if this was a better time to discuss it.

"Why don't we talk about the Club when we're not there?" she asked.

"Because at the moment it's not an integral part of your life, my darling. You're still trying to complete the course. I might accidentally say or do something that would help, or even hinder, you. You have to complete the trial on your own."

"But discussing things that have already happened wouldn't affect me," she protested.

"It's the way it always has to be. I'm only following the rules," he said regretfully. "How are you feeling this time?"

"Excited and nervous," she replied truthfully.

"The perfect combination," he said with a smile as they arrived at the now familiar high-gated entrance.

Slowly some of her excitement began to dissipate, and by the time they were inside the Dining Club and being escorted up the stairs to their usual suite, Grace was growing increasingly nervous, wishing that she had some idea of what lay ahead of her.

"How long has Amber worked here?" she asked, unpacking her suitcase.

"Five years or more. Why?"

"I want to know more about her I suppose. She's very beautiful."

David nodded. "Yes, she is. You'll learn more about her when you've completed the trials, assuming you do complete them of course," he added.

"Don't you think I will?" she asked, her already fragile confidence draining away.

David put his arms around her and kissed the top of her head. "Of course I do, darling. I certainly hope you do. Always remember, you're doing this for both of us. It matters to me as much as it does to you."

Encouraged by his words she relaxed a little. "Are we going to have a swim before lunch?" she asked, remembering what had happened the last time, and hoping he'd say yes, which would help distract her and calm her nerves.

David shook his head. "I had something rather different in mind for us today," he responded, drawing her toward the bed. "You know that you'll have unimaginable pleasures of one kind or another tonight, but what I'd like right now is for you to pleasure me."

Grace was very surprised. He'd never wanted her to take the lead in their lovemaking before. "Start by undressing me and then do what you think I'll like best," he continued, his breathing starting to quicken.

Because he'd always been in charge before, their love-making had flowed seamlessly under his skillful hands. Faced with his request, Grace was uncertain as to exactly what he'd want her to do.

"Don't you enjoy giving me pleasure, Gracie?" he asked quietly.

"Of course I do!"

"Then show me." He was watching her closely now, and she still didn't know what to do.

She realized it was ridiculous to feel shy after the things he'd witnessed happening to her here in this very house, but he wasn't making any move to help her. He was still standing by the bed, waiting.

After a few seconds' hesitation she walked up to him and started unfastening his belt. Her fingers were clumsy, and it took her far longer than she'd expected. Then, as she undid his trousers and slid them down over his hips, she began to feel more confident.

He still wasn't moving, but remained totally compliant under her hands. Next she pushed him until he was sitting on the bed. She fully expected him to protest, but he didn't. Instead he continued to watch her with a steady gaze.

The room was filled with an air of almost electric

eroticism, and Grace wanted him like she'd never wanted him before. She tore at his shirt buttons, and then when he was totally naked pushed him until he was lying widthways, facedown across the bed.

Opening the bedside cabinet she took out the massage oil that she knew was kept there, poured some into her hands and began to knead the tight flesh of his firm buttocks, squeezing and then releasing it.

He sighed with pleasure, and with rapidly growing confidence she massaged the backs of his thighs with long, sweeping strokes before turning him over. As their eyes met his sharp, bright gaze pierced right through her. It was as though he was looking into her soul, and was amused by what he saw there.

He was already fully erect, the swollen head of his penis a dark purple, and seeing a tiny drop of clear fluid at the tip of the glans she knew that he was very close to a climax, but her instinct told her that he didn't want the pleasure to end yet.

Leaving him for a moment so that she could strip down to her silk bra and panties, she then straddled his thighs and bending forward licked at his nipples until they too grew rigid and he moaned softly.

Grace had never felt like this before. David had always been in charge, always controlled their sex life, and because it had been so good she'd never felt the need for anything else. Now though she felt empowered, and finally understood why David became so aroused by watching people controlling her pleasure here at the Club.

Covering his upper body with tiny butterfly kisses, she then shook her head, letting her long hair brush over his belly. He groaned and she felt his hips move. "Not yet," she whispered, moving herself lower down his body.

Her fingers wandered through his crisp pubic hair, and then she scratched gently on the soft flesh of his inner thighs. Her nails drew swirling patterns that made him catch his breath as his excitement grew and his testicles drew up tightly against his body.

With great care she stroked the skin of his perineum, and this time he gasped aloud. Softly she let her fingers stray, stroking the underside of his hard testicles for a few fleeting seconds before moving her head so that she could cover the tip of his erection with her mouth.

Her tongue swirled around the underside of the ridge just below the swollen head, and immediately his hips jerked. Alternately sucking and licking she felt the silk of her panties growing wet between her thighs as David groaned and gasped beneath her.

Then, as her own excitement grew and she felt tingles begin deep in her own belly, David sat up. His hands gently moved her head away from him and then he pushed her onto all fours on the bed, waited for her to take her weight on her elbows, knelt behind her with his legs between hers and thrust urgently into her from behind. She realized immediately, even through the heat of her sexual arousal, that at the end he'd taken control once again.

Almost immediately he gave a shout and she felt him shuddering against her buttocks as he spilled himself into her, before slowly withdrawing and collapsing on the bed, pulling her down as well so that they were lying back to back like two spoons.

His breathing was ragged but slowly calming, but Grace was now frantic for her own climax, her body swollen and aching with desire. "I haven't come yet," she said softly.

He put an arm over her waist, his breath warm against the nape of her neck. "I know, and you won't until tonight. This was all for me, remember?"

Grace couldn't believe her ears. She was so aroused that she ignored his words, moving her hand down between her thighs, desperate to ease the ache behind her swollen clitoris.

Realizing what she was doing, David pinned her arm to her side. "No!" he exclaimed.

"That's not fair," she protested.

"You'll have your pleasure later, darling. You don't want to be worn out before the evening begins. You know how exhausting the trials can be."

"I don't care. I want to come now." She was almost crying with frustration.

"Then hopefully you're now looking forward to tonight, rather than feeling nervous about it. It's time to get dressed anyway. I ordered our lunch to be sent up at twelve-thirty."

Glancing at the bedside clock, Grace saw that it was already twelve-fifteen, and she knew then that David had planned everything. For a brief moment she'd been in control but, as always at the Dining Club, not of her own pleasure. That was always in the hands of other people.

In the evening, as she slipped into the black Grecian-style, backless dress that David had chosen for her, her body still ached with need. All afternoon he'd been touching, kissing and caressing her, even outside in the garden, yet never to the point where she could reach a climax. She hoped that whatever trial she chose, it didn't require extreme self-control, as she was sure that with the way David had teased and tantalized her body since their arrival that morning, her pleasure would spill with shaming speed tonight.

With a dry mouth but also a desperate need for whatever lay ahead, she slowly descended the wide staircase.

PART FIVE

Touch

THIRTEEN

Because she'd already been so skillfully aroused, Grace didn't take as much notice of the meal and her surroundings as usual this time. Her mind was far away, wondering what lay ahead of her, dreading and yet needing whatever the trial had in store for her.

She sipped at her champagne, and ate what was put in front of her, but her thoughts were only on the evening, and the choice of dessert cards that would soon be put before her. Laura, who was the third person at their table, ate little and said even less.

Throughout the meal, David kept touching Grace lightly on the knee, and several times he whispered in her ear, reminding her of what had happened in their room earlier. Each time he did this he would finish by swirling his tongue inside her ear, which he knew she loved, diabolically increasing her body's sexual tension.

This time it was Andrew who brought the cards to their table, and as her eyes met his and he smiled at her, Grace was surprised to realize that she hoped he would be involved in whatever she chose.

There were three choices for her: "Dangerous Damson Delight," "Masked Maple Mousse" or "Playful Profiteroles." Immediately she knew that she didn't want the Dangerous Damson Delight, and remembering how she'd felt when she'd been blindfolded she didn't think she'd enjoy the Masked Maple Mousse either. On the other hand Playful Profiteroles sounded as though it would offer all kinds of pleasures, even though she was well aware that this was a trial, and the playfulness might not all be to her liking.

"Playful Profiteroles, I think," she said slowly.

Andrew smiled at her. "An excellent choice," he said, his dark brown eyes meeting hers. "I hope you enjoy it."

"I'm sure we'll all enjoy it," said David softly after Andrew had left them.

All around them people were getting up from their tables, but Grace noticed that the woman at table four seemed reluctant to follow her partner out of the room. David saw Grace watching the other woman. "She's nearly completed the course," he explained. "Tonight is very important to her and her partner."

Realizing that if she passed tonight's trial, then that would be her next month, Grace's heart went out to the young woman. "I hope she succeeds."

"I doubt if she will. I heard she struggled last time," he replied.

"That would be so sad, to fail at the last hurdle."

"Most people do, but I want you to concentrate on this one. We're upstairs tonight."

With those ominous words resounding in her head she followed him out of the dining room and up the main staircase, but they turned left instead of to the right, which was the way to their suite.

The corridor was a long one. At the far end he opened a

thick white-paneled door and then with a firm hand in the small of her back he guided her in.

This room was almost as dark as the basement had been, but unlike that room it was vast with a very high, arched ceiling decorated with Victorian cornices. There was a beautiful Italian fireplace on the one side of the room. On the other side were two beds, piled high with cushions and pillows, positioned close to each other. Above the beds a large, gold mirror, surrounded by subdued lighting, was set into the ceiling.

"Time to start playing," said David, the excitement obvious in his voice as he crossed the room and stood by Amber's side. Grace looked at the two of them, standing so closely together, and knew, beyond a shadow of a doubt, that the blonde was her enemy, and determined to make her fail. This realization helped to strengthen Grace's resolve to succeed at all costs.

Laura, who had come up from the dining room with them, now stepped into the middle of the room and slowly stripped off her dress to reveal skimpy black and red underwear beneath it. Her large breasts were almost spilling out of the black and red bra, and the miniscule knickers were so tight that they emphasized the slight swelling of her pubic mound.

"Isn't she gorgeous," said Andrew, who was standing by one of the beds. "Would you like to touch her before we begin our games with you? She likes to be touched."

Grace swallowed hard. "I'm not sure."

"You don't have to, but she'd appreciate it, wouldn't you, Laura."

Laura nodded, and sensing that this was actually the start of the trial, Grace went up to her and lightly stroked the concave stomach with the tips of her fingers for a few seconds, causing the other girl to catch her breath with excitement.

"Excellent," said Andrew. "Now, is Amy ready?"

A door on the left-hand side of the room opened and Amy walked in. For a moment Grace couldn't make out what she was wearing, but then realized it was a black- and coffee-colored bra with a long strip of black lace down the front. It had cutout side panels and a band of lacy material around the tops of her thighs, but as she walked slowly to the center of the room it was clear that there were no matching panties.

"That outfit really suits you, Amy," said Amber, guiding Laura's twin to one of the beds. "Apron outfits are so sexy, and make it easy for us all to pleasure you."

"How does it make you feel?" David asked Amy.

"Very sexy," replied Amy enthusiastically.

"Time to do something about your outfit, Grace," interjected Andrew as he approached her. Swiftly he removed her dress, and then handed her a set of underwear.

She was nervous, but now her nervousness had a tinge of excitement. She could see how sexy Amy looked, and wondered how it must feel to be dressed in that way.

Aware that they were all watching her she tried not to show her embarrassment. Light from the one window emphasized her nakedness, and for a moment she longed for the darkness of the basement room. Quickly putting on the underwear she found that the cups of her bra were open fronted. The matching cream and black crotchless thong for some reason made her feel even more vulnerable than when she'd been totally naked, vulnerable yet sensual too.

Dressed as required, her legs trembling with a mixture of excited anticipation and fear, she mutely let Amber lead her to one of the beds. As the other woman's hand touched her shoulder Grace was surprised to realize that she was now even more determined not to let Amber win. Whatever the trial turned out to be, she had to succeed.

"Lie down," Amber said softly, "and David will explain the trial to you." Her gentle tone increased Grace's briefly subdued trepidation, because she knew how false it was, and understood that it didn't bode well for what she was about to hear.

"This evening I'm sure you'll be delighted to hear that you can both let your pleasure spill as often as you like," said David. "The only element of competition is a simple one. The first person to be exhausted, and say that they don't want any more orgasms will be the loser. If Grace loses, then she will fail the trial. Before we begin, do either of you have any questions?"

There was total silence in the room and Grace's heart sank as she realized exactly what he was saying. She and Amy were going to be brought to the peak of pleasure time after time until one of them couldn't go on any longer. This meant that the ability to slow down each orgasm, delay every climax, was vital. However, with the way her body had been teased and aroused already that day, Grace knew that her first orgasm would be very quick, putting her at an immediate disadvantage. Also, she was in no doubt that

Amy had taken part in this particular trial many times, and had been carefully chosen as her opponent.

"Why is it called 'Playful Profiteroles'?" she queried, trying to keep her voice from trembling.

"We'll be using some exciting toys on you both during the evening, and I know you'll get a great deal of pleasure from them," replied David.

"Extreme pleasure," added Amber, and Grace could hear the excitement in the other woman's voice.

"Amber and Laura will be in charge of the pleasure to begin with," added David, walking around until he was standing by Grace's head. "Amber will be working on you, darling," he added.

Putting out a hand he lightly caressed her left nipple, which was exposed due to the open-fronted bra. "So exquisite," he murmured to himself, as she tried to ignore the sensations his touch was causing her. "Remember failure tonight means you can never return for the final test, and we'll never see each other again. Don't let me down, my darling," he whispered in her ear. She shivered at his words.

With one final tweak of the increasingly sensitive nipple he moved away, leaving Grace confused by his motives for so cruelly arousing her in advance of the trial while urging her not to fail.

Amber now took David's place at her side and looking down at Grace she smiled. It was not a reassuring smile. Gently she touched the younger woman between her thighs, two fingers sliding inside the opening of the crotchless thong.

"My goodness, you're already very wet," she commented.

"Clearly you're eager for a climax, so I'll try to make this nice and quick for you."

Quick was exactly what Grace knew she didn't need if she were to have any hope of winning the trial, but as Amber's lubricated fingers moved slowly up and down the soft, damp tissue beneath her outer sex lips in a slow, steady rhythm, Grace started to make tiny mewing sounds of pleasure.

She heard Amber laugh, and now the blonde woman's other hand was at the base of Grace's gently rounded belly. She pressed the heel of her hand firmly against the soft skin above the pubic bone, while letting her fingers splay out and down so that she could trap Grace's swollen clitoris between the resulting V.

Grace could feel her breasts swelling and despite herself her hips moved urgently on the soft cushions beneath her. Her body craved this orgasm and no matter how hard she tried to control herself the need for release grew and grew.

A hot, liquid sensation filled the base of her belly, and immediately Amber's fingers pressed down harder against the area surrounding the clitoris while at the same time increasing the pace of her other two fingers moving up and down the damp inner channel.

Still Grace tried to delay the moment of orgasm, struggling not to let herself climax. She thought she was succeeding but then felt a pair of strong male hands beneath her thighs, lifting her up slightly, and she guessed that David, who knew her body so well, had joined in to make it even more difficult for her.

Amber's fingers stopped their movement, allowing the

newcomer to lightly skim his tongue along the frantic, pulsating flesh. When he swirled it around the edges of her swollen, needy clitoris Grace couldn't hold out any longer. With a scream of delight she let the pleasure flood through her, sobbing with the pleasure of such long-delayed release.

Her body continued to shudder for several seconds, until finally the spasm was over and she fell back against the bed, well aware that next to her Amy, although whimpering with excitement, had not yet had her first orgasm.

"Andrew has a clever tongue," said Amber, looking down at Grace. "You'll need a few minutes to recover, so I'll leave you for a moment while I find a toy for you."

Only then did Grace realize it wasn't David who had finally caused her body to spasm in such ecstasy. For a moment she lay quietly, but when she realized that Amy was making tiny sounds of excitement and gasping for breath as her twin worked on her, Grace discovered the sound of the other girl's rising excitement was arousing her once more.

She felt deeply ashamed. She'd never had another woman touch her intimately before, and now that it was happening, combined with the sounds of another woman reaching orgasm so near her, her body was excited by it. Not only that, she was enjoying it.

Putting her hands over her ears she tried to blot out the excited cries coming from Amy, but Andrew was immediately at her side, pulling her hands down. "That's not allowed. You're meant to feed off each other's excitement."

Gazing up at him, she could see that he was excited too, but whether by the whole scenario or her struggle with her wanton body she didn't know.

"Here we are," said Amber, returning to the side of the bed. "Andrew, turn Grace over for me, and I think the thong needs to come off now."

Gently, caressingly, Andrew pulled the thong down her legs, his fingers stroking her flesh. As he pulled it off over her feet he kissed the insides of her ankles, heightening her arousal still more. Then Grace felt Andrew's fingers parting the cheeks of her bottom and her body jerked as he moved a well-lubricated finger around the opening to her back passage. She started to tense, but then Amy gave a loud cry of pleasure, which distracted Grace, allowing him to ease two fingers slowly inside her rear opening.

The sudden sensation of fullness drew Grace's attention away from Amy, and she made a sound of protest. Ignoring her, Andrew kept his fingers still, allowing them to rest quietly against the walls of her rectum until her muscles relaxed again.

"She's ready now," he told the waiting Amber.

Lying facedown on the bed waiting for whatever was to come, Grace heard Amy say "No, please don't do that or I'll come too fast." She also heard David sharply telling her to stay silent, and realizing that he was pleasuring Amy she was almost overwhelmed with jealousy.

Lost in what was happening next, the insertion of the first anal bead by Amber took her totally by surprise, and she gasped loudly. Swiftly other beads followed, and the strange, full sensation made her restless.

"Turn on your side," said Amber. Once Grace had obeyed, the blonde woman opened Grace's outer sex lips and spread more lubricant along the inner channels, her fingers lingering lightly around the opening to the urethra for a few blissfully arousing seconds.

Immediately Grace felt her treacherous body start to respond, and an ache began way down in her belly while her breasts started to swell. All the nerves in her body were jumping, tendrils of pleasure snaking through her, but she fought hard to delay the inevitable.

"Time for another toy I think," said Amber, and without warning she eased a G-spot vibrator inside Grace and then turned it on.

Grace gasped as the most amazing sensations began to build deep inside her. Keeping the vibrator in place, Amber sat on the side of the bed, lowered her head and drew Grace's right nipple and the surrounding sensitive tissue into her mouth. Sucking and releasing it, teasing the tip of the nipple with her tongue, she soon had Grace moaning with pleasure.

Her second orgasm was building fast, and there was nothing she could do to delay it now, because of the small, relentless vibrator inside her and the added full feeling caused by the beads. As Amber nipped on the rigid nipple, causing a shard of pain to streak through her swollen breast, Grace's body convulsed as she climaxed for the second time.

This orgasm lasted longer than the first, and she thought the final tremors were never going to end. Then, as the wonderful but exhausting sensations started to ease, Andrew tugged on the cord at the end of the anal beads. As they came out slowly, each one teasing the walls of her rectum, Grace was horrified to realize that her muscles were going into a second spasm, and she gave a cry of protest as she shook from head to foot with a new, dark kind of pleasure she'd never experienced before.

Only when she was finally still did Amber and Andrew let her move onto her back, and Andrew licked at a bead of sweat just above her belly button. She jumped with shock and he smiled at her. "Wasn't that good?" he said. "And there's more to come."

She knew better than to look away from him, but despite the excitement and admiration in his eyes she felt only despair, because she didn't know if her body could manage another climax, yet Amy was still being pleasured in order to bring her to her second orgasm.

After that she lost all track of time as she was brought to peak after peak of ecstasy, fighting all the time to delay the final moment of gratification. Several times she heard Amy's cries of delight, but while they pleased Grace they also served to arouse her, and she realized how clever it had been to have the two of them side by side.

She would never have imagined that hearing another woman climax would excite her, but it happened every time. She had no idea what was happening to her opponent, or how she was being aroused. All she knew was that Amy seemed to have better control than her, and she was terrified that, as David had warned her, this might be her last visit to the Dining Club.

Then, as her body was slowly coming down from yet another intense climax caused by Amber and Andrew teasing her clitoris while it was trapped in a clitoral ring, she sensed that her exhausted body wouldn't be able to cope with any more pleasure. Amber was approaching her with something in her hands and with a heavy heart Grace was about to say she couldn't bear it when she heard Amy give a loud cry of protest.

"You're hurting me now!" she exclaimed. "It's no use. I can't come anymore."

Grace lay motionless, hardly daring to breathe. "Of course you can," said David, and Grace was shocked to hear that his voice was sharp with apparent annoyance.

"I'm sorry, but I can't," protested Amy. "Laura shouldn't have used that special lubricant on me. It makes everything too intense. I can't bear any more, and I want to stop now."

"The lubricant we import?" asked David incredulously.

"It was a mistake," said Laura. "I picked up the wrong tube. I'm so sorry, really I am." Grace could hear the fear in her voice.

"It certainly was a mistake," responded David coldly. "Leave the room. Amber will discipline you later."

A few seconds later he was looking down at the exhausted Grace, his eyes sweeping over her sweat-drenched body as he assessed her with what looked to her like dispassionate interest. "Amber and Andrew have clearly given you a lot of pleasure, Grace," he said quietly.

Grace swallowed hard. "Yes, they have," she agreed.

"Well, you heard what Amy said. She can't go on. The question is, can you manage another orgasm?"

"I don't have to!" protested Grace. "She was the first one to say she didn't want to continue."

"But my darling girl, unless you manage another orgasm it will be a draw, and the trial will have to be run again another time," he said smoothly.

Staring up into his unreadable blue eyes, Grace was totally bewildered and very hurt. "Why are you doing this? Don't you want me to succeed?" she asked, her eyes bright with unshed tears.

"Of course I do, more than anything in the world, but that's the rule. I'm sorry if I didn't explain it clearly enough at the beginning."

He hadn't, and they both knew that, but when Andrew nodded in agreement Grace knew there was no point in arguing any further. She only wished she knew whether it had been a genuine mistake by David or yet another moment of subtle cruelty by this man she loved so much.

She heard Amy get off her bed and then heard the door open and close as she left the room. Now Grace was alone with Amber, Andrew and David, and somehow she had to manage one more climax or the whole trial would be repeated. She didn't think she could face that; knowing what lay ahead the second time would make it too difficult for her.

Still puzzled and upset by David's behavior, she waited passively on the bed, as she knew was expected of her. When Andrew drew up a chair and sat down next to her, she saw the sympathy in his eyes and wondered why David couldn't ever look at her like that during trials. "I'm sorry about this. It's not like David to make mistakes, but it is the way this trial always ends," he assured her. "I'll blindfold you now. It will help to make the sensations more intense."

Grace nodded, her mind fastening onto what he'd said about David rarely making mistakes. She knew that was true, which only increased her belief that he'd done it on purpose and made no sense at all. At least, not if he wanted her to succeed. She bit on her lower lip, because the possibility that he didn't was unthinkable.

A soft black velvet blindfold was placed over her eyes, and then her hands and feet were spread out wide and fastened to rings attached to the sides of the bed.

"Let's start gently," said Amber, opening Grace up between her thighs so that her clever tongue could begin to swirl lightly over the moist flesh, but Grace scarcely reacted to the previously arousing touch. While Amber worked with her mouth male hands that Grace recognized as Andrew's opened the front fastening of her bra, allowing her breasts to be fully available to him. Then he began to massage them, lightly at first but with increasing pressure. When he let his tongue stray to the tender flesh of her armpit she squirmed, and to her relief felt a very faint stirring of desire in her belly.

"She's become a little damp now," commented Amber, letting her tongue flick at Grace's clitoris, but this time it was irritating rather than arousing and Grace tried to move herself away, pressing her back lower into the bed. With her senses heightened due to the blindfold, she heard a tiny sound of satisfaction from the other woman, and wanted to cry at the way her body was letting her down at such a vital moment.

Andrew's hands moved lower, gently stroking her around her bare waist and the soft curve of her hips, and then he began to kiss her softly in the same places. At the same time Amber tickled lightly at the inner creases of Grace's thighs, and when she did that Grace suddenly knew that an orgasm would be possible.

She could feel her body starting to respond, her hips moved restlessly on the bed as she attempted to push the lower half of her body down so that Amber would caress her clitoris with her tongue. Amber duly responded, flicking the side of the swollen nub in a steady rhythm, and now the pleasure was growing rapidly. Almost overwhelmed with relief, Grace felt her muscles start to contract.

Immediately Andrew's hands stopped moving, Amber's tongue stopped what it had been doing, moving deep inside Grace instead, and the delicious darts of her impending climax began to die away. "No, no!" she cried piteously, frantic for them to continue stimulating her in the way they had been seconds earlier.

"Oh dear," said Amber, straightening up. "I thought she was near to coming, but she wants us to stop."

"No, I don't! Please, please go on!" she whimpered, unable to stay silent as despair almost overwhelmed her as she felt the delicious sensations continuing to slowly subside.

"What a shame," agreed Andrew. "You nearly managed it Grace," he added, and she felt his hands stroking her hair.

"I didn't want you to stop!" she shouted. "I was about to come. Please, please listen to me."

"You said 'no,'" Amber pointed out.

"Only because…"

All at once, David spoke. "Be silent, Grace. I'll be the judge of who's telling the truth."

For a moment the room was silent. All Grace could hear was the sound of her own breathing, but within seconds David was at her side, and she felt his familiar touch as he stroked the side of her face. "If you were telling the truth you should be very ready, so this won't take long," he promised her.

Relief surged through her, because whatever had been happening before, she could tell that he was now on her side again.

"I'm going to suck on your clitoris now, and then stroke it with warm damp thread," he continued. "While I'm doing that, I'm going to let a small vibrator tease the surrounding flesh. Will that be enough do you think?"

His words alone were enough to arouse her. Her frantic body began to shake with excitement, and when his hands parted her outer sex lips and his mouth sucked gently on her rapidly swelling clitoris she moaned with pleasure and relief.

"Now for the thread," he murmured, and the words were so tantalizing that she felt her orgasm getting nearer even though nothing else had happened. The anticipation of the delicate, drawn-out movement of the thread was driving her out of her mind with excitement.

"Ready?" he asked quietly.

"Yes, oh yes!" she moaned, half out of her mind now as she anticipated the pleasure that was about to swamp her body.

"What a wanton young lady you've become," he murmured. Then she felt the lightest of touches as the warm, moistened thread stroked the surface of her clitoris, while a vibrator gently massaged the sensitive flesh around it, and gave a loud cry of triumph as her body was shaken by the most intense orgasm she'd ever had. It seemed to go on and on, and David continued to let the thread play over her until the last tiny tremors of pleasure died away. Only then did he stop.

"I think we can safely say you passed tonight's trial," he commented dryly.

Grace heard the door slam, and then David removed her blindfold, unfastened her wrists and ankles and looked down on her with what she thought was a look of admiration in his eyes. "You were absolutely amazing, my darling," he said, his voice husky with excitement and desire. "I would never have believed it possible."

As he wrapped her in a fluffy toweling robe and took her back to their suite, Grace knew that before tonight she would never have believed it possible either. But she'd passed, and now she would only be making one more visit to the Dining Club.

Strangely, despite everything that had happened to her there, that realization didn't bring the relief she'd expected, but instead a surprising and rather shameful twinge of regret.

Once they were in their room, Grace collapsed on the bed and within minutes was sound asleep. After he'd made sure she was comfortable, David settled himself in one of the armchairs and thought back over the evening, trying to work out why, for a time, he'd been doing his best to make sure that Grace failed tonight. Furthermore, he'd taken a perverse pleasure in it.

She was proving herself to be everything he'd ever wanted in a woman, with a body that was as receptive to the kind of sexuality he enjoyed as he could ask for, and a love for him that was beyond doubt.

He'd always wanted to find what he'd thought of as his perfect woman, yet now he seemed to have found her, he was deliberately trying to sabotage the relationship. Watching her tonight, as she reached the peak of her sexual pleasure time after time, he'd never been more aroused. He'd felt closer to her then than he'd ever felt to a woman, yet at the same time part of him hoped that she'd give in and choose to leave him. He wasn't a fool. He'd watched the way Amber and Andrew had left Grace stranded as she was about to reach her final climax, and he'd understood Amber's motive very well. It was fear. Andrew's, on the other hand, couldn't be fear, which left only one other logical conclusion. Andrew wanted Grace to fail, leaving the way open for him to ask her out.

A rival was the kind of challenge David would normally have relished, but this time a part of him wondered if it would be better if he released Grace soon, by ensuring that she failed the fourth trial, rather than ruin both their lives. And that was what would happen, he knew it would, because in truth no matter how perfect she was, or how much he loved her at the start, eventually he would tire of her.

Although not prone to self-analysis, he knew that boredom was anathema to him. He always had to find new interests: takeovers, financial ventures and of course new women. But to part from Grace now would, he realized with surprise, be impossible.

She was the only woman he'd brought to the Dining Club to pass the third trial, and for that reason alone he needed to see the game played to the finish. Tonight, at the end, as he'd enabled her sated body to be pleasured one final time, he'd also felt an overwhelming tenderness toward her.

When she'd snuggled against him, murmuring softly as he brought her back to their rooms, he'd wanted that feeling of tenderness to last, and until she fell asleep it had. It was only after that, when he had time to reflect, that the doubts surfaced again. Doubts about his ability to love, and doubts about how long she would keep him interested and intrigued if it proved possible.

As the hours passed, and dawn started to break, David remained seated in the chair, as he tried to solve a problem that, in truth, he had never expected to have to face.

FOURTEEN

The following morning, almost as soon as she'd woken up, David told Grace they'd have to leave the Club before lunch, as he needed to meet with his PA and make arrangements for a working breakfast the next morning.

"Is that Louise Penfold?" Grace asked, half-asleep but remembering what she'd seen on the television.

David was clearly surprised by her question. "Yes, as a matter of fact it is. How did you know?"

"I saw you both on TV a few weeks ago, at some charity function I think. She's lovely."

"Yes, she's very beautiful," he agreed, "but not as beautiful as you looked last night." And with that he wrapped his arms around her, kissing her passionately, until she felt him hardening against her.

Then Grace knew that Louise didn't mean anything to him now. Even if she had once, she didn't anymore. Amber was definitely her only threat to keeping this man she loved so much, Amber and the fourth trial.

She had intended to question David about the previous night, wanting to know why he'd been so angry when Amy had stopped earlier than anticipated, giving Grace a chance of winning, when he should have been pleased for her sake. She also needed to understand why he hadn't explained the trial properly at the start, but as he'd skillfully helped her to triumph at the end, and was so passionate this morning as a result, she decided it could wait. He was a very complex man, and that was part of his attraction for her.

One day she'd find out, but for the moment she'd focus on her return to the Dining Club in a month's time for her final trial. As long as she succeeded in that, she would be in a far stronger position to question David's motives about everything, and find out exactly how he felt about the beautiful, possessive blonde woman who kept him close by her expert running of this very special Club that meant so much to him.

During the drive back, David was unusually quiet and Grace chattered more than usual to fill the silence. Normally after visiting the Dining Club he was relaxed and it was a time when she felt very close to him. This time it was different; he seemed lost in thought.

They went into her apartment, and after putting her case down he caught hold of her hands, drawing her over to the window. Cupping his hands around her face he smiled down at her, and she was almost overwhelmed with relief.

"I'm so proud of you, my darling," he said softly. "You're doing incredibly well at every trial. You have no idea how much that means to me. I was sure you'd like it, but I never expected you to take to it all in the way you have. It's incredibly exciting for me, and hopefully for you too."

"I can't believe everything that's happening, or how it's making me feel," she admitted, thankful that she hadn't spoilt this moment by trying to question him about the night before during the drive back. "I'd never imagined doing the kind of things I do at the Club, and sometimes it scares me at first, but you were right. I love it, and the more things I discover about myself there, the more I want to go back."

"Want or need?" he queried quietly.

She thought for a moment. "Need," she admitted, averting her face.

"What's the matter?"

"I'm so ashamed," she confessed. "Afterwards, when I'm back in my everyday life I can't believe what's happening to me."

He turned her face back so that she was looking into his eyes. "There's nothing to be ashamed of," he assured her. "It does become a need, that's why I have to know you fully understand that before I can..."

"Can what?" she whispered.

His expression changed. It was obvious that there was some internal battle going on in his mind, as his eyes left hers and looked into the distance.

"Please, tell me," she begged, longing to hear some words of love from him.

"Before I can tell you about table five," he said at last.

She was so disappointed that it took a moment or two for his words to sink in. "Amber's table?"

"It's where Amber sits, yes." He glanced at his wristwatch. "Look at the time! I'm late for Louise now."

Grace desperately wanted to ask him more questions, but she realized that he'd already said more than he'd intended before they came inside, even though he still hadn't said the words she longed to hear. Neither, she realized, after he'd gone, did she know what he'd meant when he'd spoken of table five.

"That was an absolute disaster!" said Amber furiously that evening. "I could kill that stupid Laura!"

Andrew tightened the cords fastening Amber's ankles to the spreader board and looked at her lying spread-eagled on the king-size bed. "She made a genuine mistake. If you punish her too severely she'll leave, so you'd better control yourself. We need her. The twins are a big turn-on for the men here, and some of the women too. Are we going to test this trial tonight or not?" he added. "If not, I'm going to find someone who'll be more fun tonight."

"If we're not careful I'll lose my place here, which will be a far bigger loss than the twins going," snapped Amber. "I saw the look in Grace's eyes when she triumphed over Amy. She's the first of David's guests to reach level four, and he'll soon be starting to think he can't live without her. So, if you want any chance at all with her, you should be worried too."

"I'm not pleased, but losing my temper won't help matters. Can you move at all?"

Amber tested the spreader board, and also tried to sit up, but a thick leather strap around her waist made it impossible. "No, I can't. So do you have a brilliant scheme up your sleeve to make sure Grace fails the fourth trial?" Her breathing was quickening now.

"I wasn't thinking about the trial, more about what she'll be doing this coming month. David's away on business in Europe for three whole weeks. She'll be alone, and would probably be pleased to see a familiar face one evening."

"What do you intend to do, go and knock on her front door? I'm sure David would be delighted if he learned about that."

"That's just silly, Amber," said Andrew, and without warning he brought a multi-thonged leather whip down hard across the blonde woman's lush, creamy breasts. Amber gave a cry of pain, but Andrew knew she liked pain, and swiftly whipped her three more times, until her upper chest was covered in thin red lines.

"I know where Grace is going to be next Friday night. I shall meet her there, ostensibly quite by chance, and try to get her interest. I'm sure she likes me. It won't be difficult." With that he lowered his head and started to run his tongue over Amber's marked breasts. She shuddered with rising excitement at his touch.

"She probably likes a lot of people, but it's David she's in love with," she gasped, finding it hard to concentrate now.

"At the moment she is, but the next trial is spread over the whole weekend. I bet he hasn't told her that. I might let the information slip out during our chat, along with a few other things she may not know yet. Time to move between your thighs I think. Should I say out loud what I'm going to do? Tell me if that increases the excitement for you."

Amber didn't answer. "I think I should," said Andrew. "I'm going to whip your inner thighs now, and then cover the marks with your own juices, but I don't want you to come yet."

"You bastard!" retorted the gasping Amber.

"We are testing out a trial," Andrew reminded her, letting the whip fall expertly on each of her inner thighs before thrusting his fingers inside her and spreading her love juices over the marked skin.

Amber's stomach muscles bunched tightly as she fought to stop herself from climaxing. "And you think that's enough to stop her loving David and fall for you?" she said, her voice shaking as Andrew's naked body crouched over her and he pushed two fingers into her rear opening while at the same time letting a vibrator play over her tight stomach. "No, but it's a start. You need more faith in my ability to get a woman I want," he murmured. "Do you have a better plan?"

"God, I need to come," said Amber breathlessly.

"I think this is turning out well," murmured Andrew. "Perhaps a touch of the whip on the stomach now? Would that trigger an orgasm already, even in you?"

"I don't know, just do it!" shouted Amber.

Andrew dropped the vibrator, and whipped Amber's heaving belly hard before gripping her swollen breasts firmly in his hands and thrusting himself urgently into her.

Amber tried to get him off her, she hated it when he took over like this, but she was helpless to stop him, and the harder he thrust, moving against her bruised thighs, hands gripping her marked breasts, the closer she came to reaching her orgasm. Finally, with a scream of relief the pleasure flooded through her, and she tightened her muscles around Andrew, milking him hard even after he'd come, until he cried out with pain and withdrew rapidly.

"That was good," she said after her breathing had calmed down. "It will test table three's guest to the limit next month."

Andrew padded off to the shower room.

"If Grace succeeds next month, she'll want to challenge me, because she knows now that I'm her enemy. I saw it in her face last night. I felt it in the way her body reacted to my touch," said Amber the moment he returned.

"Hardly surprising; you're not exactly subtle," Andrew pointed out, releasing her from the bed.

"Listen, if this so-called plan of yours fails, all you lose is the chance to move in on Grace. I could lose everything. Where would I go if David got rid of me? What could I do?"

"You could set up your own Club, with a similar theme. Be your own boss. That would suit your sexual preferences very well."

"But I'd never see David again. We've been together for ten years now, and he does care for me."

Andrew looked genuinely sad. "Surely you're not in love with him? You of all people should have known better than to let that happen."

She bit on her lip. "I didn't mean it to, but it was impossible to keep totally detached and despite all the women he's dated, he's always ended up coming back to me. He told me he'd never find anyone else who matched him so perfectly."

"But did he tell you that he loved you?"

"Of course not! I've already told you, David doesn't fall in love."

"Maybe he never has before, but Grace is different. He's different when he's with her too."

"He nearly made her fail last night," protested Amber.

"Yes, but in the end he helped her succeed. That's when I knew how much she meant to him."

"But you still want her?" Amber sounded desperate now.

"Yes, I want her and I think I'm half in love with her already. The irony is that I've never felt quite this way about a woman before, yet she's in love with the only man I know who always gets what he wants and who's also my closest friend."

"Then fight for her," Amber urged him. "If you fight for her as strongly as I'm going to fight to keep David, we won't fail. Play to your strengths. You're the polar opposite of David, and right now she's probably torn between desire for him and her newfound sexual needs and fear of what a future with him might mean. You can satisfy her sexual desires but you're less complex than David.

"Right now I'm sure she's in a state of total confusion about what's happening to her. I can tell she likes you, and with David out of the way these next three weeks are your best chance of success."

Andrew nodded. "You're right. It's now or never for me. I'll get things organized. We'll leave that enema trial for another time."

Amber watched him leave. She hoped he'd be success-ful, but if he failed, then she would need to have a fallback plan, to make it very difficult for Grace to take her place.

Thoughtfully, squeezing her still sore breasts to keep herself aroused for as long as possible, she began to watch all the film that they had of Grace from her first visit to the Dining Club.

At ten o'clock on the Friday night, Grace and Fran walked through the black doors of the King's Head theater in Islington into the light and noise of the pub bar. As always the cramped pub was packed full of people, but Fran ruthlessly elbowed her way toward the fireplace as Grace collected the drinks they'd ordered in the interval.

To her surprise, by the time she'd been served and got through the crowd, Fran had found two seats at a table, which was nothing short of a miracle.

"How did you manage that?" she asked in astonishment.

"All thanks to this nice gentleman sitting beside me," said Fran with a smirk that made it clear she fancied the nice "gentleman."

Grace set their drinks down and settled herself in the remaining empty seat before looking at the man sitting next to Fran. "Andrew!" she exclaimed in astonishment, feeling the color rush to her cheeks.

Fran raised her eyebrows. "You two know each other?"

Andrew looked equally astonished. "Grace! How lovely to see you again!"

Grace didn't think it was lovely at all. "Have you seen the play?" she asked, hoping they could talk about that so that Fran didn't start trying to find out how they knew each other.

Andrew pulled a face. "No fear; I'm not a great fan of Shakespeare, and I don't like *The Winter's Tale* at all. I'm too old for fairy stories!"

"I love it," said Fran. "Every time I see it I'm reminded of the power of jealousy to ruin even the strongest love."

"I find the fact that it shows how even the closest male bond can be ruined by jealousy more interesting," said Grace, directing her comment at Andrew.

"It's only a play!" he responded, smiling at her, and despite her shock at seeing him, and a suspicion that it wasn't a chance meeting, Grace couldn't help smiling back.

He was so relaxed, and totally at ease in his surroundings. He was also even more handsome than she'd realized, and judging by the way Fran was hanging on his every word she hadn't failed to notice that either.

Grace liked him a lot, but she couldn't help worrying that for some reason David had sent him, although why he'd want her watched she couldn't imagine, since he was the least jealous man she'd been out with.

"How do you two know each other?" Fran asked. "Clearly it's not through work if you hate Shakespeare, Andrew."

"Grace isn't only interested in Shakespeare surely?" he asked, with a quick teasing glance across at her.

She felt herself tensing, remembering the last time he'd seen her and what she must have looked like as she struggled to reach that final elusive orgasm. "No, I like all theater, and I specialize in the work of new playwrights. Fran's a playwright," she said, trying desperately to push Fran in Andrew's direction and distract him.

"Then how do you know each other?" persisted Fran, who was like a dog with a bone once she got hold of something, and it was plain she now thought she was onto something very interesting.

"We work out at the same club," said Andrew.

Fran looked at Grace in astonishment. "You've joined a gym?"

"Yes, but I don't think I'll be going there much longer."

"It was a special offer; one she couldn't refuse!" laughed Andrew.

The three of them made desultory conversation for a few minutes, but when Andrew went up to the bar to get himself another drink, Fran began to gather up her things. "Don't go!" protested Grace.

"Look, he clearly fancies you and I'm not sitting here like a spare prick at a wedding. We can talk about the actress who played Hermione when we meet on Monday. You two have a nice evening. Does your financier lover know about him?" she added curiously.

"There's nothing to know! We're just friends."

"Maybe, but he definitely wants to be a friend with benefits! Phone me over the weekend and tell me all about it. You're certainly good at keeping secrets these days. You never talk about David and now up pops a handsome hunk with a body to die for!"

If she knew exactly how good she was at keeping secrets, Fran would be stunned thought Grace to herself.

"Where's your friend gone?" asked Andrew when he got back.

"Home, she wanted an early night…Do you come to the King's Head a lot?"

"Yes, I like the atmosphere."

"I've never seen you here before, and I come at least once a month," said Grace, still convinced he was only there because David had asked him to come.

"Maybe we've always come on different nights then. You don't look very pleased to see me," he added. "I'm quite hurt."

He didn't look hurt, because his eyes were dancing

with amusement, and now that Fran had gone, Grace began to relax a little and reluctantly smiled back at him. "I was embarrassed. I didn't know how I was going to explain knowing you."

"I thought I did that quite neatly for you."

"Yes, but now Fran will expect me to be super-fit!"

They both laughed, and for a time Andrew chatted in a way that Grace realized David never did, telling her amusing anecdotes about things that had happened to him. He made her feel attractive and amusing too, and when they left the pub together, with Andrew insisting he must see her safely back to her apartment, she noticed the look of envy in the eyes of several women in the pub.

She wasn't surprised. His broad shoulders and powerful physique were emphasized tonight by his tight-fitting jeans and short-sleeved shirt. His thick, dark hair was as tousled as always, and again she was struck by how easy he'd be to cast if he were an actor. He'd certainly attract a huge fan base, and if she weren't in love with David she knew that she'd be enjoying his attention this evening.

"What are you thinking?" he asked as they waited for the next tube train.

"That you'd be a great hit with the women if you were an actor."

"Maybe a career change is called for!" he said with a laugh.

"Tell me what you were thinking," said Grace.

"That David isn't being fair to you," he said quietly, just as the train appeared out of the tunnel.

Shocked to the core, Grace didn't speak at all during the

journey. On the short walk from the underground to her apartment, she still felt too shaken to make conversation, and when they stopped at her front door she didn't know what to do or say.

Andrew put his hands gently on her shoulders. "I'm sorry, I shouldn't have blurted it out like that, but it upsets me. I know he's my friend, but I care about you Grace, and I don't want to see you hurt."

"He's not hurting me," she protested. "The Dining Club has made a huge difference to my life, a positive difference, and it's brought us closer together as well. I don't know why you're doing this, but the fact is that I love David and I want to be part of his life, all of his life."

"I know you do, that's why I think you need to hear what I've got to say."

Grace hesitated. She didn't know what to do. She liked Andrew, and felt instinctively he could be trusted to speak the truth. If he wasn't there on David's behalf, and she didn't think David would need to test her loyalty like this after their sessions at the Dining Club, then obviously Andrew was genuinely worried about her. On the other hand, having seen the play tonight, the power of jealousy was still fresh in her mind.

"At least hear me out, Grace," said Andrew urgently. "If you don't believe what I tell you, or it doesn't make any difference, then no harm's been done. If you do believe me, then you can make an informed decision about any future with David. All I'm asking is that you hear me out, for your own sake."

Still Grace hesitated. A part of her didn't want to let

Andrew inside the front door, and didn't want to hear what he had to say. But, and she was honest enough to realize this, that was only because she already had some subconscious doubts after the last weekend, and was terrified that Andrew was now going to prove them right.

For a few more seconds Grace waited. "All right, you'd better come in," she said at last, turning her key in the lock but hoping against hope that what he was about to tell her didn't mean that she would never return to the Club with David again.

Once in the apartment she turned to face him. "Right, you'd better tell me what it is that you think I need to know."

PART SIX

Caress

FIFTEEN

The atmosphere in the flat was so highly charged that it seemed to have affected Andrew. "Is it okay if I take my jacket off and sit down before we start to talk?" he asked.

"If you must," said Grace, realizing she sounded ungracious but desperate to hear what he had to say.

"I could do with a coffee too," he added.

"I'm sorry, you must think me incredibly rude, but I need to know what..."

He nodded. "Sure, I understand, but it's not easy for me either."

Reluctantly Grace made them both coffee, and by the time she handed him his mug he seemed more relaxed, but was plainly still uncomfortable.

"This is no fun for me either, Grace," he admitted. "David's been my friend for years."

"Then why are you doing it?"

"Can't you guess?"

"No, I can't," said Grace.

"Because I care for you and don't want to see you hurt by him. Believe me he will hurt you eventually. He doesn't know the meaning of love."

"And you don't seem to know the meaning of loyalty," she pointed out. "Just tell me what you think I need to know. I can't stand all this waiting." She cupped her hands around her coffee mug so that he couldn't see how much they were shaking.

"I want to talk to you about the last girlfriend he brought to the Dining Club."

"You mean Louise Penfold?"

Andrew was clearly taken aback. "He's talked to you about her?"

"Not in detail, but I believe she went to the Dining Club and that although she failed she's still his PA."

"Yes, she failed the trial that you've now passed, and she failed it because David made it too difficult for her to have any chance of succeeding."

"And how did he do that?"

"By giving Amber information about her sexual preferences in advance. She was worn out very quickly, which was his intention. He wanted her to fail."

"Why did he take her there if he wanted her to fail?"

"At first I think he wanted her to do well, but as the months went by he realized success would change the balance of their relationship. She was gaining in confidence all the time, and he decided he'd preferred the dynamics the way they were before."

"Then why did he stop going out with her after she'd failed? The dynamics, as you put it, wouldn't have changed then."

"The Dining Club changes everyone, Grace. Surely you've realized that by now? It changes the guest and it changes the person who's brought them. The member of the Club starts to see their lover in a different light. That's not always a good thing. Watching a woman you make love to regularly having a wonderful time with other men and women can stop you from feeling you're special to them.

"Of course that doesn't always happen, but it can. It can cement a partnership, but equally it can tear one apart even though the guest does everything that's asked of them in order to keep their lover. It's a dangerous game."

"You're saying David felt inferior to Louise after she passed three trials, and so he tried to make her fail the fourth?" queried Grace incredulously. "I can't imagine David ever feeling inferior to anyone."

"Perhaps he preferred her as a PA rather than a lover after that," said Andrew. "I don't know what goes on his head, I only know what he did."

"Well he didn't do it to me."

"Didn't he, Grace?" he asked gently.

Her mouth went dry. "No, at the end he helped me."

"But he wasn't pleased when Laura made a mistake which meant Amy couldn't climax anymore was he?" said Andrew. "Why not? He should have been delighted."

Grace hated hearing her own doubts about that voiced aloud. "Perhaps he felt it wasn't a fair contest anymore," she suggested.

Andrew looked thoughtfully at her. "You must really love him a lot; you don't want to face any of this do you? Why didn't he explain the trial properly at the beginning then? Do you really think that was a mistake?"

"I don't know," she confessed. "It's hardly a big deal though. I passed, and that's what matters. He was very happy afterwards."

"He was?"

"Yes," she said firmly, remembering how close she'd felt to him, and how near she was sure he'd come to saying he loved her. "And since you seem very keen on talking about the last trial, you and Amber both tried to stop me succeeding."

"How?"

Her cheeks felt hot. "You stopped what you were doing to me just when... Look, I'm really not comfortable talking about this here. It's different at the Dining Club."

"Yes, because that's not the real world. Don't ever forget that. All right, I admit I didn't play fair either, but I did it because I like you so much. I'm only human. I don't have David's skill at remaining detached during all the trials, not when I have feelings for someone."

Grace looked across the room at him. He was as flushed as she was now, but not with embarrassment. She realized that thinking back to the trials had aroused him, and that he wanted her.

"If I weren't with David, would you want to go out with me?" she asked slowly.

Andrew nodded. "Yes, I would," he said, his deep voice tender. "I realize that's not the way a best friend should behave, but I can't help it. I think I'm falling in love with you, Grace."

"But your motive for warning me off David is still purely for my own sake, is it?"

"Yes, hard as it may be for you to believe, it is. I know you don't feel the same way about me at the moment, and if you leave David you still might not, but despite that I don't want to see you hurt."

"I think I'll take my chance on being hurt. I'm not a fool, Andrew. David's very complex, and I don't pretend to understand him all the time, but I love him and I want him to love me too. The Dining Club is my only chance of making that happen. He's made that very clear."

"Even if you're right, and he does fall in love with you, it won't last," said Andrew slowly. "I've never known anyone who gets bored of things as quickly as David. I think he's one of those men for whom the conquest is all."

"The only certainty in life is that nothing stays the same forever," retorted Grace. "There are never any guarantees of anything, least of all love."

"But you think you could hold his interest for several years?"

"I don't know, but Amber seems to have done."

"He's not in love with Amber," Andrew pointed out. "That's why their relationship has lasted. Even if he does fall in love with you, Grace, when it's over and his love for you has died, Amber will still be in his life. Can you cope with that knowledge?"

"I'll do my best, although thank you for the warning."

"Good luck for the next trial then," said Andrew. "A lot of people find the prospect of a trial that lasts a whole weekend very daunting. Clearly you don't."

"The whole weekend?" she asked, unable to hide her surprise.

"Yes, didn't he tell you?"

"No, he must have forgotten," she said, suddenly remembering that David had suggested they meet up on the Friday night, something they'd never done before a visit to the Club before. Her mind raced as she realized that if the Friday evening ended with them making love, she'd already be quite tired before the long weekend began.

"I shouldn't have said anything then," said Andrew. "I simply assumed..."

"I don't see why it's important," she interrupted, not wanting him to know he'd already shaken her confidence.

"At least you know now, and can make sure you get an early night. That's what I'd suggest if you were my girl-friend, anyway."

"Well I'm not your girlfriend, I'm David's, and I'd like you to leave now," said Grace.

Andrew got out of the chair and put his jacket back on. "You're angry with me, aren't you? That's the last thing I wanted, but since you clearly don't choose to listen to me there's nothing more I can say. Remember though, if things do go wrong and you need me, I'll still be there, Grace. My feelings haven't changed, especially as I'm so certain you're making a terrible mistake."

"If you're right, then you'll know you did all you could to stop me won't you," said Grace quietly, wishing she'd never let him come back, forcing her to listen to words that she didn't want to hear, especially as some of them had merely reinforced fears she was already trying to bury.

"You don't hate me for this, do you?" asked Andrew when they reached the front door. "You're so special to me and..."

"No, I don't hate you," she assured him, kissing him lightly on the cheek. "On the contrary, I think you're a very nice if misguided person, and you're totally wrong about David."

"I doubt it, but for your sake I hope so," he replied as he left.

Grace closed the door gently behind him, wondering why she couldn't have fallen in love with such a handsome, open and caring man but instead had lost her heart to someone as complicated as David.

⁘——⁘

"I blew it!" said Grace's open and caring man furiously, walking into Amber's office an hour later. "I think if anything I've made matters worse. She knew some of the things I was saying were true, but she's pretending they're not. She's so besotted with him that there's no reasoning with her. All I've done is messed up my chances if something does go wrong at the next trial."

Amber looked thoughtfully at him through narrowed eyes. "I suppose you were fool enough to tell her how you felt about her?"

Andrew shrugged. "Yes, sort of."

"Idiot! That means she'd have put it all down to jealousy, the truth and the lies. You men are so stupid. Why couldn't you have kept that nugget of information to yourself for the moment? Did you seriously think she was going to give up David and throw herself into your manly arms the moment you'd finished telling her a few home truths about him?"

"She's bright, I thought she'd already have some doubts."

"I expect she did, until you barged in, making your own interest in her only too clear. She was bound to rush to his defense then. Mind you, some of what you said will

probably sink in later. I imagine you've given her something to think about."

"Not enough to make her withdraw from the next trial."

"Then we, or rather I, will have to make absolutely
certain that she fails it won't we?"

"She already knew about Louise."

"What, that David made her fail?"

"No, but she knew she'd been here."

Amber tapped her pen against her notebook. "She's
done her homework well. I doubt if David would have told
her about Louise. Luckily I've had a more productive few
days than you."

"Why, what have you been doing?"

"It's all in here," she said with a tight smile, locking
the notebook away. "All her weaknesses, all the things she
struggled to do, and I've had a nice long chat with David
about them as well. I can tell he's still not sure whether he
wants her to succeed or not."

"That doesn't change her abilities, or her determination
to succeed," said Andrew.

"Be thankful I put together another plan, since yours
seems to have backfired so badly," said Amber.

"I've less to lose than you," he snapped, still smarting
from his time with Grace, when her love for David had
become all the more obvious.

"Yes but something tells me that you'll now be even
keener for her to fail, so I know I can count on you during
the whole weekend," retorted Amber.

"As long as it's in the trial, and David's approved it, I'll be on your side," Andrew promised her. "I think I'm in the mood for testing that other trial now."

"That's fine by me," said Amber with a thin smile. "As you're the one who's just made a mistake, I think you should be the one on the receiving end this time. We often use it in men's trials, so it will be better all around."

Andrew shook his head. "I don't like..."

"It will be more like a real trial then. I'll call Will and Amy."

Before Andrew could protest, Will was at the door and they hustled Andrew into the basement. Stripped of his clothing, his hands manacled to a bar above his head, he waited, the sound of his heavy breathing filling the dark room.

"You're not at all aroused," said Amber, running her fingernails around the sensitive rim of his glans. "Let's hope Amy can help change that."

Andrew's body tensed as he felt Will parting his buttocks and then Amy's small fingers were probing softly at the entrance to his rectum, pressing against the inner walls and then moving until they located his prostate gland. He drew in his breath sharply, but after a few seconds she stopped. Then, as Amber's mouth closed over his rapidly hardening erection, he felt a thin tube being inserted between his buttocks.

"I don't want to do this!" he protested.

Amber smiled at him. "You sound just like a guest! Besides, your body is saying something totally different."

He wished that it wasn't, and felt his bowels churn as

warm water slowly filled him and the pressure built in his pelvic area. Amber lifted her head for a moment, staring into his eyes. "You love this," she said softly. "Don't try to pretend you don't. Let yourself go."

"It's too intense," he protested. His erection was so hard that it was hurting him, but still he couldn't come. Then the tube was withdrawn, the water slowly left him and once again Amy started massaging his prostate as Amber closed a warm mouth over his purple glans, letting her tongue flick into the tiny slit at the top. With a deep moan he felt the pleasure rising up and then it was spilling into her mouth and she sucked so hard on him that the pleasure only lasted a few seconds before turning to discomfort and then pain.

Still Amy continued to stimulate him from behind, and now as his hard cock began to shrink, Amber's mouth closed around the head again, only this time her mouth was ice cold, and he shouted with shock, even though he could feel himself stirring again and his testicles started to tighten once more.

"That will do," said Amber, and immediately Amy withdrew her fingers, Will untied him and the two of them left him alone with Amber, alone and still not totally satisfied.

"Excellent!" exclaimed Amber. "A suitable punishment for your stupidity, and a successful test for a trial. If you want my opinion, you need a different kind of woman from Grace anyway, someone more sparky, less easily shocked perhaps. You should find someone and bring them along as a guest once Grace's time with us is over."

Driving back to his home as dawn was breaking,

Andrew remembered her words. Despite everything, he still thought it possible Grace might well succeed, and that Amber was right to be afraid of the curvy, dark-haired girl with the long-lashed brown eyes and deceptively innocent smile.

If she wasn't right, but Grace didn't turn to him when David discarded her, he thought he would like to bring a guest to the Dining Club sometime in the future.

He wanted to experience what David was feeling, but he could never do that with Grace because she wouldn't be allowed to do the trials again. So, should he be thwarted in his efforts to make Grace fall in love with him, it would be exciting to find a woman he felt deeply about. However, finding the right person would be very difficult, and it was still Grace he dreamed about at night.

That night Grace was woken from a deep sleep by the sound of her phone ringing. Virtually no one she knew used her landline these days, and she fumbled with the switch on her bedside lamp and then nearly dropped the receiver because the phone cord was tangled.

"Hello?" she said breathlessly.

"Grace darling, it's me. Are you all right?"

"David?" she asked incredulously. He'd never phoned her from a work trip abroad before. "Is something wrong?"

"Of course not, I just wanted to hear your voice. Did I wake you?"

She glanced at her bedside clock. "It's three in the morning, of course you woke me!"

"Sorry, I lose track of time when I'm working. How was the play?"

"The play?" she queried, quite forgetting having seen *The Winter's Tale* and worried that somehow he knew about her meeting with Andrew, which she sensed wouldn't have pleased him.

"Yes, at the King's Head. You went with Fran to check out an actress as I recall. Was she any good?"

Grace was totally bewildered. Although he did take an interest in her work, it was totally out of character for him to ask her about such a relatively unimportant theater trip. "Not brilliant, but adequate," she said, still struggling to emerge from a deep sleep.

"What did Fran think of her?"

Grace didn't have a clue, because they hadn't yet discussed it. "We're going to talk about it more next week. Fran wanted an early night and the play went on quite late," she explained.

"Are you missing me?" he asked tenderly.

Immediately she was certain that he knew. Somehow he knew that she'd met up with Andrew and that he'd come back to her flat. Despite being half-asleep she had to decide quickly what to tell him. "Yes, I am," she said truthfully. "It was made worse tonight because I saw Andrew at the King's Head. He was there drinking when Fran and I came out of the play."

There was a moment's silence at the other end of the line. Clearly David hadn't expected her to tell him the truth. "And that made you miss me more?" he asked.

"Yes, it did."

"How much do you miss me?"

Grace wished she wasn't so tired. She felt she needed to be more alert to cope with the conversation, but her brain wouldn't function properly. "A lot," she said.

"Then touch yourself for me."

She couldn't believe what she was hearing. "David, I'm half-asleep, I..."

"Darling, I want to think of you touching yourself."

Even though she was half-asleep she noticed that he didn't sound aroused or excited, it was more as though he was determined to remind her that she was his.

"This isn't the Dining Club," she pointed out. "I don't have to do what you want."

His voice softened and deepened, and she felt a flicker of excitement. "I know that, and if you don't want to do it then that's fine. I wish I was with you and could touch you myself. I'd begin by running my fingers along the insides of your arms and the backs of your knees. Then I'd kiss the sides of your neck, before moving lower to lick your nipples as they hardened. Are they hardening now, as I talk? Tell me the truth, Gracie," he urged her.

"Yes," she whispered.

"Excellent. Now let your fingers stray over your stomach, moving slowly down to where you're starting to ache and feel heavy. That is happening, isn't it?"

She could hardly answer she was so aroused as she obeyed his instructions. "It is," she said at last, feeling a heavy pulse beating between her thighs.

"Press the palm of your right hand over your pubic bone, and let your fingers part your sex lips," he urged her. "Isn't that good?"

She heard herself make an incoherent sound and then whimpered with pleasure at the blissful feelings the pressure of her palm was causing her. Her skin seemed too tight for her body, and she was damp with desire.

"Tell me how wet you feel," he said, his voice like velvet now.

"I'm very wet," she said breathlessly, letting her fingers slip and slide over the throbbing area around her clitoris.

"How wet?"

"Very wet," she admitted, her voice little more than a whisper.

"And you like the way you feel?"

"Yes, yes!" She could hardly wait for his next instruction.

"Good girl," he murmured. "You're wonderfully easy to arouse these days. I can't wait for our next weekend at the Club. You get back to sleep now, my darling. It was selfish of me to phone you at this hour." With that, he put down the phone, leaving her unbelievably aroused, soaking wet between her thighs and with the sound of a dead phone line in her ears. She wanted to weep with frustration.

So that had been his way of punishing her, she thought to herself. The call was a punishment for chatting to Andrew, and perhaps for taking him back to her apartment, since it was possible that somehow he knew that as well. Now she was fully awake, aroused and alone again. Yet, despite what he'd done she felt elated. For the first time he'd shown that he was capable of jealousy, which in her mind could only mean one thing. That he was falling in love with her.

SIXTEEN

It was the day before Grace's final trial at the Dining Club, and she'd spent six hours in a small, airless room with Fran interviewing possible lead actresses for Fran's play.

"That was the last of them," she said with relief, stretching her arms above her head and tilting back her chair. "I still think the one who played Hermione at the King's Head will be best. The fact that she'll be playing David Tennant's love interest in a TV series only weeks before we open is good too."

"Yes, definitely bums on seats if viewers like her," agreed Fran.

"So you're happy if we go with her?" asked Grace, glancing at her watch.

"Very happy; are you in a hurry to go somewhere? I thought we'd have a coffee down the road and chat a bit more. It's too early for a drink, more's the pity."

"I'm out for a meal tonight, I don't really have time," apologized Grace.

"With David?"

"Yes of course, who else?"

"I wondered about the hunk from the pub."

"Fran, he's not for me. He's good-looking, fun and I like him, but I'm in love with David. You know that!"

"Good," said Fran with a grin. "Give me the address of the Club then."

Grace looked at her in total shock. "What do you mean?"

"Just what I say; if you don't want him, I'll have him! Where's the Club?"

"I can't tell you that," protested Grace weakly.

"Why the hell not? Is it some kind of posh gym that you have to be invited to join? If so, and if it's expensive, you're being robbed because you don't look any different from the days when your idea of exercise was stumbling to the tube station early in the morning!"

Relief washed over Grace. She realized how stupid she must have sounded, but for a moment she'd thought that somehow Fran had heard about the Dining Club. "You do have to be invited," she said quickly. "It's only a small gym and membership is limited."

"So how did you get in?"

Grace's mind raced. "David has a stake in it," she replied.

"Well fancy that! I bet he's got a finger in more pies than Little Jack Horner ever ate. You must be mad going out with someone like that. Do you do weights or cardiovascular stuff? I remember even yoga made you put your back out!" she added, laughing at the memory.

"I really only use the swimming pool, that helps my back," said Grace, thinking that she should be the one writing plays if she could invent things this quickly.

"Damn, I really fancied him. Maybe you could sound him out about me? On second thoughts though, don't. He fancies you, so that wouldn't help me at all."

Grace gathered up her notes and slung her bag over her

shoulder. "I've got to go. We're out to dinner tonight and then away for the weekend. Let's meet on Monday and we can talk about Sandra Fisher a bit more before we actually contact her agent."

Fran looked at her thoughtfully. "You're obsessed with David, aren't you? I've never known you like this before. Is he really hot in bed? Sometimes those cool, controlled types can be dynamite when they let themselves go."

Grace didn't answer.

"You're actually blushing!" laughed Fran. "I bet I was right the first time, when I said I'd heard he was into some pretty extreme stuff. You are a dark horse," she added. "Who'd have guessed it? Now if it was me, no one would be surprised, but you!"

"You're talking rubbish," said Grace. "You're just fishing, but I'm not biting! My private life is staying private. I might as well tell the Town Crier as tell you anything!"

"See you Monday then, and you can just say hi to Andrew for me when you next have time for a leisurely swim at your posh gym."

"Will do!" promised Grace, dashing out of the door and into the gloom of a wet Friday afternoon in London.

⌫⎯⎯⎯⎯⍟

"You didn't eat much, darling. Are you nervous about the weekend?" asked David, watching Grace push her almost untouched plate of food away from her.

"A bit," she confessed. "I think I'm also too tired to eat. We were auditioning almost all day. I'll need an early night," she added.

"Sounds good to me," he said with a grin as the waitress cleared their table. "Shall we spend tonight at my place and then pick up what you need for the weekend tomorrow morning?"

After what Andrew had told her, Grace knew that he was deliberately hoping to tire her, so that when she arrived at the Dining Club and had to face a two-day trial she would struggle. She wanted to ask him why he felt the need to make it extra difficult for her, and if he wanted her to succeed or fail, but she couldn't. That would mean admitting Andrew had broken the rules and told her about the weekend in advance, and she didn't want to get him into trouble. The realization troubled her, niggling away at the back of her mind and unsettling her.

"I don't think I could cope with sex tonight and the weekend," she protested.

"We'll just hold each other and sleep then," said David.

She glanced across the table at him. He was wearing a dark blue shirt, open at the neck, and light gray trousers. The blue of the shirt emphasized the blue of his eyes, and just looking at him made her stomach tighten with desire.

"I don't know if I could manage that," she admitted.

He smiled. "You mean I have to sleep alone because you can't control yourself? That's not kind of you! We haven't seen each other much this month, and it's not exactly private at the Dining Club."

Grace wanted him as much as he seemed to want her, and she couldn't keep refusing, because he was bound to become suspicious if she did. Anyway, to her shame she was finding it difficult to control her need for him.

"All right, but I will need some beauty sleep," she said firmly.

"Of course, that's a promise."

All the way back to his flat he kept touching her lightly on the knee, telling her how much he wanted her. Her excitement grew as he told her what he wanted to do to her, and how he'd touch her. Then, the moment they were in the front door he pulled her to him and started kissing her, his hands expertly removing her top and bra, so that he could lower his head and let his tongue roam over her naked breasts.

Her nipples grew so tight they were painful, and she could hear the sound of her own breathing, ragged and fast. Pushing her up against the wall, he unzipped her jeans, and his tongue played over her stomach as he pulled them down around her ankles, along with her panties.

Grace slipped off her shoes so that he could lift her off the floor, freeing her legs. He was moving so fast, so urgently, that she could feel her orgasm starting to build. Pausing only to tear off his own clothes, David drew her into the bedroom then fell backwards onto the bed, pulling the now naked Grace on top of him. His right arm reached around behind her, pushing her up his body until she was straddling his face.

With his head buried deep between her thighs he let his tongue tease and tantalize her, and she fell forward so that her hands were flat on the bed each side of his head, supporting the weight of her upper body.

She was frantic now, moaning and crying out as the pleasure grew and grew. Still his tongue teased her, flicking around her swollen, aching clitoris before thrusting deep inside her for a few seconds, then returning to the clitoris again.

Every time she felt she was about to come he would change what his tongue was doing, and the breaks in rhythm meant that she remained balanced on the edge of her orgasm for what seemed like an eternity. Then, as her cries grew more frantic he drew her clitoris into his mouth, sucking gently on the mass of nerve endings while at the same time slipping a finger between her buttocks and caressing the paper-thin skin around her second opening.

As her climax exploded, the pleasure spread through every inch of her body and then she screamed with delight. Without pausing, he rolled her onto her back, hooked her legs over his shoulders and thrust himself deeply inside her.

The last tingles of her long-delayed climax were still dying away as he moved in and out of her, his movements slow and steady at first but then quickening. She felt the sparks of pleasure reigniting and once more her muscles contracted in a spasm that was so intense it was almost painful.

Her back arched off the bed as she climaxed for the second time. Now his hands gripped her hips, and he continued to move in and out of her, rotating his own hips until he found her G-spot. To her surprise she realized that her body was tightening once more, the heavy pressure building deep within her belly until, with a groan of pleasure mixed with despair, she was shaken by another intense orgasm.

She heard herself cry out, and then heard David gasp loudly as finally he allowed his own pleasure to spill, and she felt him shuddering above her, until finally he too was still.

Rolling off her he then pulled her against his damp, sweat-soaked body. "You were wonderful, my darling," he murmured, "absolutely wonderful. Now you'd better get that beauty sleep I promised you."

As her breathing slowed and her sated body lay limply on the sheets, Grace was keenly aware that although it had been some of the best sex they'd ever had, David had got his way. Her body would definitely be tired when they arrived at the Dining Club the following morning.

By ten the next morning they'd already called in at Grace's apartment and were on their way. Waiting at some traffic lights, David saw that Grace was almost half-asleep beside him, and felt a fleeting moment of guilt about what had happened the previous night.

He'd known full well that what he was doing wasn't fair on her, but hadn't been able to stop himself. When he'd learned that she and Andrew had met at the King's Head, and that Andrew had gone back to the flat with her, he'd experienced a moment of jealous fury that was totally new to him. Even though she'd been open and honest about it when he'd phoned her, the jealousy had lingered all the following day, distracting him from his work, and he hadn't liked it. Possessing her last night had been both a primitive need to reaffirm that she was his, and also a punishment for her, because of what he knew was waiting for her at the Club.

If jealousy was the price of love, then that was another reason for trying to avoid it, he thought to himself, yet Grace already meant too much to him. Somehow she'd found her way under his skin and into his heart, and he'd never felt so vulnerable before. The only way he could stop their relationship now was if she failed this weekend. Then he would have to walk away, but he was torn between his need for her and his fear of how his life would be changed once he admitted his love.

If she succeeded this weekend, he would then have to tell her about table five, because that was in the rules. Normally no one was interested in table five, but he knew her well enough to be fairly certain that now, after all she'd seen and done at the Dining Club, she would be interested, because of Amber, who hadn't managed to hide her determination to make Grace fail.

That inability to conceal her feelings had almost certainly allowed Grace to realize the full extent of the other woman's importance to him. His feelings for Amber were nothing like his feelings for Grace, but he liked the security of knowing that with her running the Dining Club he would never be sexually bored.

If Grace should succeed in both the trials then David's life would change radically, and he didn't know how he'd cope with that. He'd always liked the sheer animal magnetism and wonderful perversity that Amber brought to the sexual challenges at the Dining Club, as well as their occasional private moments, and didn't believe that any one woman was capable of being all things to him. There had been times during the last week when he'd faced the fact that perhaps he couldn't ever fall in love in the way that other men did, yet he didn't want that either. If Grace failed this weekend he wouldn't have to keep turning the problem over and over in his mind, which might well be the best solution, and not impossible to arrange.

"Each man kills the thing he loves," he murmured to himself.

"Oscar Wilde," said Grace sleepily.

"What?"

"Oscar Wilde wrote that. He said the coward does it with a kiss."

"Did he indeed," said David, wondering why she'd quoted that particular line. "We're nearly there now, darling. How do you feel?"

"Still nervous, but sad in a way too. I think I've become addicted to the Club, although I might change my mind after tonight I suppose."

David stopped the car at the gate at the end of the road and waited for the man to let them through. "Actually, this trial is in two parts. It begins after lunch and then concludes tonight," he explained. "Obviously as it's the last one it's more complicated."

"And more difficult?"

"Well yes, of course."

"It's spread over two sessions in one day and yet last night you…"

"I got carried away," he said apologetically. "Here we go," he said, and eased the car down the road and into the drive of the Dining Club. Once parked, he turned, and took hold of Grace's hands. Whatever happened, whatever he decided to do as the weekend progressed, he wanted her to understand the depth of his feelings at this moment, and he knew that she needed to hear it too.

"I really want you to succeed, darling. I know you may be doubting that now, but I do. Success for you this weekend will make me happier than I've ever been in my life before.

"Also, if you succeed then I can tell you about table five, and table five is very special to me."

"Does table five involve another trial?" she asked nervously. "I thought that there were only four."

He felt another twinge of guilt. "Only if you choose; it's an option that's rarely offered and has never yet been taken up."

"Why?"

"Sweetheart, I can't tell you yet. Just remember, if you succeed this weekend I'll be happier than I've ever been in my life before. That's all you need to think about over the next two days. Whatever happens, however difficult it is, think of us and remember that's why you're doing it, for us and our future."

With that he leaned over and kissed her gently on the lips, just as Oscar Wilde's coward had done.

SEVENTEEN

Sitting on the end of the bed watching David unpack, Grace wondered what lay ahead of her and if she would ever return to the Dining Club after this weekend. For the moment she was pushing all thoughts of table five to the back of her mind. This weekend was what she'd always thought of as the top trial.

She remembered the woman who'd hoped to marry her lover, and how she'd failed. So many sensual struggles had already taken place, and yet two more sessions of pleasure mixed with frustration or pain still lay ahead of her. Two more tests of her ability to control her own sensuality, a sensuality that had been honed and heightened by the three trials she'd already passed.

"When does the first trial begin?" she asked.

"At two o'clock," replied David. "I'll have a sandwich sent up to you soon."

"Aren't you eating?"

"I've got to help make sure everything is ready for you," he explained. "I'll come and fetch you when it's time."

"So, I have a test this afternoon, and then another one after dinner tonight?"

"That's right."

Grace bit on her lower lip, wanting to know more, but

well aware that he couldn't tell her anything. She must remain in their suite and wait for everything to unfold.

When David finally came for her, he was brisk and businesslike. All traces of the affectionate lover had disappeared. "Here's what you're to wear to begin with," he said, holding out a small black and red garment. "Take off your clothes," he added. "It's time. The twins are waiting."

The change in him made Grace even more nervous, despite the fact that she realized this was the intention. When she was naked he helped her into the tight-fitting bondage body-shaper, which thrust her breasts upwards while the bones of the corset nipped her in at the waist. Where it flared over her hips the material fitted so tightly that she could feel the pressure on her naked stomach and hips.

It ended at the top of her thighs. When she was standing still with her legs together, she looked perfectly decent, but the moment she started to walk she knew that she was no longer totally covered either at the front or the back, as she felt the air against her pubic hair and the bottom of her buttocks.

"Very nice," said David appreciatively, running his fingers over her naked shoulders and upper chest. Lifting her hair he kissed her softly on the back of her neck, and then his teeth nipped sharply at the flesh at the top of her spine and she squealed with surprise. With a light laugh he let her hair fall back into place. "This should be very interesting," he promised her. "Let's go downstairs."

On the way down they passed several members of staff, all of whom smiled at Grace, but every time they did this she averted her head, aware of how indecent the costume was.

"Stand up straight, be proud of your body," David instructed her. "You look sexy and you're meant to arouse excitement and interest in people. Don't forget that, or you'll be punished."

Pushing her shoulders back, Grace obediently lifted her head high, and heard him make a sound of approval as he led her into the room where she'd met the twins on her arrival for the very first trial.

This time the twins were standing naked, apart from a black strap around their waists, standing side by side with their backs against two poles that had been lowered from the ceiling. Moving nearer she realized that the black straps were keeping them fastened to the poles, so that they couldn't move away.

Amber and Andrew were sitting on the sofa where she'd first had to touch Laura's breasts. They both smiled at her. "Welcome back, Grace," said Amber sweetly. "You should enjoy this. All you have to do is bring both of the twins to orgasm within thirty minutes. You can use anything that's on the side table over there, plus any part of yourself you choose of course. The only thing you can't do is unfasten them."

"Not too testing, is it?" said Andrew.

Grace didn't reply. She was too busy looking at the twins and realizing that since they must have done this many times before, it wouldn't be an easy task. Neither was it one that she felt in the least bit comfortable doing.

"The three of us will stay and watch," added Andrew. "We have to make sure that the game is played fairly."

Amber glanced at her wristwatch. "Any questions before you begin?"

Grace shook her head.

"Excellent, then we'll start the clock. Oh, and remember twins, if Grace succeeds, whichever one of you came the quickest will be punished by me afterwards."

"In your own time, Grace," said David. "The clock starts now."

Grace's mind began to race. From everything she'd seen and learned of the twins, she was sure that Amy would be far more difficult to bring to orgasm than Laura. So, if she started with Laura, then Amy would have to listen to her twin's rising excitement, and hear her having her climax before Grace got around to touching her. By then she should already be a little aroused.

She hesitated, wondering what she should do to Laura to get her to climax quickly, unsure that she could even manage to touch either of the girls in the way that was being asked of her. Then, as she heard the clock ticking she felt a sudden surge of determination. Having come this far, she had no intention of failing, and the sooner she started the sooner she'd discover what she needed to do in order to tease an orgasm from Laura.

Quickly she went to the table Amber had mentioned and picked up a tube of scented lubricating gel. Pouring some into the palm of her hands she began to massage Laura's heavy breasts. She didn't dare stop to think about what she was doing, or what she must look like to the three people watching her, because she knew she had to concentrate on the task she'd been set.

As her fingers massaged the undersides of Laura's gradually swelling globes, cupping and lifting them as she worked, she was shocked by what she was doing, but even more shocked to discover that as Laura's large nipples hardened and the tips turned bright red, she herself was excited.

After a few minutes Laura's breathing quickened slightly, so Grace teased each of the nipples in turn, rolling them between her thumbs and index fingers, and she saw Laura swallow hard, trying to subdue her quickening flesh.

With the ticking of the clock sounding loudly in her ears, Grace poured some more of the gel into her hands before smoothing them down each side of the twin's body. As the palms of her hands skimmed Laura's hipbones, Laura instinctively pushed her lower body forward as far as the imprisoning strap would let her.

Sitting on the floor, feeling the soft carpet brushing against her own naked vulva, elated and astonished by her own success, Grace pushed Laura's legs apart and ran her fingernails up and down the insides of the girl's thighs. At first she moved them in straight lines then, just as she judged Laura was adapting to that sensation, she traced tiny circles on the twitching flesh instead.

Laura's breathing quickened, the sound loud in the silent room. Now Grace hesitated. She knew that she had to open the twin up, part her outer sex lips and touch her in her most intimate area, but she didn't know if she could do it.

As she froze into stillness, out of the corner of her eye she saw Amber move, leaning eagerly forward. Remembering what was at stake, and what David had said to her before they'd entered the Dining Club that morning, she tentatively let her hands open Laura up, and saw immediately that the girl was already highly aroused.

She let her fingers move softly along the damp flesh, while avoiding the swelling clitoris, and Laura let out a tiny moan of pleasure. Immediately Grace let the tip of one finger brush against the side of the swollen nub, swirling Laura's own juices around the area before touching it once more.

This time Laura gasped loudly, but then the sound abruptly ceased and Grace knew that the twin had remembered she shouldn't climax too soon. Desperate not to let the sexual tension in the girl's body decrease, Grace picked up what looked like a child's paintbrush, almost hidden beneath other items on the table. While she was doing that, Laura moved her legs together again, but with the ticking of the clock loud in her ears, Grace roughly pushed them apart and reached up, caressing Laura's hips with one hand while swirling the tip of the brush around and around her needy, damp clitoris. Almost immediately, with a loud despairing cry, Laura's body went into a spasm as her climax flooded through her.

Watching Laura, and imagining only too well how she must feel, Grace was shocked to realize that she was becoming aroused herself. Giving the other girl such pleasure had made her own body feel heavy, and the stimulation of her vulva by the carpet was increasing her excitement.

Quickly she got up and moved across to Amy. Approaching the other girl she saw that Amy's top lip was already beaded with sweat and her chest showed the pink flush of sexual arousal. Grace knew then that her decision to work on Laura first had been right.

"Laura, you only lasted fifteen minutes," said Andrew, his voice breaking the silence in the room. "Hopefully you can do better, Amy."

The tension in Amy's body increased, and Grace realized she could use that to her advantage. Swiftly she massaged Amy's breasts and body in the same way as she had Laura's, but when she parted her thighs and opened her up, her own fingers trembling with a mixture of fear and shameful excitement, she saw that Amy still wasn't as aroused as her twin had been at this stage.

Again she repeated the previous pattern, letting her finger brush against the side of the as yet relatively small clitoris, but Amy was still nowhere near an orgasm.

Grace tried to put herself in Amy's position, working out what would work better, as she was obviously controlling her well-trained body with every ounce of willpower she possessed. After a pause, Grace knew what she had to do, but wasn't sure she could make herself do it. Before her initiation into the Dining Club she could never have imagined herself making love to another woman, but she had no choice if she wanted to pass this part of the trial.

Holding Amy open with her hands, she buried her head between her thighs and let her tongue do the work, running it softly up and down the increasingly wet flesh, then swirled it around the now rapidly swelling clitoris. Amy was breathing heavily by this time, and Grace sensed that it wouldn't be long before she climaxed.

"Only five minutes to go," said Andrew.

Grace realized that hearing his words, Amy had let her guard down. Quickly she drew the sensitive clitoris into her mouth and sucked on it very lightly. This delicate pressure on the mass of highly aroused nerve endings caught Amy by surprise and with a protesting cry of "No!" her whole body convulsed. The wide strap fastening her to the pole dug deeply into her tender flesh as she doubled forward.

Watching Amy's pleasure spill, and hearing her tiny cries of delight mixed with frustration, Grace realized she was close to an orgasm too. Quickly she started to get up, but the soft carpet brushed against her open, damp vulva as she moved and her body trembled as the hot pleasure engulfed her.

Andrew released the twins, and glanced down at Grace, appreciation and admiration in his brown eyes. "You clearly enjoyed yourself too," he said with a half-smile.

"Make the most of it," said Amber, leading a downcast Amy out of the door. "I trust you enjoy this evening as much. Being hooded and bound isn't to everyone's taste."

Suddenly the room was silent. The clock had stopped, the twins, Andrew and Amber had left and Grace was alone with David. "What does she mean?" she asked fearfully.

"She shouldn't have said anything," replied David, looking down at her sitting on the soft carpet. "You have no idea how exciting that was for me. I've never wanted you as much as I do at this moment," he added, his voice thick with passion. "At least you're mine until dinner, and I know exactly what I'm going to do with you." His eyes were bright with a strange, unsettling excitement.

"Shouldn't I rest?" asked Grace.

"My darling girl, surely you understand by now that

what you want this weekend doesn't matter, and we have two hours before you need to dress for dinner."

Grace began to shake, stumbling twice as she climbed the stairs, her mind full of dark images conjured up by Amber's words and the expression on her lover's face a few minutes earlier.

"Time for you to change," said David, pushing her into their bedroom. Swiftly peeling off her corset he opened a bedside drawer. "This is what you'll be wearing for the next two hours."

PART SEVEN

Submit

EIGHTEEN

G race looked at the dark red leather outfit he was holding in his right hand, noticed the rings and straps and felt her flesh tighten with a mixture of fear and anticipation.

"It's only a body harness, plus one small extra," said David. Looking at his right hand she saw that he was holding what looked like a matching leather cap. "I don't think I want to do this now," she said nervously. "Not with tonight's trial coming up."

"I thought I'd already made it clear that everything that happens here this weekend is part of the trial," he said impatiently. "You should be grateful. I've chosen something that will help you tonight."

Grace wasn't certain that she believed him, but had no choice other than to obey or leave. As she had no intention of leaving, she walked slowly toward him, remembering to keep her head up high, and with a few deft movements he soon had the body harness on her.

The leather rings encased her breasts, and the strap that was attached to the leather collar ran from the back of her neck down her body, then came up between her thighs where it divided. The division left a gap over her sex lips, then closed again so that it was like an open crotched bikini bottom. Leather straps also supported the cheeks of her bottom, and more straps shaped like a triangle joined a metal ring in the middle of her stomach.

After studying her thoughtfully, David tightened the strap between her legs until she felt it pressing hard against her vulva. Her breath snagged in her throat as tingles of pleasure throbbed beneath the strap, and he nodded to himself. "That's better," he murmured. "Now for the hood."

Standing in front of him, silent and unblinking, Grace tried to stop herself from shaking as he pulled what at first seemed like a tight-fitting red leather cap over her head, releasing a few tendrils of hair so that they fell to her shoulders, making her jump nervously. Next he pulled hard on the leather and when it covered her face she began to panic. Terrified, she moved back, hitting herself against the foot of the bed.

"Keep still, Grace," said David sharply, and instinctively she obeyed him. "That's a good girl," he murmured, his voice now gentle as he pushed the edges of the hood back into place. His change in tone confused her, and it was a moment or two before she realized that now her eyes and nose were free again, but the lower half of her face was totally covered except for a gap over her mouth.

The leather was tight, and she was more afraid than she'd ever been, but she didn't know why. Although her ears were covered, she could still hear David's muffled voice, and she was able to see and speak. It was the pressure, and the realization that this, combined with the body harness, had taken away her sense of self. It was as if she, Grace, no longer existed. Instead she was simply a helpless plaything, for David to use as he liked.

She wondered how she'd ever let it come to this. How she, Grace, a well-respected theater director who'd been in the *Sunday Times* list of most promising new directors the year before, had allowed herself to be in this position. Tears of humiliation and disbelief filled her eyes.

"What's the matter?" asked David quietly. "If you want this to stop now, all you have to do is say so. That one word will end it all. Say 'stop' and it's over, Grace. You must choose to do this yourself."

"For us," she replied, struggling to regain her composure. "This is for us."

"But the choice is yours. Now, do you want to stop?"

Grace shook her head.

"You have to say it."

Her tongue moved over her dry lips. She hadn't come this far to be defeated now. "I don't want to stop," she said clearly.

"Excellent. Walk around the room for me. I want to watch your body as you move."

She did as he'd commanded, feeling the metal-rimmed leather rings encasing her breasts as they moved, while the tight leather strap between her legs pressed on her vulva, and every movement meant all the tiny nerve endings beneath tingled and sparked.

"I think one thing is missing," murmured David, putting out an arm and pulling her toward the window as she passed him. He made her stand facing the garden, caught in a ray of bright June sunlight, while he opened the bedside drawer again. After a few seconds she realized that there were couples walking in the garden, and some of them looked up at her, pointing her out to others walking by.

She knew she couldn't move, that she had to wait. "That was very useful," said David, fastening small rubber cones with hanging tassels on them over her rapidly hardening nipples. "Seeing you like this should help get everyone in the mood for their own tasks tonight."

The rubber cones fitted tightly, but weren't painful. For a few more minutes Grace continued to walk around the room, while David watched closely. Then he sat on the side of the bed and pulled her onto his lap. One hand went between her thighs, and he slid two fingers inside her. "You're certainly ready for me," he remarked, and she felt her cheeks go hot with shame. His other hand touched one of the hanging tassels, squeezing a tiny bulb on the end. At once the cones tightened on her nipple, and then he relaxed his grip and the pressure released again.

Working his fingers around her inner walls, letting the pad of his index finger glide over her G-spot every few seconds while at the same time pressing and releasing the bulbs on the tassels, David teased her already jangling nerve ends.

She could feel her whole body tightening now, and drew in her breath sharply as her stomach muscles began to bunch up ready for her climax. Immediately David stopped and laid her facedown on the bed. Grace turned her head to one side, as the effect of the hood was increased by the soft coverings on the bed. She was gasping now, partly out of fear and partly because her whole body was so tight that she longed for some touch to trigger the moment of release.

"You need to come don't you?" asked David, his voice deceptively kind. The words alone were enough to increase her arousal. "Answer me."

"Yes," she moaned, wanting to feel his fingers inside her again but knowing that it wasn't going to happen.

"This will help," he promised her, and she wished she could see what he was doing.

Suddenly she felt the cold touch of the end of a whip on her upper spine. She wanted to cry out in protest, but managed to stay silent. The cool, slender cord trailed gently downwards, lingering over every disc until she could feel the bed shaking she was trembling so much. Trembling not with fear but with a desperate need for release from the sexual tension that was being so cruelly heightened.

"Not long now, my darling," he murmured, letting one hand stray over her buttocks, his fingers warm and reassuring. When he let his hand stray to her sensitive hip-bone she felt the pleasure build still more, and a moan escaped her.

"Yes, you need to come," he whispered, and again his words aroused her more than anything else could have done, keeping her poised on the brink, frantic for the hot waves of pleasure to engulf her.

The tip of the whip trailed down the backs of her thighs until, without any warning, David brought it down sharply right across the middle of her buttocks. With a scream of shock and pain her body jerked violently, and she was about to shout at him to stop when suddenly the pain changed, turning into a hot, liquid sensation that spread through her whole body, triggering the most intense climax she'd ever experienced.

She shook violently from head to foot as wave after wave of muscular contractions swept through her. As she shuddered and cried out, she felt David lying naked on her back, his erection hard against her buttocks.

"Stay with me," he murmured, reaching under her and pulling back the hood of her clitoris so that he could continue to stimulate it lightly with one hand. Swirling two fingers of his other hand around in her juices he then inserted them into her rectum. She made a sound of protest as a sudden pain seared through her, but his other hand continued to play skillfully between her thighs until she was almost out of her mind with the conflicting sensations of red-hot pain and exquisite pleasure.

"I can't wait any longer," he said thickly, as slowly and carefully he eased himself inside her tight second opening.

She felt too full. It was too much to bear, and she wanted to cry out and tell him to stop yet at the same time she didn't want to lose this new sensation that was filling her with a dark, forbidden ecstasy.

David moved very carefully inside her, his own gasps mingling with hers, and then he tapped one of the fingers that were between her thighs against the side of her pulsating clitoris. With a scream of relief she came again, and as all her muscles contorted and tightened she realized that she was tightening around him as well and with a muffled groan he spilled himself into her while her whole body was still in the throes of her third orgasm of the afternoon.

For what seemed a very long time he continued to lie on top of her, as she waited for him to move. He was heavy against her trembling flesh, but at that moment she felt closer to him than she ever had before.

"You see," he whispered in her ear. "There are many pathways to pleasure."

When David eventually moved, he pulled her up off the bed and removed the harness and hood. "Time to take a bath and then change your clothes," he said briskly. "We're due down to dinner in just under an hour."

Grace looked at him, longing to hold his naked body against hers, to smell and touch him. "I've never..." she began.

"It's all part of your trial, we can't discuss it," he said abruptly.

She could have wept at the change in him, but these days she knew better than to let her feelings show during a trial. She was also coming to realize that this change actually increased the eroticism of the sex during the tests.

With the marks of the harness still imprinted on her skin she walked past him and down the few steps to the luxurious bathroom that she loved. When she came back, David had already showered and changed in another part of the Club.

"Here's your dress. I think you'll like it," he said, handing her a floor-length, split-front, peach-colored asymmetric dress, with one strap over the right shoulder and a thin silver chain belt that emphasized her slender waist. "No underwear tonight," he added.

Slipping it on, Grace discovered that the split at the front was so high she would have to be very careful how she moved if she didn't want to reveal everything to all the diners tonight.

"Perfection," he murmured, when she was ready. "Let's just pull your hair around so that it falls over your left shoulder. It makes you look sophisticated and yet wanton. My favorite look."

"Then I'm happy too," she replied quietly.

David's eyes widened for a second, as he tried to work out whether she meant it or not, and that helped give Grace the courage to face what lay ahead of her. If she'd come so far that she could take David by surprise, then nothing was going to stop her tonight. "Shall we go down?" she asked him, and with a nod he held the bedroom door open for her. The final stage of her last trial was about to begin.

NINETEEN

B y the time they entered the dining room, all the other tables were full, and several people turned to watch as Grace walked to table four. She kept her back straight and her head high, the feel of David's guiding hand in the small of her back giving her some badly needed reassurance. No matter how much she tried, she couldn't forget Amber's words earlier, and the thought of being hooded and bound terrified her.

She saw several men glance at her appreciatively as she passed, but concentrated her gaze on Andrew, who was already sitting waiting at table four. He smiled warmly at her and stood up as David pulled out her chair.

"You look stunning," he said appreciatively.

"Indeed she does," responded David. "Now, let's look at the menu."

Food was the last thing on Grace's mind, and she settled for a cheese soufflé and green salad. Then, as the meal progressed and the men chatted, she sipped her champagne, waiting nervously for the cards to be brought around.

It was Amber, dressed in a tight-fitting pale green silk sheath dress who brought them to the table, but there were only two. Grace looked at them in confusion. One said "Club Sandwich" and the other "We hope you have enjoyed your time with us."

"I don't understand," she said to David. "There isn't a proper choice."

"It's a choice," said David, watching her with interest.

Without another word Grace picked up the "Club Sandwich" card and handed it back to Amber.

"I'm sure you'll enjoy this," said the blonde woman with a smile of satisfaction. "It's one of my favorites."

Grace knew then that it certainly wasn't going to be one of hers.

For this fourth trial she was taken down two flights of steps, and when she stepped inside the door David was holding open for her she noticed how cool the air was. It felt as though the room should have been used as a wine cellar. It was very dark, and her eyes took time to adjust, but eventually she saw that the ceiling was very low, there was only one small window set in the farthest corner, and several shadowy figures were seated on small sofas set around the perimeter of the room.

An oak beam was suspended from the ceiling in the middle of the room, with something hanging from it. Her first instinct was to turn and run. There was a darkness here that scared her. Not the darkness of the room, but the darkness of the atmosphere. With so little light, everything and everyone looked menacing.

"Take off your shoes and walk into the middle of the room," said David. "Then turn and face me. Throughout the trial speak only when asked to speak, unless you want to stop the trial. If that happens you can, of course, say 'stop' at any time. You will then go back to our rooms, change back into your own clothes and be driven away as quickly as possible."

"On my own?" she whispered.

"The trial has begun. I didn't invite you to speak," he replied. "Now, take off your shoes."

This was worse than anything Grace had ever imagined. Her legs began to shake, but she slipped off her shoes and made her way to the center of the room, which had been marked with a large circle on the plush carpet.

Standing there she was able to make out the faces of some of the people sitting watching her. The twins were there, as was Andrew. Will was also back, and of course Amber, plus a man she didn't remember seeing before.

"Take off your dress for us, Grace, but slowly," said Andrew. "We want you to excite us."

Obediently Grace removed her chain belt, holding it in her hands for a few seconds before allowing it to fall to the floor. Then she unfastened the strap of the dress, easing it off her shoulder and pausing before letting the bodice fall forward, exposing her breasts to the watchers in the shadows.

Finally, after waiting a few seconds, she let the dress fall into a pool around her ankles, before stepping out of it and standing facing everyone, her nipples already hard due to the cold air. For a fleeting moment, hearing the sounds of their breathing in the otherwise silent room, she felt a sense of power at the way she'd clearly affected them.

"Now stand under the beam," said Andrew, and as she obeyed she was aware of some people moving, getting off the sofas and approaching her.

As soon as she was in place a switch was flicked and tiny lightbulbs set in the ceiling above her were switched on. The lighting was subdued and soft, but she realized that now everyone could see her clearly. She wanted to cover her breasts with her arms, or move out of the light, but instead she stood as tall as she could, determined not to let anyone see how scared she was becoming.

Amber and David emerged out of the shadows, Amber's eyes gleaming with excitement. Working quickly the pair of them spread her legs wide, fastening a spreader board to her ankles to keep her legs from moving. Then David fixed another board between her wrists. Once she was securely fastened with her arms wide apart, he finally spoke.

"Raise your arms above your head, I need to fasten the cuffs to the beam."

Obediently Grace obeyed, but she was too short and it wasn't possible. "I'm afraid you need to balance on the balls of your feet," he said, sounding far from regretful. As soon as she did this he clicked the grips from the beam into her wrist cuffs. "Excellent, we're almost done," he said to Amber, who nodded before moving away.

"You look incredibly sexy," said David appreciatively, running the palm of one hand over her breasts. "Just arch your back a little. You'll be more comfortable, and it will push your stomach forward, which will help us all. Remember, if you want to end the trial, you merely have to shout 'stop,' and no matter what's happening we will hear you."

Wondering what he meant by the last part of his sentence, Grace did as she was told. Now he ran his fingers down the tightly stretched flesh of her inner arms, making the muscles twitch beneath his touch. "So delicious," he said with satisfaction. "Have you got the finishing touch there, Amber?"

With every muscle in her body stretched and taut, Grace waited tensely as Amber and David walked around behind her. Then Amber gripped Grace around the waist to keep her still as David dropped a loose black hood over his lover's head.

The soft dark material brushed against her face, and suddenly she was in pitch-black darkness. She twisted wildly in panic, causing pain to shoot through her arm muscles. Her first instinct was to shout for the trial to stop, but a pair of strong hands steadied her around the waist, and while that was happening someone else's hand stroked her back gently, as though calming a frightened animal.

Forcing herself to breathe slowly and deeply she realized that there were holes over her ears, so while she couldn't see, and her voice would be muffled, she could at least hear what was happening in the room.

"How lovely she looks," said a man's voice. "I wish I'd been involved in some of her earlier trials."

"But you always like to be at the fourth trial," pointed out Andrew. "You can't have everything I'm afraid, not even at the Dining Club. Perhaps you'd like to begin Grace's evening?"

"Yes, I would," said the unknown man, and Grace tried to remember what his face had looked like in the shadows, then jerked in shock as he blew gently on her breasts. "She reacts quickly," he said with obvious satisfaction. "Her nipples are extremely responsive. Tonight is going to be very exciting for us all."

She could feel her nipples hardening, and when he then blew gently on the soft undersides of her arms she jerked again, but this time the result was a sharp flash of pain on the muscles that were being held so tightly by the board and cuffs. A whimper of pain escaped her lips, and she heard the man laugh softly.

For what seemed an eternity, but was probably only a few minutes, he proceeded to cover her body with his warm, gentle breath, avoiding only the area between her thighs. The contrast between his breath and the cool air in the room was so great that her body overreacted each time, her muscles twitching and jerking.

When he finally stopped, Grace didn't know if she was glad or sorry. For several minutes she was left alone, and she strained her ears to try and make out what was happening. Suddenly, two pairs of hands started spreading a warming gel all over her body. She thought it was the twins at work, one concentrating on her front and the other her back.

Only after the first couple of minutes did she realize that the warmth was a stimulant of some kind, and her whole body felt as though it was swelling. She wanted desperately to be touched, to feel fingers on her breasts and thighs, and twisted herself slightly in her desperate need to have her throbbing breasts touched again.

"Keep still, Grace!" said David harshly. "Tonight we choose how to pleasure you, and we decide when to let you come."

The hands stopped moving over her, their work finished, and she was left suspended and alone as the warm glow spread through her. She was breathing heavily, feeling the heat of her breath against the material of the hood, and gradually the hot swollen feeling moved lower. Although no one had touched her there, she felt hot and heavy between her thighs, and could feel her sex lips swelling and opening. She moaned quietly to herself, almost overwhelmed by the desire for a touch of any kind on her throbbing vulva.

"See how needy she is," said Amber, and Grace could hear the pleasure in the other woman's voice. "You'd love to have someone stroke the side of your clitoris now, wouldn't you, Grace? Think how that would feel, and how quickly you'd be able to come. Oh, the bliss of release. Imagine it, how wonderful it would be."

Tears of frustration fell from Grace's eyes, trickling down her hooded face, as she bit on her bottom lip to stop herself from responding to Amber's words, skillfully chosen in an attempt to trigger the forbidden orgasm.

A hand moved inside the hood and fingers stroked her damp cheeks. "She's crying," said Amber, satisfaction clear in her voice. "What can we do to stop those tears?"

"She's done very well," said Andrew. "Perhaps she should be allowed her first orgasm now. What do you think, David?"

Grace held her breath, waiting for her lover's reply. "In just a moment," he said, and within seconds he was standing behind her, his mouth close to her ear. "We're going to smooth some ordinary lubricant between your thighs now," he whispered. "Then we'll slide some tiny love balls inside you and after that, when you feel so full and aroused that you're almost out of your mind with pleasure, I'll give you permission to come. Do you understand?"

His words were almost too much for her. She felt little tremors of an impending orgasm sparking deep within her belly, and drew in her breath sharply.

"Answer me," he ordered her.

"Yes, I understand," she gasped.

Drawing the tips of his fingers across her painfully hard nipples, which forced another sharp intake of breath from her, he moved away. Immediately she felt the cool lubricant smothering her already damp inner sex lips, fingertips brushing the sides of her clitoris yet still she managed to control herself. Then she felt a man's hands easing the smooth love balls inside her, before closing her up and then gently rotating the palm of his hand over Grace's entire vulva.

"Oh no, no!" she protested, feeling her belly heave as her orgasm built, the relentless pressure making her stretched and fastened muscles quiver and shake as her need for release threatened to overwhelm her too soon.

"Just a few more seconds," murmured David, his fingers moving knowingly up her inner thighs before coming to rest at the base of her belly, his fingers spread upwards over her pubic bone. As he began to increase the pressure there she knew that she was lost.

Every nerve ending in her body was now tingling, the pressure so great that she knew she couldn't control her response anymore. The tightness drew up into a tight knot below David's hand, and then, finally, he spoke.

"You may come now," he said calmly, pressing his fingers hard against the throbbing flesh above her pubic bone. Immediately Grace's head went back as the so cruelly delayed orgasm tore through her, causing her to twist and turn on the beam in endless spasms of ecstasy. She thought the pleasure would never end, but eventually the last flickers died away until she became limp and still, suddenly aware of the aching in her arms and legs.

"She's very good," said Andrew, and to Grace his admiration sounded tinged with disappointment.

"Excellent," agreed the other man. "She's quite a find for you, David."

"She'll get cold," said Amber, annoyance clear in her voice. "We need to warm her up quickly."

Grace's mind raced as she wondered what was coming next.

"This is the final test, Grace," said David. "It comes in two parts. First we warm you up and then you sample our Club Sandwich, which you chose earlier."

Grace, trembling after the intensity of her orgasm, her whole body aching due to being suspended and cuffed for so long, yearned to hear some note of encouragement in his voice, but she couldn't. In any case, having passed the first part of her test, she was growing in confidence. She'd come so far, learned so much about herself and her sexuality, that failure was no longer a consideration for her.

Lost in her thoughts, she was totally unprepared for the sudden jet of warm water that hit the front of her body. It was moved with great precision over every inch of her, and then another jet hit her back. This time she gave a scream of shock as her body swayed as much as her bonds would allow under the force of the twin sprays. Then, as suddenly as it had started, it all stopped.

For a few seconds there was silence in the room and

her body tensed. "We need to make sure you're quite clean for the final part of this," said Amber, and now Grace felt soapy bristles moving over her tender breasts.

The brush moved briskly across her aching nipples and around the areola. Grace's flesh cringed, but there was no escape, and other people quickly joined in, meaning that every centimeter of her was brushed and stimulated.

Gradually, her flesh began to react to the stimulation. Her nipples hardened, her breasts began to ache again, and when someone swirled the brush into her belly button her stomach muscles jumped and tiny tendrils of pleasure began to snake through her.

She heard the sound of soft laughter. "Fantastic," said the unknown man. "I envy you, David. She's incredible."

Hearing him speak again, Grace wondered if he could be the owner of this Club that meant so much to her lover.

"She'll like this," said Amy, swirling a brush along the back of Grace's knees and the back of her tightly stretched thighs.

Grace did like it, but she was becoming rearoused far too fast, which worried her.

"That will do," said David after a few more minutes. "Rinse her off now."

At once all the brushes stopped moving, she heard people moving away from her and then warm water was sprayed over her suspended body once more. She waited tensely for whatever was to happen next, but to her horror heard the door open and close and then there was nothing but silence.

She wanted to call out and ask if anyone was there,

but didn't dare. She had the feeling that if she did then she would have failed the trial. All the same, as the silence continued, the sense of loneliness and terror was so great that tears rolled down her face again. She didn't think she'd ever been so terrified before.

Suspended, bound, wet and still semi-aroused she was desperate for someone to touch her, or speak her name. She wondered how long they'd stay away, and as her body began to cool down from the warm water all her muscles started to shake. She longed for any kind of human contact, the touch of a hand on her abused flesh, the sound of a voice in the empty room, but there was nothing. She was alone, and all she could do was trust in the man she loved.

For what seemed an eternity she remained there in the dark silence, and she couldn't suppress a tiny whimper of fear as the sense of abandonment increased. Bereft of human contact she waited, unable to judge how long she'd been alone and battling to stop herself from shouting for help, because she knew that then the trial would end and she would have failed. As the pain from her tortured muscles threatened to become overwhelming she forced herself to breathe slowly and deeply, relaxing her body as much as possible.

Even so, the terror of her situation was overwhelming, and now she understood why no one had ever succeeded in passing this final trial. As she strained her ears, hoping against hope to hear the door open again, the silence was suddenly broken.

"Your time of solitude is up," said David, his voice seeming to come from a corner of the room. She heard him

moving across the floor and, feeling his cool fingers running down the length of her spine, her body jerked and she
realized that he must have been in the room, watching and
listening to her, the whole time.

Then she heard the door opening and the sound of
more voices as everyone returned.

"As you all doubtless saw on the camera, she never
called for help," said David. "Now get her down, and
quickly."

Grace nearly fell to the floor as the two spreader boards
were removed and she was finally released from the torture
of the beam.

"I've got you," said Andrew, his arms gripping her
tightly. "This can come off now too," said David, removing
the hood.

Grace blinked, her eyes trying to adjust to the dim lighting in the room after the total blackness of the hood. The
twins were busy working on her aching, chilled body with
warm, fluffy towels, their hands lingering between her
thighs and around the cleft at the base of her spine.

After all she'd endured she was amazed to find that her
whole body soon reacted to their touch, as though the fear
she'd endured had heightened her responses, and increased
the sexual tension within her.

"And now for the Club Sandwich," said Amber. "Bring
her over to the bed."

Now Grace saw that a drop-down bed, previously concealed in one of the walls, was ready for use.

"Make yourself comfortable in the middle, Grace, and
lie on your side," said her lover.

Without a word she walked proudly toward the bed, knowing that after all that had happened to her, this was the moment when she could finally prove to both David and herself that they were right for each other. She no longer cared about the other people, the watchers in the shadows; all she cared about was their future.

Naked and still aroused by the brushes she lay on her right side and waited. Andrew was the first to approach the bed, and he lay naked behind her, wrapping his arms around her waist. "You may not enjoy this quite as much," he whispered quietly in her ear.

She tensed, then saw David approaching the bed. He was already naked too, and visibly aroused. Joining the two of them on the bed he lay in front of her, his hands on her shoulders as he looked deep into her eyes. "I hope you find our club sandwich to your liking," he said. "Remember though, you can only come when I give you permission."

Grace nodded, acutely aware of Andrew's erection nudging against her buttocks while his hands fondled her hips and thighs.

Now David began to caress her breasts, first with his hands and then with his tongue. His erection pressed against the base of her stomach, and she could feel tiny beads of moisture from the tip against her hot flesh.

The two men worked smoothly together, their hands and mouths arousing and stimulating her until she was trembling with excitement, her hips twitching as her need to climax increased.

Then, lost in the sensations David was arousing in her, she was suddenly aware of Andrew inserting something between the cheeks of her bottom, and then her rectum was flooded with a lubricating gel, clearly intended to ease the way for him to enter her there.

Only then did the full realization of what was happening hit home. She was going to be filled by two men, one her lover and the other a man who had wanted her to be his. Both of them were sensuous sexual libertines and together they would bring her to her final peak of ecstasy at the Dining Club.

As Andrew began to push his way into her she tensed. He felt too big, and was moving too quickly. A shaft of pain shot through her, and suddenly she was afraid, but David's hands were gentle on her waist and he held her steady, while his tongue teased each of her nipples in turn until they were fully erect.

At the exact moment that Andrew entered her fully from behind, David closed his teeth over her left nipple and bit on it. She gave an instinctive cry of pain, but almost immediately the pain turned to a dark pleasure, as it had in his flat the first time he'd done it to her.

His timing meant that she began to writhe with pleasure, forcing Andrew to hold her still, and now she realized that he was fully inside her and the full feeling was becoming pleasurable.

"My turn I think," said David, his voice thick with desire, and finally he thrust urgently into her, rotating his hips so that her G-spot was stimulated and her internal muscles tightened around him and around both men.

Hearing them breathing heavily as they controlled themselves in order to test her to the limit, she felt her own pleasure rising and rising. With a huge effort she subdued it and instead tightened all her internal muscles around them again. She heard Andrew give a low moan, and then he was spilling himself inside her, his body shuddering violently.

With her own orgasm perilously close now, Grace looked into David's eyes and saw a mixture of pride and love in them that she'd never seen before. "You can come now, Gracie," he whispered, and they climaxed together, their bodies shuddering in mutual ecstasy.

Exhausted, Grace remained on the bed as the others left. Amber slammed the door shut behind her, leaving the two of them alone together.

"Congratulations, my darling, you've succeeded!" said David, pulling her against his chest. "I knew you could do it. You were magnificent."

She cuddled against him, loving the warmth and strength of his body. "I did it for us, but I enjoyed it," she admitted. "I've never felt so alive before. In a way, I feel sad too, because now it's over. I'm going to miss the Dining Club."

"It may not be over, it's up to you," he said softly. "After your display tonight, you've definitely earned the right to be told the whole truth about the Club, and the secret of table five. Let's go to our rooms, and after you've rested I'll explain what I mean."

PART EIGHT

Surrender

TWENTY

Looking at Grace, freshly bathed and sitting curled up in the large armchair by the long window of their bedroom in a toweling robe, David felt a rush of tenderness toward her. She'd achieved so much during the four months they'd been visiting the Dining Club, and this weekend she'd amazed him by her capacity for controlled pleasure.

He could no longer deny, even to himself, that he was in love with her, and it scared him. He'd never wanted this. He'd expected her to fail, then he would have had nothing to fear, for love and tenderness were the only things that did scare him. They left him vulnerable, and they would leave Grace vulnerable too because, no matter how much he was in love with her now, he knew that eventually he would tire of her.

"What are you thinking about?" she asked.

"How you looked earlier," he said, not yet able to commit his love to words. She smiled at him, and he realized that, possibly even more worryingly, she was beginning to understand him. Joining her in the armchair, and settling her comfortably on his lap with her head against his shoulder, he stroked her long, dark hair. "Are you ready to hear about table five now?" he asked.

Grace nodded. "Yes, and everything else that you think I should know about the Dining Club."

Holding her close to him, his fingers still playing with her hair, he struggled to think how best to explain it to her. After all she'd been through, she deserved the truth, but the truth might hurt her and she didn't deserve to be hurt at this moment, when she'd passed her final trial so triumphantly.

"Have you ever wondered who owned the Club?" he asked.

"I did, but now I think it's the new man who took part in tonight's trial. He seemed to have authority, and he knew what he was doing too."

"He's a business partner of mine, but you're wrong, he doesn't own the Dining Club. I do."

Grace looked at him in astonishment. "You said you had money invested in it, that you..."

"I do have money invested in it. I own it."

"Then all along you've known what was going to happen. You must have planned the evenings right from the start. Everything that happened to me was designed by you." She was clearly both shocked and hurt.

"That's not true, Gracie. Amber designs all the trials, I merely approve them. This weekend you've just finished never varies. If people reach the fourth table then that's the trial they all take, which is why despite what I feel for you, I need Amber in my life too.

"She understands what turns me on, what excites me and relieves the boredom of..."

"Of being in a loving relationship?" asked Grace quietly.

For the first time in his adult life, David wanted to lie. He wanted to tell this woman he was in love with that their relationship was all he needed, and all he would ever need, but he couldn't do it. She'd earned the right to total honesty, even if that meant he destroyed their love at the very start. "Yes," he admitted.

Grace sighed softly, but curled herself more tightly against him. "I see. Please tell me about table five now."

"Table five is where Amber, as the hostess, always sits. You see, the Dining Club doesn't only open one weekend a month. There are themed weekends in between; bondage, S&M, and dominatrix breaks. Amber oversees them all."

"Do you come to any of them?" asked Grace.

"I used to come quite a lot, but since I've met you I only come here if you're working on a weekend. I prefer your company," he added with a half-smile.

Grace didn't smile back at him. "Do you have sex with Amber? Privately I mean, not in the context of a specialty event."

"Yes, we've been lovers on and off for several years now. She fulfills a need in me that not all women would want to satisfy."

"What sort of need?"

"Darling, I don't think..."

"I want to know everything," said Grace firmly.

"It's only the darker side of sex, more pleasure pain than tenderness. Amber doesn't do tenderness, as you've probably gathered."

"And table five belongs to her?"

"Yes, unless someone wants to challenge her for the role of hostess here. The problem is that even if you do want to, and I believe you'd be a worthy opponent, it's a full-time job running the Club. You already have a good career. You can't want to give that up."

"I might," said Grace. "I'd bring a lot to it, given my line of work. I'd be able to look at it with fresh eyes, make it even more exciting. After several years, Amber is bound to be stuck in a rut."

David knew that he had to be honest. "Not really, she's very inventive."

"Don't you want me to challenge her?" asked Grace, sounding hurt.

"I don't know," he admitted. "I'm used to the Dining Club being a retreat from my everyday life. If you challenged her and won, then the two would merge, and..."

"And you'd never be bored again!" exclaimed Grace. "I want to do it, David. I want to take the final step. Would it be like the other trials?"

"No, it's a head-to-head competition, and the result is decided by a vote."

"Who votes?"

"The men who've taken part in the evening; they're all connected to the Dining Club in one capacity or another. Andrew will be there of course, as he's my manager, and Lucien, the man you noticed tonight."

"Don't women take part in the evening?"

"Only to assist with things; they don't vote."

"How many times has Amber been challenged?"

David thought for a moment. "Three times in all, but no one has ever come close to defeating her. In truth, I think you have a chance. You're possibly more suited to the theme of the trial than she is, but Amber likes her job and will do anything to keep it."

"I only need to know one thing," said Grace, and he could feel her body trembling slightly. "Do you love me, David? If you do, I need to hear you say it."

Caressing the nape of her neck, he kissed the top of her spine, and heard her sigh with pleasure. "Yes, Gracie, right now, at this moment, I do love you," he said truthfully.

Slowly she slipped to the floor, shrugged off her robe and then unzipped him, bending her head toward his rapidly hardening penis. "That's all I needed to know," she said. "I definitely want to challenge Amber for table five." With that she started to run her tongue around the underside of the ridge below the head of his erection and with a soft sigh he gave himself up to the pleasure of her skillful tongue, and was equally aroused by the prospect of what lay ahead following Grace's totally unexpected but exciting decision.

"She passed!" exclaimed Amber, hurling herself at Andrew and punching his chest with her fists. "No doubt David is telling her all about table five at this very moment too. Why didn't you stop her? You said you'd help me!"

"I tried to make her fail, but nothing worked," protested Andrew, grabbing her wrists to protect himself. "She was pretty amazing this weekend. I don't think anything could have stopped her."

Amber wriggled in his grasp, trying to free herself, but

he was too strong for her. "What am I going to do?" she cried. "I hate the challenge for table five."

"Well you're just going to have to learn to be more submissive, if it ever comes to that," replied Andrew. "Personally I don't think she'll give up her career in the theater for the Dining Club."

"She might not want to, but she won't fancy sharing David with me either, so what choice does she have?" retorted Amber, landing a kick on Andrew's shins in order to break away from him.

"That hurt!" he exclaimed.

"Good, it was meant to hurt. You've let me down, and all because you're secretly in love with that wretched girl too."

"Pull yourself together," he snapped, pinning her to the wall by her shoulders and dodging her flying fists and feet. "You really do need to learn to control yourself," he added, grabbing the neckline of her dress and tearing it open down to the waist, leaving her perfect breasts exposed.

Amber continued to fight him, but he knew better than to stop now. Bending his head he bit her shoulders and breasts, jamming one knee between her legs so that his thigh was pressing against her pubic mound.

Her breathing grew ragged and Andrew put his left forearm against her throat to keep her against the wall, while reaching down with his right hand and pushing the leg of her panties aside before thrusting two fingers inside her.

Amber began to writhe with excitement. Her face was flushed, her eyes bright and when Andrew rotated his thumb on her clitoris while pressing firmly against the internal walls of her vagina with the two fingers, she started moaning.

Lowering his head he drew her left nipple into his mouth, sucking on it hard then releasing it for a few seconds. "Don't stop!" she shouted, thrusting her hips forward to try and precipitate her climax. Now he used his body to pin her to the wall, freeing his left hand. Swiftly he gripped her right breast and began to squeeze it, softly at first but then harder and harder until she gasped with pain.

Pain was an aphrodisiac for Amber, as Andrew knew very well, so he kept his grip steady, moving the fingers of his other hand in and out of the soaking wet opening between her legs until, with a scream of excitement, her body jerked and shuddered as her orgasm swept through her.

Quickly Andrew unzipped his jeans and entered her with hard thrusts that made her gasp for breath. His body slammed into her and he rested his hands on the wall for support as his testicles pulled up tight against him and then he was emptying himself inside her as she climaxed for a second time.

After that she was quiet. Her breathing slowed, and eventually she sat down, pulling the tattered pieces of her dress up. "What will become of me if I have to leave here?" she asked despairingly.

Andrew had never heard her so despondent. "You must make sure that doesn't happen," he said firmly. "You've seen off three challengers since you started here. You know what's involved. Grace doesn't have a clue. You hold all the cards."

"You're wrong," said Amber. "This challenge suits her, that's what worries me."

"Then you have to learn to control yourself better," said Andrew. "I'll help you practice if you like. I'd rather enjoy seeing you obeying orders."

"You'll be one of the judges, and anyway I'm not sure where your loyalty really lies," retorted Amber. "Perhaps you'd better go away and think about that before next weekend."

"What do you mean?"

"I mean you should consider what would be best for you. Do you really want to work with Grace, knowing she can never be yours? Or would you prefer things to stay as they are? If that happens, then eventually David will tire of Grace and things will return to normal here. If she wins, she'll change everything. She's clever and ambitious, there may not even be room for you by the time she's reorganized things."

She was right, thought Andrew as he was driving home. He couldn't affect the outcome of the challenge, but he did need to think about what he would do if the once-unthinkable happened, and Grace replaced Amber as the Dining Club's hostess.

———

"What do you mean, you can't make Sunday?" asked Fran in disbelief. "What the hell's more important than a first read-through that's taken weeks to set up?"

Grace didn't know what to say. "I've no choice, Fran. It's something that's come up unexpectedly and..."

"Unless someone's bloody dying I can't imagine what it can be," snapped Fran.

"I'm sorry, but I have to be somewhere else. I can't explain more, and I'm really sorry. I know it's terrible timing."

Fran laughed bitterly. "That has to be the understatement of the year. Just don't let it be something you have to go to with David, because if it is I'll never forgive you."

Grace didn't answer.

"It is, isn't it? You're swanning off to some posh event with Mr. Moneybags and abandoning MY play. Go on, admit it."

"It's not like that. If I could get out of it I would, but I can't," said Grace, feeling close to tears.

"Then explain to me exactly what it is that you can't get out of, because I can tell you right now that this is so unprofessional I can't believe you're doing it."

"I can't tell you. I'm not allowed to tell you," said Grace.

"Not allowed? Is it some Masonic function, where they're admitting women as a treat for being good girls? God, what's happened to you? We used to laugh at people like that."

"People like what?" asked Grace. "You don't know anything about David, so don't try to judge him."

"I know he's changed you," retorted Fran, picking up her jacket and shoulder bag.

"Please don't walk out on me, Fran," begged Grace. "I don't want us to fall out over this."

"Well tough luck, because we just have. I'll tell everyone you're sick, which is true in a way, as you seem to be lovesick. Don't expect to be welcomed back with open arms when you and David break up though. I thought you valued our friendship, but clearly I was wrong.

"You know, if you were head over heels in love with that chap we met at the King's Head I could understand it better, he was a real hunk, but I have no idea what you see in David. All I can say is, he must be bloody good in the sack."

Grace felt her cheeks flushing, and hastily turned away from her friend. "I'm truly sorry, Fran," she repeated. "And I wish I could tell you more, but I can't. I should be able to get your play up and running though. It's probably only Sunday I'll have to miss."

Fran was speechless for a moment. "You 'should' be able to get my play up and running? Fine, but remember this. If you want to screw up your entire career through lust or whatever you choose to call it, it's up to you, but lust doesn't last. What will you do when David tires of you and you're just another forgotten director who was once tipped for great success?"

"You don't know what you're talking about," responded Grace, stung to anger by her friend's words, which were too close to home to be comfortable. "I won't let him tire of me."

Fran raised her eyebrows. "Really? Well short of casting some kind of spell over him, I don't know how you can possibly say that. How can any of us know that someone we love will never tire of us? We all change, Grace. It's called growing up, I believe. I'm beginning to feel really sorry for you."

"There's no need," retorted Grace. "I've never been as happy as I am at the moment."

Fran looked at her thoughtfully. "Yes, you do look happy; different, but happy. I still think this is a disgusting way to treat a friend, but if you've discovered the secret to eternal happiness, then feel free to let me in on it sometime. Until then, I'm leaving." With that she walked out of the flat, banging the front door shut behind her.

Alone and shaken, Grace turned her thoughts to the coming Sunday. Now, more than ever, she knew that she had to succeed in the challenge. After everything that Fran had said, she was even more certain that her decision was right. What she really wanted to do was to run the Dining Club, and make a life for her and David that would totally fulfill them both. The moment she'd set foot in the Club her life had changed irrevocably, and she was now so consumed by her love for both David and the Club that nothing else mattered, which meant that Amber definitely had to go.

TWENTY-ONE

On the Sunday morning, David collected Grace from her flat at six-thirty in the morning. She'd already been awake for over two hours, her mind racing as she tried to imagine what might lie ahead of her, and how she could summon up the skills necessary to defeat Amber in the challenge for table five.

"Dark circles?" he queried, touching her face with the tips of his fingers. "I hope you haven't been awake all night?"

"No, although it would have been nice if we could have spent the night together."

"Unfair to Amber, don't you think?" he queried.

"You really are totally impartial about this aren't you," she said incredulously. "I thought you said you loved me, and that you wanted me to do this."

He cast a quick sideways glance at her. "I certainly said I loved you, because I do. I think the decision to take on the challenge for table five was yours alone though."

"But we agreed it would be good for us, for our relationship. We talked about that."

"Damn these lights, they're all on red," was his only response, and she realized that he didn't want to talk about it.

"David, please tell me that you want me to win," she begged him. "I need to know that."

"I've known Amber a long time, and we've a lot of

shared memories, Grace. I'm one of the judges in this competition, and I take part in the challenge. It wouldn't be fair if I was more in favor of one of you than the other."

"But..."

"Close your eyes and rest. We'll be there soon enough and the challenge begins straight away. You're nervous, which is understandable, and..."

"I'm doing this for us!" she exclaimed. "I've missed the first read-through of Fran's play to be here today. All I want is to know that you're pleased. Is that too much to ask? What's happened to you?"

"Nothing's happened to me, my darling. You're the one who's decided on a major career change."

Suddenly Grace felt incredibly alone. "Please, say something nice," she begged him. "I'm scared."

He put a hand on her knee and squeezed gently. "Just remember how much I love you, Gracie. In all fairness to Amber, I can't say anything more."

She realized then that her final visit to the Dining Club as a client was to be no different from her first. David had switched off emotionally, his mind focused entirely on whatever the day held for her and Amber.

"I understand," she said softly.

"I knew you would. That's part of why I love you," he said quietly, and finally she felt both comforted and reassured by his words.

There were already several cars in the driveway of the Club when they arrived. Laura opened the front door to them. "Everyone else is already here," she said to David. "They're waiting for you both in the drawing room."

Walking in ahead of David, Grace saw Andrew sitting opposite the door. Glancing around the room she saw Will was there too, and also five other men that she didn't know.

"Laura, take Grace upstairs and get her changed, then collect Amber and bring them both back to us," said David, walking across the room to greet one of the men.

Grace's mouth went dry as she realized that for the men in the room, the challenge had already begun. She followed Laura up the stairs to a small dressing room. "You'll need to take all your clothes off," said the blonde twin. "You and Amber have to wear the same outfit for this."

Opening a wardrobe door she took out a black and gold dress, except that when Grace put it on she realized it wasn't really a dress. The tight-fitting leather basque was laced up at each side, and the halter neck had a tiny black and gold collar attached to it. Black silk hung from the bottom of the basque to Grace's heels, but only at the back. At the front there was one thin strip of silk that hung between her bare legs, brushing lightly against her skin.

"You need these too," said Laura, unwilling to meet Grace's gaze as she handed over a tiny pair of black bikini bottoms and a black and gold metal bracelet. "The bracelet goes around your left wrist. The pants will feel tight, but that's how they have to be."

Once she'd put everything on, Grace looked at herself in the full-length mirror set in the door of the wardrobe. "I look like some kind of slave girl!" she exclaimed.

"We'd better go down now," said Laura.

"Am I?" asked Grace, fear rising in her. "Is that the

theme of this trial? Do we have to be some kind of sex slave to those men down there?"

"I don't know," said Laura. "I wasn't here when the last challenge for table five took place. We must go down now or I'll get into trouble."

At the top of the stairs, Grace came face to face with Amber, who had Amy with her. Looking at the blonde woman, so poised and confident, her slender, honed body shown to perfection in the same outfit as she was wearing, Grace felt a moment of doubt. How could she hope to defeat such a sexually skilled woman, who even now was looking supremely confident while she, Grace, was filled with fearful foreboding?

Amber's eyes swept over Grace. "The costume suits you," she said silkily. "I always knew you were naturally subservient."

"In that case, I might do well," responded Grace, as they descended the wide staircase together.

The men had gathered in the hallway, watching the two women with excited anticipation in their eyes. When they reached the bottom step, David stepped forward. "It's time for me to explain the rules of the competition now. If there's anything you don't understand you can ask me, but no questions are permitted once the challenge begins.

"For the rest of the day you will both become our sex slaves, showing total obedience to our desires at all times. You will be allowed sexual satisfaction, but only when we give permission. Should you get satisfaction before gaining permission you'll be punished. Punishment must always be followed by an expression of your gratitude. You will thank

us for showing you the error of your ways. You won't speak
at any other time unless you are invited to do so.

"During the course of the challenge you will both be
evaluated by each member of the committee. At the end of
the trial a vote will be held in private, and whoever has the
largest number of votes will be the winner. Do either of you
have any questions?"

"I do," said Grace, her nerves jangling after hearing him
speak of punishments. "What do we do if we want the trial
to end?"

"Naturally the normal Dining Club rule then comes
into force, and you simply say that you want it to stop,"
said David. "There will be no attempt to coerce either of
you into continuing if you no longer wish to. Naturally we
hope that won't happen, and that you both complete the
challenge. If there's nothing else you want to know, we'll
begin."

The men split into two groups. Andrew, Will and one
of the strangers gathered around Grace, and a lead was
clipped onto the collar around her neck. Instinctively she
flinched away in shock, before being led along the hallway
into the room where she'd first met the twins, while David
and the other men brought Amber along close behind.

Then the leads were unclipped and the two women
were told to wait by the door. Grace's legs began to tremble, until she was afraid they would give way beneath her.
David's words, delivered in a crisp, dispassionate tone, had
been a salutary reminder of how intense and challenging
the day was going to be, but she knew there could be no
going back now.

After a few minutes, Will and one of the strangers came over to them. Will hooked his fingers in Amber's collar and led her across the room while the stranger indicated with his head for Grace to follow him.

Two deep chairs had been moved into the center of the room. Andrew was sitting naked in one while another stranger was naked in the other.

"Your first task as personal sex slaves is to bring your man to a climax without the use of sex toys. There's a tube of lubricant beside each chair, which is allowed to be used. Naturally there is an element of competition involved. The winner will be the one who is successful first. Naturally you yourselves are not expected to reach orgasm through this.

"Before you begin, there is something else that needs to be added to your costumes, which Amy and Laura will put in place now."

Standing naked before the unknown man, who was lean but well-toned, Grace realized he was very attractive, with dark hair and deep brown eyes. However, he had the same detached expression that she'd often seen on David's face.

Amy was quickly by her side, sliding the tight bikini-style panties down Grace's legs so that she could reach inside them, and now Grace could feel something smooth and cool pressing against her vulva.

"Excellent," said David. "You may both begin now."

Grace hesitated. She'd never touched a stranger in such an intimate way before. For her this act had always been an expression of love and trust, but she knew nothing about the man sitting waiting expectantly, and she didn't know if she could do it. Then she heard a soft sigh from Andrew, and realized that Amber had already begun.

Seeing that the stranger was already semi-aroused, she swiftly unfastened the halter top of her clothing, then put some lubricant on her breasts before lifting them to form a shelf for his testicles.

He gave a sharp intake of breath as she arched her body, and his testicles slid through the channel between her breasts. Cradling his shaft in the gap between them she stroked his glans with the tips of her fingers, letting her long hair brush his straining stomach. He was breathing heavily now, the testicles swelling and tightening.

With increasing confidence she closed her mouth over the tip while letting her left hand stray beneath him so that she could lightly caress his perineum. His hips jerked and she tasted the first drops of pre-ejaculatory fluid in her mouth. Encouraged she swirled her tongue around the tip while at the same time pressing her breasts tightly around his straining shaft.

Small sounds of rising excitement escaped from his mouth, and his hips moved upwards, pushing his erection further into her mouth, but still he didn't come, and Grace could hear Andrew moaning with ecstasy.

Then the stranger's testicles tightened and she knew that within a few seconds he would come. Relief surged through her, but to her horror, just seconds before he did Andrew gave a loud shout of pleasure and she realized that she'd lost. She wanted to weep with disappointment, but remembered that the stranger's pleasure was still paramount.

Flicking her tongue over the tip of his glans she moved

her right hand until it enclosed his shaft, so that she could stimulate that as well. Immediately his body jerked and shuddered and then he was spilling himself into her mouth, groaning with pleasure, and immediately she felt a surge of power and excitement.

Settling back on the carpet, Grace now became aware of an intense, vibrating pressure against her vulva. Pleasuring the stranger had aroused her, and she didn't want any more stimulation. Confused, she started to move a hand to ease the pressure.

"Don't touch anything, Grace," said David, his voice harsh in the silence of the room. "Your vibrators are controlled by us, and you must both learn to cope with the stimulation. Regrettably you lost the trial to Amber. What do you want to happen to her, Lucien?"

So she'd been right, thought Grace. This man was David's business partner.

"She was very good," said Lucien. "Excellent in fact, but unfortunately she did lose, and a losing slave girl reflects badly on me. Three strokes of the whip will be sufficient, I think."

Before Grace had time to protest, Will lifted her up and placed her facedown across Lucien's thighs. With the pressure of his thighs against her body, the incessant, insidious arousal caused by the vibrator and the added stimulant of fear, Grace was terrified she'd climax during her punishment and then be punished again.

Lucien was mercifully quick, and within seconds he'd pushed the black silk away from her buttocks and three sharp, burning blows of a riding whip fell on her exposed buttocks. Pain streaked through her body and she couldn't stop herself from crying out, but as the vibrator continued to pulsate the pain changed to a strange, dark pleasure, her nerve endings jangling as a result of the different sensations.

Abruptly, Lucien pushed her off him and she tumbled to the floor, but she was grateful that her belly was no longer being stimulated, and slowly the orgasm that had been building abated.

"Lucien is waiting," said David.

Only then did Grace remember the rules. "Thank you for punishing me," she said, shocked to find that suddenly she was perilously close to tears. "I'm sorry I failed you," she added.

Lucien said nothing. It was as though she no longer existed. Feeling strangely bereft and lonely she pulled up the halter neck of her dress and looked around her. All the others had left the room leaving her alone with Amber, but neither woman spoke.

Eventually the door opened and the twins came in. "Massage time," said Amy. "Follow us."

This time they were taken to a high-ceilinged fitness room that Grace had never seen before. Andrew was standing by two massage tables, while the other men were standing close by, their eyes watching the women closely. "You first, Amber," said Andrew. "Up on the couch, this won't take a minute."

Grace watched as the blonde woman lay flat on her back, her head supported by a small pillow while Andrew pushed her feet up toward her body until her knees were pointing to the ceiling. Then he pushed her knees sideways, drawing the length of silk cloth to one side, leaving her sex fully exposed to the watching men.

"This little internal massager works very well," he explained to them, parting Amber's sex lips. "It consists of three small gold balls on a cord. During exercise, the pelvic muscles will massage the women internally. It massages them with any movement, but exercise increases the sensations."

While he was talking, Will slid a small pillow beneath Amber's hips, making it easy for Andrew to slide the gold balls inside her until only the end of the cord remained outside her body. "There, that's done," he said, pressing his hand against her vulva until Grace heard the other woman's sharp intake of breath. "Yes, working well," he added. "Your turn now, Grace."

Grace obediently took Amber's place. She wanted to close her eyes, to blot out the watching men and hide her shame at being exposed in this way, but she knew it would count against her. Andrew expertly eased the balls inside her and she relaxed a little. Then, when he pressed against her vulva she felt a coiling sensation in her stomach, and her eyes widened in fear as she realized exactly how stimulating they were. Finally, released from the couch she stood next to Amber, her eyes cast down as seemed right to her given the role she was playing.

"You may look at us now, Grace," said David, and she obediently raised her eyes, hoping that Amber had been looking at them all the time. "I'm sure you'll both be relieved to hear that this time you may climax as often as you wish. The winner will be the one who manages the most orgasms in forty-five minutes. You will both begin by using the treadmill, but we'll remove your costumes first as they're not suitable for this test."

Silently, with total obedience, Grace let Will and David remove her costume and then walked naked to the treadmill and David switched it on. "Naturally we control the machines," he added.

As the speed of the treadmill increased, and Grace's muscles had to work harder, she could feel the first tingles of pleasure deep inside her, and within only a few minutes she shuddered as her body contracted in a deep, satisfying orgasm.

Immediately she was moved across the room and made to sit on a large exercise ball. She struggled to stay on it, forced to tighten her muscles in order to keep her balance, and this time the balls pressed heavily against her G-spot and her body went into another spasm of blissful release.

She lost track of what was happening to Amber as she was made to ride the exercise bike, return to the ball and then finally ordered to lie on the couch again. She no longer knew how many orgasms she'd had, but she felt exhausted. Her last spasm had been painful as well as pleasurable, her tortured muscles forced into yet another climax.

Now, lying on the bed, she felt hands moving over her hot, sweat-soaked body. They teased her nipples, stroked her stomach and kept her whole body aroused. Shamed by her capacity for pleasure she was relieved to be told to close her eyes.

She was aware of Amber lying on the adjacent couch, but had no idea how the other woman was doing. Slowly the last embers of arousal began to die away and then with shocking suddenness, a drop of ice-cold liquid fell on her breasts and she screamed with surprise.

"Stay silent," said Andrew.

Tensely she waited, eyes closed, but for a long time nothing happened and then, just as she thought it was over, another drop fell, landing just above the dent of her belly button and making her lower body jerk. Now the drops came more frequently, sometimes singly, sometimes two or three at a time. She began to ache between her thighs and realized that every time she jumped with shock, her muscles contracted and the massage balls worked their insidious magic on her. She wanted, needed, to come yet again, but the stimulation wasn't quite enough. Frantically, with no thought for the watchers, she pushed her hips upwards, trying to make one of the drops fall between her needy thighs.

Then someone pushed a cushion beneath her hips, her legs were parted by firm hands, another pair of hands held her sex lips open and she waited longingly for a drop of the cold water to fall. When it did, it fell directly onto her swollen clitoris and she screamed with ecstatic delight, writhing on the couch and moaning "Yes, oh yes!"

As soon as the words were out of her mouth she felt the sting of a crop falling over her unprotected breasts, and stifled a moan of pain as the crop fell four times as punishment for her cry of pleasure.

"Forty-five minutes," said Lucien. Immediately all hands were withdrawn and Grace was left alone.

"She's wonderfully wanton!" said one of the men. "I hope she's mine for a time this afternoon."

"We draw lots I'm afraid," said Andrew.

"Dress quickly," said David, his voice clipped. "There are only two hours before we make our decision."

Once dressed Amber and Grace had to stand in the middle of the room again while David looked at his notes. "We have a clear winner for this trial," he said briskly. "And that winner was Grace. Amber, you..."

"It can't be!" exclaimed Amber. "Someone's made a mistake. I've always been multiorgasmic. I had numerous orgasms."

"Be silent!" said David. "As I was one of the people watching you, you're suggesting that I made a mistake. Clearly you've forgotten your place and you'll be punished for your outburst after lunch, when you've had time to recover some of your strength. You must both be in the dining room in fifteen minutes," he added, and with that he left the room.

Fifteen minutes later Grace and Amber arrived at the entrance to the dining room. During the short break, Grace had reminded herself that in two hours' time it would all be over. It seemed a very short time in which to achieve her aim of ousting Amber, especially as they were equal at the moment, but following her victory in the fitness room her confidence had improved.

She knew that what she needed to do in order to win was actually become a slave girl in her own mind. Invest herself with a background story, as actors had to do. She must imagine how a female slave in Roman times would have felt when fondled and used by her master and his friends.

The twins led them in and told them to serve the guests. All the food was on a side table, and Grace immediately collected a plate and placed it in front of David, who was sitting at the head of the table.

Without looking up at her he idly pushed the piece of silk that was between her legs to one side and caressed the inside of her smooth thighs. "Remember, your pleasure is only to be obtained with permission," he reminded her, and as she moved away she felt the vibrator that was pressed against her sex lips start to throb gently.

As she and Amber moved along the table, the men all let their hands touch the exposed areas of their bodies, and as the meal progressed so the vibrator's pulsations increased.

By the time Grace poured the dessert wine for Andrew, her eyes carefully downcast, she was highly aroused. Pulling her onto his lap he tipped the contents of his glass down her left side, so that it trickled into the spaces between the tight lacing, then licked at it with the tip of his tongue.

The sensation was intense, and she shivered with excitement. She could hear the buzz of conversation around them, but was only aware of his delicate tongue, and the incessant arousal of the vibrator, now pressed even more tightly against her vulva by his hard thighs.

"You want to come, don't you?" he whispered in her ear. "I can tell you're ready. Tell me the truth."

"Yes, I do," admitted Grace.

"What a shame that I forbid it," he said, abruptly pushing her off his lap.

Grace scrambled to her feet, picked up the decanter and keeping her eyes down, moved on to serve Will. He contented himself with caressing her breasts, his fingers tweaking her nipples so hard that she struggled not to cry out. Passing Amber she saw that her adversary's top lip was beaded with sweat, and realized that the ordeal was proving just as difficult for her.

When all the men had been served she went to put the decanter back on the sideboard but then David spoke. "My glass needs topping up, Grace. Pay attention."

Swiftly she went across to him, and this time he too pulled her onto his lap, parting her legs so that she was balanced on his left thigh. Casually he slid a hand up under the bottom of her tight-fitting basque, spreading one hand wide over the base of her stomach. His fingers were firm and she wriggled to try and ease the rising spirals of excitement.

"Keep still!" he ordered her.

"Forgive me," she begged him and he glanced at her in surprise.

"I think I will," he murmured. "Would you like to come now?"

Grace was totally lost in her role-playing, and words flowed easily from her. "Only if you wish," she replied subserviently.

"I do."

As he spoke he pressed the heel of his hand hard into the base of her stomach, and the pressure there combined with the sensations from the vibrator were enough to trigger her climax. With a muffled groan of pleasure her body trembled violently.

As soon as she was still again she was ordered to continue her work, but she nearly stumbled as she moved away from him, just regaining her balance before she fell. At that moment she heard Lucien give Amber permission to come, and watched her opponent's head go back as with a loud cry of satisfaction she climaxed, standing in front of him.

Clearly they had both been watched and judged by all the men during their brief moment of pleasure, but the thought no longer worried Grace. She was proud of what she'd done, and elated that she'd clearly surprised David by her response.

"Time for the final test," said Andrew, pushing back his chair, "and then the vote will be held."

This time the women were led down to the basement room, and Grace tensed. She'd hated the shadowy darkness and claustrophobic atmosphere there. Two long couches were in the middle of the room, and the twins swiftly stripped the two contestants of their clothes before pushing them toward the beds.

"You must both lie on your backs, and keep your eyes open during this trial," said David. "We will draw lots for who is to make love to each of you. As he does, you must keep perfectly still, moving only when you're moved by your partner, never visibly or verbally responding to what's being done to you. You must behave as though you've been drugged, and are totally helpless, and can only climax after your partner. Such self-control is needed by anyone who believes they are suitable to be in charge of the Dining Club.

"However, before we begin, Amber will receive her punishment for this morning's outburst. Andrew will administer that."

Amber stepped forward, looking mutinous. Watching

her, Grace knew that no slave girl should ever look like that, which boosted her confidence.

Andrew ordered Amber to kneel on all fours, then trailed a leather strap the length of her spine, so that her slender figure began to quiver. Grace watched wide-eyed as the strap fell with considerable force across Amber's buttocks, and the blonde woman gave a cry of pain.

Swiftly and dispassionately, Andrew let the strap fall three more times, leaving four clear and separate red lines on her golden skin, and then he moved the strap underneath her, pulling the ends up tightly above her back, trapping her breasts beneath it.

The watching Grace realized that Amber was now trembling with excitement, not distress. "Don't come," said Andrew, "or you'll be punished again. Now apologize."

He was twisting the ends of the strap, so that Amber's breasts were squashed hard against her body, yet still she seemed to find it impossible to utter the words required of her.

"You have ten more seconds to apologize," said David, standing watching in the shadows. "If you don't, the challenge will be over."

"I'm very sorry," said Amber quickly. Andrew released her, but neither her expression nor her tone of voice had made the apology seem sincere. However, as she was clearly aroused by the punishment, Grace hoped this would be to her advantage.

As the two of them lay on the couches, the men drew lots, then Grace heard someone approaching her. She waited anxiously to discover who had drawn her name.

With eyes wide open as instructed, she didn't dare turn her head, but then sensed a figure standing beside her.

"Time to begin," said a familiar voice, and she realized that it was David who would decide her fate. David, who knew her body so well, and wouldn't hesitate to use that in order to make things even more difficult for her. Keeping her gaze fixed on the low ceiling she waited for him to begin.

The silence in the room only added to the tension as his hands roamed over her shoulders, skimming the sides of her neck and then moving down the insides of her arms. She tried not to think about what was happening, but it was impossible. When he lay down naked next to her she longed to wrap her arms around him, but all she could do was lie motionless.

"So beautiful," he murmured, tracing patterns around her breasts. "And so wonderfully responsive as well." Lowering his head he licked beneath her armpits, and she struggled to keep still. With diabolically cruel slowness he covered her whole body with butterfly kisses, then dipped his tongue into the tiny dent of her belly button. This always made her body jerk with rising passion, but she switched her mind to Fran's furious response when she'd let her down and slowly the reaction to his caresses faded.

Moving down her body he opened her unresisting legs, parted her outer sex lips and let his tongue move up and down the damp, aroused flesh beneath. It was impossible to stop her body from trembling, but she didn't move a muscle or utter a sound.

"I know how much you like this," he murmured. "Your

clitoris is very swollen. I'm sure it would like to feel my tongue against the side of it."

Grace wanted to cry with despair. His words were driving her out of her mind with excitement, and there was a tingling beginning in her toes that she knew would soon spread upwards.

With a superhuman effort she managed not to move or make a sound as his tongue flicked at the aching little nub, and then she felt his fingers stroking the top of the inner creases of her thighs. As he pressed more firmly there she wanted to cry. It wasn't fair, because only he knew that this could sometimes trigger an orgasm for her.

Staring up at the ceiling she concentrated on how their life together would be once she took over from Amber. Removing herself mentally from what was happening she began to make plans about the future of the Dining Club and the changes she'd make.

"What a clever girl you are," said David as she remained motionless. "Only one trick left, I fear."

With that he rolled her over onto her face, lifting her hips up so that he could enter her from behind. This was her favorite position for sex, because he always reached around her body and teased her clitoris with his fingers as he thrust in and out of her. It never failed to bring her to a climax, but this time she knew that she had to make sure he climaxed first.

With the top half of her body flat on the couch, he positioned himself against her, stroking her buttocks with one hand, then entering her slowly, while at the same time caressing her clitoris with his free hand. She remained

totally still, desperately fighting back the wonderful sensations that were threatening to overwhelm her.

"You may speak now. Tell me how much you want to
come," he said, his voice as caressing as his fingers. "I need
to know."

Grace didn't want to speak, she needed to concentrate,
but had to obey or she would fail. "I'm so close that I want
to come more than ever before, but I can't because I love
you," she admitted despairingly. To her relief and astonishment her words proved to be the final trigger for him and
with a loud groan he spilled himself into her.

"You can come now," he whispered, slumping against
her, and when his fingers pressed the side of her clitoris
she finally relaxed and a wave of pleasure so intense she
thought she might pass out swept through her tight, frantic
body.

"Your usual clothes have been left here," said David,
his voice controlled once more. "Get dressed when you're
ready, then wait with Amber in the small drawing room."

As she slumped onto the bed, her muscles aching with
the power of her orgasm, she realized he'd gone, taking
the other men with him, and leaving the two women alone
together.

They dressed in silence, before Amber led the way to a
small, sunny room on the first floor. Exhausted, Grace sat
down in one of the plush, red, high-backed Regency chairs.
Amber was the first to break the silence.

"Even if you win, David won't be yours, you know.
He can never be what you want him to be. He may love
you, but you'll never be the center of his world. His work,

this Club and extreme sexual pleasure dominate his life. Because I'm not 'in love' with him, he can never disappoint me. He'll always be disappointing you. Why can't you settle for being a part of his life, instead of wanting to invade it all?"

"It's because I'm in love with him that I want to be part of his entire life," explained Grace. "I have embraced and understand everything about him, and in a strange way I've fallen in love with the Dining Club as well. I've learned so much about myself here. I believe that I can make it even more exciting for him and everyone else too."

Amber shook her head. "You may tell yourself that, but deep down you think this is the only way you'll keep him interested in you, but you're not like me. You don't truly love all the aspects of sexual pleasure that he does. Your capacity for pleasure pain is very limited, as you'll discover if you get your way and replace me."

"I know I've still got a lot to learn," admitted Grace, "but that's part of the excitement. He loves me, I know he does, and he'll enjoy teaching me, just as I'll enjoy making changes here."

"Changes?"

"Yes, I've got a brilliant idea for…"

At that moment David and Andrew came into the room together. Both women tensed, waiting to hear the result. Grace couldn't remember ever being as nervous before. She felt as though she couldn't breathe as they waited for the verdict. If Amber had won, then all her hopes and plans for a future with David would be destroyed, and everything she'd learned here at the Dining Club would have been for nothing, because in order for her dreams to come true, Amber had to lose.

"It was a close vote," said David quietly, "but we do have a clear winner." He paused, and Grace felt physically sick. "That winner," he continued in the same even tone that gave nothing away, "is Grace. Amber, unfortunately you'll need to pack your things and be ready to leave by tomorrow morning. A house will be available for you to live in until you find new employment, but your time at the Dining Club is over."

As Grace tried to take in what he was saying, she heard Amber gasp.

"Why did I lose?" she cried, clearly close to tears. David didn't reply.

"The problem was that you failed to look or behave like a true slave girl," said Andrew gently.

"Really? I think the problem might have been that you decided to change your mind and vote for Grace," said Amber, her quick temper rising.

"Before the vote we had a general discussion, which is where the comment Andrew has mentioned was made," said David smoothly.

Amber looked directly into his eyes. "You'll miss me," she said quietly.

The watching Grace saw his expression change for a moment as he considered the beautiful blonde woman's words, but then he moved away and stood looking out of the window, his face hidden from both women.

With a shrug, Amber walked toward the door, pausing as she passed Grace. "Be careful," she whispered. "At the moment you're a novelty, but one day you'll be in my position. No one can hold his interest forever." Andrew followed her out of the room, and Grace's first instinct was to rush into David's arms, but instead she stood very still and waited for him to come to her.

Turning to face her he smiled warmly. "You did incredibly well, my darling. You were amazing. I was so proud of you. Even Andrew voted for you, and I wasn't expecting that."

"Why not?"

"I'm not stupid, Gracie. I know he's attracted to you and asked you out. He could have got his revenge by voting for Amber, but the prospect of working alongside you as manager was clearly a more attractive alternative. Plus it was clear you deserved to win, of course."

Hearing his words Grace took a step toward him, and finally he took her in his arms. His grip was tight, almost possessive, and he kissed her passionately as he whispered words of love and desire.

Despite all that had happened throughout the long day, Grace both wanted and needed him. When he finally led her upstairs to the suite of rooms where it had all begun and started to make love to her, he was more tender and gentle than ever before, and afterwards she fell into a deep, dreamless sleep in his arms.

Later, as they were drinking champagne in the small drawing room where she'd waited for the result of the contest, he looked thoughtfully at her. "So, do you have any suggestions about the future of the Dining Club yet?"

Grace hesitated, unsure for a moment as to how he

would react if she told him. Then, knowing that she had to have confidence in her ideas if their new relationship was to work, she nodded.

"Yes, I do," she said eagerly. "I think it should be expanded. Perhaps there could be a small, private hotel in London, hidden away in an exclusive back street, where people who've enjoyed the Club experience can go for a whole week at a time."

"A hidden hotel? Yes, I like that idea," he said, leaning forward.

"And I think it would be exciting to have themes at the hotel. There could be a Victorian week or an Ancient Roman week, for example. It would open up a whole range of exciting new sexual possibilities.

"Also, schooling women to prepare them for those weeks could take place here at the Dining Club beforehand."

David's eyes darkened with excitement. Putting an arm around her waist he kissed the side of her neck. "Brilliant!" he exclaimed. "The possibilities are endless. No wonder I fell in love with you!"

Later that night, Andrew came to see them leave. "I'm pleased you've decided to stay on," said David, shaking him by the hand. "I think you'll find your work even more interesting from now on."

"I'm sure I will," agreed Andrew. "I'm hoping to introduce a guest of my own before too long. In fact, I'm off to the King's Head in Islington to meet up with her now."

"That's great news," said David to Grace as they drove away. "I wonder what she'll be like?"

"I'm sure she'll be interesting," said Grace, knowing

perfectly well who Andrew meant, but uncertain how she felt about it.

David glanced at her. "Lucien liked you," he said. "What did you think of him?"

"He was interesting," she admitted.

David raised an eyebrow. "Interesting? Well, the interest is definitely reciprocal."

"I didn't feel attracted to him," she said hastily.

"My darling girl, there's no need to worry. I thrive on challenges. Tomorrow morning I shall start looking for a suitable building for our hidden hotel."

His excitement was contagious, and Grace was overwhelmed with love for this handsome, complex man, who had finally committed himself to her.

As their car sped through the night, Amber picked up her bedside phone, wondering who could be calling her at such a late hour. "Lucien? I never expected to hear from you again. What do you want?" she asked and then, as she listened intently, a slow smile spread over her face.

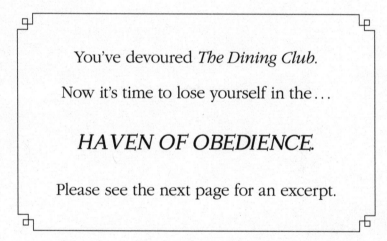

You've devoured *The Dining Club*.

Now it's time to lose yourself in the...

HAVEN OF OBEDIENCE.

Please see the next page for an excerpt.

ONE

On a Sunday night in April, twenty people were assembled in the reception area of The Haven. Rob Gill, the owner, was addressing them as they listened attentively. 'I trust you've enjoyed your stay over the past three days,' he said, a half-smile playing around his lips. 'At the very least I'm sure that you've all learned something new about yourselves.'

Jan Pearson, a twenty-eight-year-old freelance casting director, felt herself start to blush. She glanced at the rest of the group, all of whom were watching Rob. They looked so conventional now: the women in their trouser suits or designer leisure clothes, most of the men smartly suited. This was in sharp contrast to the way they'd looked over the past weekend. For example, she'd last seen the man standing next to her—now safely encased in his three-piece suit, white shirt and dark blue tie—kneeling submissively at the feet of a voluptuous blonde, his hands tied behind his back as he waited, trembling with excitement and need, for her finally to allow him a cruelly delayed climax.

'What it's important for you to understand,' continued Rob, 'is that you are now part of a very select and secret society. When you arrived here you signed a form, swearing to keep our code of silence. You may find this difficult once you start mixing with friends from your everyday life again.

But if any of you should break your vow, then you will be ostracized. In other words, you won't be allowed to visit us again.'

Jan's mouth went dry. Even after just one weekend she was addicted to the pleasures that she'd learned to enjoy here, at this very special retreat. If anyone had told her how erotic she'd find it to be forced into obedience and submission she would have laughed at them. In all her relationships she'd been in control, and that was the way she'd liked it. However, her stay at The Haven had changed her completely.

Rob was still speaking. 'I'm sure that many of you here today will want to stay in touch with each other, and that's how we like it. You're all like-minded people now. The only people here that you're not free to continue seeing are any of your tutors. You have to remember that for us this is a job of work. It isn't personal.'

The nipples beneath Jan's V-necked, semi-fitted ribbed cardigan suddenly stiffened and she felt the caress of the material against the rigid tips. It was Rob's fault—his words had reminded her of the previous evening.

She'd been lying on her bed in an exhausted, sated heap after a long session with one of the other tutors and two of the guests when Rob had entered the room. He'd been accompanied by a trainee tutor, a young lad who hadn't had anything to do with Jan before her visit. Rob had told her that they were there to pleasure her for an hour. At first she thought there'd been a mistake, and she'd explained that she'd already been very well pleasured. It was then that his expression had changed, changed to one that she'd become used to over the weekend. His piercing blue eyes had narrowed.

'I hope you're not still trying to tell me what to do, Jan?' Rob had asked. Remembering the punishments she'd endured before she'd come to understand the rules of The Haven, Jan had hastily shaken her head. 'That's good,' he'd continued. 'Because as you know, here you're expected to be obedient to our wishes. It's Marc and I who wish to pleasure you: *your* wishes are of no importance.'

To Jan's surprise, Rob's words had excited her. All the same, she had felt certain that her tired body would be unable to respond no matter what the two men did. How wrong she'd been, she thought now as memories of the intense orgasms that they'd wrenched from her rushed through her mind.

Jan recalled the way Rob had sat astride her, his hands kneading her breasts with sweet-scented oil, while Marc had kneeled at the foot of the bed, parting her legs and using his tongue with incredible skill on the soft centre of her. She'd lost count of the number of times her body had contorted, arching upwards in spasm after spasm of helpless pleasure. It had been an incredible experience, and when Rob had finally climbed off her and run a hand over her sweat-streaked flesh she'd thought that for a brief moment there had been something personal in his gaze. Now it seemed that she'd been wrong. Or, even if she was right, she would never be able to find out.

'I hope that we'll see you here again some time,' said Rob as his speech drew to a close. 'I suggest that those of you who've learned that there can be pleasure through pain should exchange phone numbers. For most of you, your new sexual preferences might come as something of a shock to the people you've previously been intimate with.' A ripple of uneasy laughter spread through the room.

Jan's buttocks clenched beneath her ankle-length pencil skirt as she recalled the hot, stinging sensation caused by the latex whip, wielded so expertly by Simon, Rob's second-in-command. She'd cried out with shock and anger the first time it had happened to her. But as she'd been spread-eagled on a large wooden table, her wrists and ankles held firmly by other guests, she'd been unable to do anything about it.

Slowly, as her 'punishment' had continued, she'd been surprised to realise that the discomfort quickly passed whilst the heat from the lashes seemed to race through her flesh, causing her breasts to burgeon and her belly to swell. Yes, she must certainly exchange some telephone numbers before she got into her car and set off again for London, and her busy work schedule.

'And now it's time for you all to go,' said Rob, with a smile. 'Remember everything you've learned here. You don't want to waste your money, do you?' Again there was laughter, but this time it wasn't embarrassed laughter. Jan tried to catch Rob's eye for a moment, wanting to prove to herself that she'd been right and that she was special to him. But without another word he turned and left the room. With a start she realised that the crotch of her panties was damp. Just thinking about the things that had happened to her had excited her again.

A man of about Jan's own age approached her. She remembered him from the Saturday. He'd been an amazingly adept lover, although at that stage she still hadn't mastered how to hand over control completely. Now that she had, sex with him would probably be even better so when he asked if she'd like to give him her phone number she accepted eagerly.

'I was thinking of having a party some time soon,' she told him.

'That's a good idea. I hope I'll be on the guest list.'

Jan smiled, tucking her short, sleek brown hair behind her ears. 'I thought eight would be an ideal number. What do you think?'

He nodded. 'Yes, eight sounds about right. It's been an interesting weekend, hasn't it?' He stared intently at her.

A shiver ran through her. 'Very interesting,' she said softly. As he touched the side of her face lightly with his fingers Jan remembered the way the same fingers had forced her hands above her head, and how his mouth had fastened around her left nipple, sucking cruelly at the delicate skin as he ignored her protests—because that was what the weekend was all about. Suddenly she wanted him again, there and then, and she could see from the look in his eyes that he knew it.

'Don't wait too long before you ring,' he commanded her. Whereas before her stay at The Haven she would have resented his tone, now it excited her.

'I won't,' she assured him. Then, reluctantly, Jan picked up her cases and began the journey back to London.

TWO

By the time Natalie Bowen arrived home at her small but expensive flat on the outskirts of London it was nearly nine o'clock. A tall, slim and typically cool English blonde, she realised that she was in danger of having nothing in her life apart from her magazine. Admittedly the magazine was a great achievement. She'd started it eighteen months earlier, deliberately targeting women in the twenty-five-to-thirty-five age group, single and working in high-powered jobs. She felt that most magazines were trying to teach women how they could juggle home, children and work, but she wasn't interested in the home-and-children side. She dealt with fashion, health and relationships, both in and out of the workplace, and the magazine's success had exceeded even her expectations.

All of which was very pleasing. But somehow, despite all the articles in her magazine aimed at helping women like her, Natalie had got lost. Her tendency to be impatient, and her ability to cut straight to the heart of the matter, were assets at work—but not when it came to staying in a relationship. She had no trouble in attracting men, but was beginning to find little satisfaction in short-term affairs, which were pleasurable enough sexually but left her feeling empty.

'Do as the editor says, not as the editor does,' Natalie

muttered to herself as she opened her front door. Glancing at the answerphone she was disappointed to see that no one had called while she was out. There were several people she half expected to hear from, including Philip, although she was beginning to suspect that she'd been politely ditched by him. But it was Jan she really wanted to ring her: Jan was her best friend and until a month ago they'd met up at least three times a week.

Because Jan too had a busy professional life and struggled to find a man that she considered good enough for herself, the two of them always had plenty to gossip about. Also, they shared the same sense of humour and the same love of Italian food and good wine. Natalie couldn't understand why Jan had stopped phoning her. It wasn't as though there'd been an argument, or even a disagreement. At their last meeting Jan had mentioned that she was going away the following weekend but had promised to call Natalie as soon as she'd got back. The call had never come.

Too tired to cook herself anything, Natalie took a bottle of wine from the fridge and poured herself a large glass. Then she chopped up some feta cheese in a bowl, threw in some black olives and some tomatoes and sat down in front of the television. After the meal her hand started to move towards the phone. Then she drew it back again. She didn't know why, but she was reluctant to call Jan herself. There had to be a reason for her friend's silence and she wasn't sure that she wanted to know it, not if Jan was going to end their friendship.

It was only after two more glasses of wine that she finally found the courage to dial the number. The phone rang for a long time. She was about to hang up when Jan answered.

'Hi!' Her familiar voice was slightly breathless, as though she'd had to hurry to get to the phone.

'Jan? It's me, Nat.'

'Nat.'

There was an awkward pause, a pause that Natalie rushed to fill. 'Yes, you remember me, I'm the one whose shoulder you cry on when men disappoint you.'

'God, look, I'm really sorry I haven't rung you,' babbled Jan. 'The truth is I've been incredibly busy casting for a new historical drama. I haven't had a moment to myself for the past few weeks. I was going to ring you tonight, but I seem to have gone down with some kind of virus.'

Natalie frowned to herself. She thought that she could hear people in the background, people laughing and chattering. But it was always possible it was the television that Jan had put on to cheer herself up. 'How was your weekend away?' she asked brightly.

'What weekend away?'

'You know, the one you took just after we last met. You told me you were going to a retreat or something like that. What was it like? Did it do you any good?'

'It was all right,' said Jan hesitantly.

'What do you mean, "all right"? I got the impression it was going to be something special.'

'Did you? I don't know why. It was just a weekend in the country.'

Natalie knew that Jan wasn't telling her the truth. 'If you say so,' she said stiffly, annoyed at being lied to. 'Well, shall I come round and see you tomorrow? I'll bring some chicken soup and grapes.'

'No, you can't come tomorrow,' said Jan. Now she sounded panic-stricken.

'Why not? You're not infectious, are you?'

'My mother's coming over.'

'From Paris? You really must be ill.' Natalie could hear that she was getting an edge to her voice and she knew that Jan must be able to hear it too.

'Look, I can't talk now,' said Jan, suddenly lowering her voice. 'We'd better meet after work one night next week.'

'How about Tuesday?' suggested Natalie.

'No, sorry I can't do Tuesday, I've got some friends coming round.' 'Anyone I know?'

'No, people in the same line of business as me. I tell you what, Thursday's clear. I'll see you at our usual Italian place at seven o'clock, okay?'

'You're sure you can spare the time?' asked Natalie coolly. At that moment she heard a man's voice calling Jan. It was clear that he was impatient. 'It sounds as though the doctor's arrived,' Natalie said sharply. 'I'll see you on Thursday.' With that she slammed down the phone. At least she'd made contact with Jan again, and it didn't sound as though she'd done anything to offend her. What hurt was the realisation that Jan suddenly appeared to be having a far busier social life than Natalie was. She'd have to ask Jan about that when they met.

Jan put her cordless phone down on the kitchen worktop. Natalie couldn't have rung at a worse time. She felt terrible about the way the conversation had gone, but she hadn't been able to say any more because Richard had been standing right behind her, listening to every word.

'Who was that?' he asked, running a finger down her spine.

Wearing only a black leather thong and high-heeled shoes, Jan felt incredibly vulnerable—which was how she was supposed to feel. It was also how she liked feeling, when she wasn't at work. That was what they'd taught her at The Haven, and they'd taught her well. 'No one you know,' she said lightly. 'Only a friend.'

'And is your friend pretty?' asked Richard, placing his hands on each side of her waist with his fingers splayed out over her belly.

'Yes, but she wouldn't interest you. She's a high-powered businesswoman who likes to be in control of her men.'

'Perhaps she should go to The Haven for a weekend,' murmured Richard, his voice growing husky with desire. 'We're going upstairs now and while I'm making love to you, you're going to describe her to me.'

'I am not!' retorted Jan.

She felt Richard's left hand move to the nape of her neck and he gripped her tightly. 'I hope you're not going to slip back into your old ways, Jan,' he whispered. 'Don't forget that the men are in charge here this weekend. As long as you do as we say, you receive as much pleasure as you can bear, remember?'

Her whole body tightened with desire. 'Of course I remember,' she whispered. Then she walked up the stairs in front of him, past other guests—some of whom reached out to caress her as she and Richard made their way to her bedroom. Once there she knew that soon, desperate to feel the delicious hot liquid pleasure rush through her, she would be doing as he'd said. She knew it was a betrayal of Natalie but, shamingly, the dark perversity of what she was about to do only increased her excitement.

Natalie arrived at Mario's before Jan. Watching her friend arrive she noticed that Jan was looking tense. When Natalie waved to her, Jan's answering smile seemed strained. 'Sorry I'm late,' she said breathlessly, sliding into the seat opposite Natalie. 'The damned casting session ran overtime, as usual.'

'I've only been here five minutes,' said Natalie. 'I've ordered a bottle of the house red for us but thought I'd wait for you before I ordered any food.'

'Fine,' said Jan vaguely. 'I'll have the spaghetti al pomodoro.' She then began to flick through her pocket diary.

Natalie decided to have the fresh pasta filled with spinach and ricotta in a tomato and basil sauce, her favourite meal at Mario's. Since Jan showed no inclination to eat she had to catch the waiter's eye and order for them both.

'Don't you ever get tired of having the same food?' asked Jan, putting her diary away.

Natalie shook her head. 'No, I know what I like.'

'I thought I did.' Jan's tone was strange.

'What do you mean?'

'Nothing. How's the magazine, then?'

'Taking up far too much of my life, as usual. Philip's dumped me, in case you wanted to know but didn't dare ask.'

Jan looked sympathetically at her. 'Bad luck. Did he say why?'

'Oh, the usual stuff about not wanting to get involved, feeling that I deserved someone better. It's not what he meant, of course. It went wrong the last time we had sex. I said that I wanted to be on top because my orgasms are always better that way and...' She stopped as the waiter arrived and they both had to stifle their giggles. 'He must have missed us,' laughed Natalie as they began to eat. 'I'm sure no one else has such interesting conversations.'

'Go on with what you were saying,' commanded Jan.

'Oh, that. Yes, well, he didn't like me saying that I knew best. He pretended that it was all right, that he liked a woman who knew her own mind and understood her own body. But it put him right off.'

'You mean although you had a better time, he didn't?'

Natalie nodded. 'Exactly. God, the times that's happened to me. Still, it's happened to you too, hasn't it? That's some comfort to me. I'm not alone in this.'

'No,' murmured Jan.

'Is that all you've got to say? Haven't you got any interesting gossip for me? How's *your* sex life at the moment?'

'It's okay,' said Jan, with a shrug.

'What do you mean, "okay"? Are you seeing someone special?'

'No.'

'Are you seeing anyone at all?'

'Yes, now and again.'

'Is there some reason why you can't tell me about him?' asked Natalie. 'Is he married or something?'

'No, it's just that it isn't very interesting.'

Natalie couldn't believe her ears. 'Your sex life's *always* interesting. What's the matter? You're keeping something back from me, I know you are. Is this why you haven't rung me since your weekend away? Did you meet someone dishy there, someone you want to keep secret?'

'Oh Nat,' said Jan sadly. 'I wish I could tell you about it, but I can't.' She lowered her voice. 'You see, it isn't allowed.'

'Isn't *allowed?*' shouted Natalie.

'Ssh!'

'Why do you keep whispering and why have I got to keep my voice down? I don't understand what's happened to you,' said Natalie. 'You've changed completely since we last met. Have I offended you or something?'

'No, you haven't done anything,' said Jan firmly. 'Please, can we just change the subject?'

Natalie sighed. 'If that's what you want. But the evening won't be as much fun as usual. You'd better tell me about this place where you went for your weekend. You're look-ing really well, so it must have done you good. Perhaps I should go there. Where is it?'

'It's, uhm...sort of in the country.'

'That's a *great* help. I should be able to find it easily from *that.*'

'I can't tell you where it is,' said Jan, the exasperation clear in her voice.

Never before had Natalie felt uncomfortable when she was with Jan. They'd always been like sisters, able to talk about anything and everything. Obviously, for reasons known only to Jan, that was no longer the case. Suddenly Natalie just wanted the meal to be over and to escape back to her flat. She felt incredibly hurt. 'I think you'd better choose what we're going to talk about,' she snapped. 'Nothing that I pick seems to be right.'

'Nat, I *am* sorry,' responded Jan, leaning over the table towards her friend. 'I'd like to tell you, truly I would, but I'm not supposed to.'

'Then don't. I don't think I want a pudding. Let's just have coffee and then split, shall we?'

'Oh, blow them,' said Jan. 'Listen, Nat.' She dropped her voice. 'I *will* tell you about my weekend away but you must never talk about it to anyone else. If you do, you're going to ruin everything for me. So will you promise me that before I start?'

Now Natalie was intrigued. 'Of course. You know me, I'm good at keeping secrets.'

'Yes, well you'd better be because I'm risking everything in telling you this. The place I went to was called The Haven. It's in Sussex. A girl at work told me about it. You see, they don't advertise. People have to hear of the place by word of mouth, and their names must be put forward by someone who's already been before they can actually go there to stay.'

'But why?' asked Natalie in astonishment. 'Do you have to be incredibly fit or something?'

'Hardly, or I wouldn't have got in. No, it's really a weekend seminar.'

'A business seminar? I don't want a weekend away working. I want a break.'

'It's a seminar in sex.'

Natalie couldn't believe her ears. 'What on earth do you mean?'

'Exactly what I say. People go there to learn how to fulfil their sexual potential, but it's a very special kind of potential. You see, it's for women like you and me, or for men who spend all their time controlling people at work. They teach you how to hand control over to your partner in order to gain your pleasure. I heard one of the tutors refer to it as "the haven of obedience", which sums it up.'

'I can't believe I'm hearing this right,' said an astonished Natalie. 'You're not telling me—'

'For heaven's sake keep your voice down.' Jan looked nervously around her.

'Sorry. You're not telling me that you became a submissive, are you?'

'Yes,' confessed Jan. 'It was incredibly difficult at first. To be honest, I didn't think that I was going to make it through the first day and night but I was determined to try. Let's face it, my sex life's hardly been that wonderful, running it the way I wanted to, so what did I have to lose? Anyway, once I started to give in and do what they wanted me to, it was so fantastic that I just wanted to learn more and more.'

'What do they make you do?'

Jan shook her head. 'Now that's something I *really* can't tell you.'

'I can understand that they might want to keep the place a secret,' said Natalie. 'What I don't understand is why I haven't heard from you since you got back.'

'Because I'm still seeing loads of the people who were at The Haven when I was. We have parties at each other's houses, and meet up for dinners that always turn into something rather more exciting. The trouble is, we're not allowed to invite people who've never been to The Haven, which is why I haven't been able to include you. The awful thing is, Nat, I've got so caught up in it that I can hardly bear to take an evening off even to see you, my best friend.'

Natalie could see that simply thinking about it was exciting Jan. Her cheeks were flushed, her eyes bright and her hand, gripping the stem of her wine glass, wasn't quite steady. Suddenly Natalie wanted to feel like that, to have something to be excited about—and, more to the point, to have truly satisfying sex. 'Do you think I could go there?' she asked.

Jan frowned. 'I honestly don't think you'd like it. I've rather simplified what goes on there. The place is very strictly run and if you don't do as you're told, well...' Her voice trailed off.

'Well, what?' demanded Natalie.

'You get punished,' whispered Jan.

'Punished?'

'Yes. But even the punishments are designed to turn you on, only in a completely different way from anything you've ever experienced before. I really don't think it's for you, Nat.'

'I wouldn't have thought that it was for *you*. But you seem to have enjoyed it. Surely they'd take me if you put my name forward?'

'I suppose so, but I don't want to.'

Natalie felt as though her friend had slapped her. 'I think you're being incredibly selfish,' she said finally. 'You've been there and come back a totally different person. You admit that your sex life's now fantastic and that you're seeing people nearly every night of the week. Do you know what *I* do when I stop work each day? I go home, drink too much wine and go to bed with only the cat for company.'

'But if I did put you forward and then you didn't like it once you got there, it would reflect badly on me,' explained Jan. 'I don't want that to happen. I don't want to spoil what I've got, and they'll start questioning my judgement if I send the wrong person along.'

'I honestly can't see what can be so bad about the place,' said Natalie. 'I'm not some naive eighteen-year-old. I'm twenty-seven, and I've had a fair bit of experience. I doubt if anything they suggest is going to shock me.'

'Oh Natalie, you have absolutely no idea of what I'm talking about, do you?' said Jan. 'You're the same as I was. You've always liked being in control, both at work and in bed. The older the pair of us got, the more dominating we became. That's why we frightened all the men off, only neither of us realised it. At least, I know I didn't—not until I went to The Haven.'

'I accept all that,' replied Natalie. 'If you're truly my friend then prove it to me by putting my name forward. I promise I won't let you down, no matter how much of a shock I get.' She laughed.

Jan hesitated for a few more seconds and then shrugged. 'On your own head be it, then. The only thing is, knowing you, and knowing what it's like there, I want you to take the two-weekend option. I don't think you'd be able to put up with the intensive course.'

'Whatever you say,' agreed Natalie hastily. Privately she thought Jan had gone mad. She couldn't imagine any sexual situation where she wouldn't be able to cope. 'You'll do it, then? You'll put my name forward?'

'I've said I will, haven't I?'

For the first time in months Natalie felt excited about something other than her work. 'How long will it take before I hear from them?'

'I had to wait several weeks.'

Natalie groaned. 'Oh, no. I was looking forward to going next weekend.'

'They're booked up a long way ahead. Now I have to go. I've got someone coming round for the night.'

Natalie didn't mind any more, not now that she understood why Jan was so busy. Soon she would be as well. 'That's all right,' she said with a smile. 'Don't forget to ring them up about me tomorrow, will you?'

'No, I won't,' Jan assured her. As the pair of them stepped outside into the fresh air she glanced at Natalie. 'I really hope I'm doing the right thing for you,' she said slowly. 'If you don't like it, you won't hold it against me, will you?'

'I'm going to love it,' said Natalie confidently. 'I wanted my life to change, but I didn't know how to do it. Now you've solved the problem for me.'

'Give me a ring when you've finished the course,' said Jan, hailing a taxi.

'Aren't we going to meet again before then?' asked Natalie.

'No,' shouted Jan, climbing into the cab. 'I haven't got an evening free for the next two months.'

As the taxi sped away, Natalie shivered with a mixture

of nerves and anticipation. She realised that Jan was right. She was more private than her friend, and the two-weekend option was probably the right one for her. She also realised that she'd now taken the first step on a journey that would lead her to discover new things about herself sexually. Unexpectedly, she was already aroused by the thought of learning to relinquish control and be dominated in bed. It was something that she would never have considered for a moment before hearing about The Haven from Jan and seeing what a difference it had made to her friend.

ABOUT THE AUTHOR

Marina Anderson is the pseudonym of a British author. Her novels have sold over half a million copies worldwide and she is a *Sunday Times* bestseller.